Prove

Steven F. Galloway

ISBN: 9781086575927

3805970007768 0

PROVENANCE

First published 2019 by Circle Line Books

Thanks to Victoria for cover photography and moral support…

www.bobbieprint.com

@StevenFGalloway

Prologue

There are many stories I want to tell, but this isn't one of them.

I don't really want to have to write this at all, but it's becoming ever more pressing that I put it all down on paper - or in this case, on a laptop - and make sure it gets somewhere safe.

Somewhere that those who seek to suppress it will never find it.

No, I don't want to tell you this story at all.

I need to...

I don't even know who you might be, but somebody else needs to know what happened, because I might not be around to tell the story for much longer.

STEVEN F. GALLOWAY

Part One:

<u>'A Good Place to Die'</u>

STEVEN F. GALLOWAY

1

London, January 2019

The day everything changes starts so normally...

It's my first winter in London, and the capital is beginning to lose its sparkle. Literally. The Regent Street lights have all been packed away for another year and Trafalgar Square's Christmas tree has long been fed into a chipper and returned to mulch. The place no longer twinkles with excitement, and there's nothing to look forward to, except another few months of cold. It's January, and nothing's happening anywhere. We're all just working. Working and waiting…

I walk along a grey Whitehall, heading into a West End which sometime in the last few months has stopped being somewhere I go as a wide-eyed occasional visitor and started being *somewhere I go to work.*

I veer left at Trafalgar Square - barely registering Nelson's Column - and head into the National Gallery. Within minutes I'm in my uniform and ready to start my shift.

It was only ever supposed to be a temporary job. But somehow, six months after Siobhan and I left the Sussex coast for South London, I'm still employed as a lowly Gallery Assistant, working eight-hour shifts for what can generously be described as a pittance.

That's right - I, Charlie Marks - English graduate and general undiscovered genius, have spent half of my first year in London working as a glorified security guard.

It's at times like these that I'm thankful my father isn't around to see what I'm doing with my life.

Move to London. Find a job. Write the next great screenplay. Make millions.

The plan isn't quite working out just yet...

Still, the job has its benefits. The 10am start isn't exactly too frightening, for someone as 'artistically inclined' as me, and I get to spend my eight-hour days surrounded by some of the most beautiful works of art ever made.

Fortunately, this is a thrill that is still yet to wear off...

On this particular morning I'm working in Room 44 - home to Paul Delaroche's The Execution of Lady Jane Grey, among others. I stand in a corner and study it closely, as I tend to do nowadays.

I'm the first to admit that my knowledge of art is paltry, to say the least. Before taking this job I barely knew my Titians from my Turners. It had always been film posters that lined my student bedroom walls, not Salvador Dali prints. But somehow, my job in the National has stirred some sleeping art enthusiast inside me, and I now find myself gazing at the assorted works for hours, trying to make use of my time by understanding how the great artists managed to do what they did. After all, it will all surely help me with the *next big screenplay,* someday...

In the painting, Lady Jane Grey kneels in front of the execution block, a pale, red-haired teenager in a white dress, facing the last few seconds of her short life. You can't see her eyes, but somehow you *can* still see the fear in them. That was clever. I wonder how Delaroche had done it...

"Excuse me..."

Lost in the painting, I don't notice him at first, but an elderly gentleman approaches me from the left. He's old. Late 80s is my immediate guess, and he is smartly dressed in salmon chinos and a pale blue shirt under a cream blazer, matched with the distinctive red and yellow striped tie of the Marylebone Cricket Club. His unkempt white hair is thinning but still rather plentiful for a man of his age. He looks up at me and I glance down at him. He's thin and slightly stooped but retains an air of wiry strength rather than fragility.

"Good morning young man," he says in a clipped accent that makes me think of army parade grounds. Not that I've ever been on one.

"Er, morning, sir," I reply.

"When was this one painted?" he asks.

He's looking towards Lady Jane Grey.

"1833," I reply, without bothering to look at the information label.

"I see," says the man, gesturing back towards the label. "Would you humour an old man and read the rest for me? The eyes aren't quite what they were."

He taps at a pair of round spectacles balanced owlishly on his nose.

"Certainly," I say.

I move closer towards the canvas. The man follows me and leans in; his ear almost touching my head. He smells of aftershave and black coffee.

I begin to read:

"Lady Jane Grey was Queen of England for just nine days until she was driven from the throne and sent to the Tower of London to be executed. Jane became queen after the death of her cousin, Edward VI, in 1553. As a Protestant, Jane was crowned in a bid to shore up Protestantism and keep Catholic influence at bay.

The plan didn't work. Jane's claim to the crown was much weaker than Edward VI's half sister Mary. Mary, a Catholic, had popular support and soon replaced Jane as queen.

Lady Jane Grey was executed at Tower green on..."

The man's hand grips my arm firmly and sends a jolt through my body. I stop reading and watch his eyes as they roll upwards towards the ceiling. His strong hold on my arm slackens and his body seems to crumple beneath him. I stare helplessly as his head thumps against my chest, at which point I'm shocked into action and grab hold of his flopping arms. I try to prop him up, but he's surprisingly heavy, so all I can do is break his fall and help him gently to the floor.

He lies there at my feet, still, his eyes closed and invisible. Just like those of Lady Jane, who still looms large above us.

2

The National Gallery is a quiet place. Usually.

Hordes of visitors file in and out every day - generally featureless and unremarkable - hushed into a silent respect by the masterful artworks that surround them. It's a place where the paintings on the wall are more powerful and permanent than the people who gaze upon them. These are pictures that have been around for centuries and will still be around long after the last visitor has turned to dust. The crowds seem to acknowledge that - unconsciously perhaps - with their sober reverence.

But now the spell is broken, and the drama becomes the old man on the floor - rather than the art on the walls. A crowd gathers around me as I kneel over his limp body. I look at his chest. He's still breathing - very faintly.

"Hello sir," I say. Nothing.

I turn to the room.

"Is there a doctor here? Or a nurse?"

A sea of blank faces stare back at me, and I deduce that none belongs to a medical professional. I grab my radio…

"Medical emergency in Room 44. Send a first-aider immediately."

I look back at the man. His lips are curled up at the sides, almost in a smile. He seems oddly peaceful, like he's enjoying an afternoon nap.

"Er, sir, can you hear me?"

He groans, and opens his right eye so it's just a slit, then closes it again as if the effort is too much.

I try to recall what the recovery position looks like… I'm sure it involves putting the person on their side, but the finer details escape me. I decide to leave him where he is. As I wait for the first-aiders, I try to remember some of those TV documentaries about Accident and Emergency Departments that Siobhan insists on watching. The paramedics always seem to ask the patient their name… to establish a rapport, or something.

Worth a go...

"Sir, can you tell me your name?"

"Urgh."

Well, that went well.

He breathes in slowly and makes a muffled, two-syllable sound which might be:

"Victor…"

I take a chance.

"Victor? My name is Charles. Charlie… You're going to be OK, a first-aider's on their way."

"Urghhh."

"Please, don't try to say any more. You're going to be fine."

Actually, I have no idea whether he's going to be 'fine' or not. It's a good thing I never considered going to medical school… not that I had the grades anyway.

Victor groans again, then speaks…

"Where am I?"

"Please, don't try and speak…"

"Where am I?" he repeats, faster, straining with the effort.

"The National Gallery. Room 44. Opposite the Execution of Lady Jane Grey."

Victor rolls his head backwards, his mouth still upturned at the sides.

"A good place to die."

"You're not going to die, Victor, just hold tight. Don't speak."

He grins again, his eyes shut:

"You're a good man, Guy. A good chap."

Guy? Is he delirious?

I watch silently as his chest rises and falls. After what seems an age, a first aider runs in with some suit from the management team. I stand up.

"What happened?" asks the suit.

"Er, he just collapsed."

"Get them out of here" he hisses, nodding at the gathered crowds of tourists.

I clear my throat and try to sound authoritative.

"Ladies and gentlemen, I need you to all step outside of the room, thank you very much."

Most of them start to shift towards the doors, but I see that a young man in a blue hoodie has his camera-phone pointed at the scene and shows no sign of moving. I raise my voice…"

"Now! Thank you."

He pockets his phone and heads to the doors. I follow him, taking up a crossed-arm stance in the doorway, channelling my inner nightclub bouncer and hoping this wins me brownie points with management. I need them.

Over my shoulder the first-aider is saying the same things to Victor that I had been saying moments before…

"Please don't try to speak. You'll be fine…"

It doesn't take long for the paramedics to turn up, and the rest of the morning becomes a blur. Victor is wheeled away in an oxygen mask and I am sent on a break. I make my way to the staff room and dig my e-cigarette out of my bag, but proper tobacco seems more appealing right now. I hunt down a smoker colleague and cadge a real cig, heading out onto Trafalgar Square where I light up in the shadow of Horatio Nelson.

As I inhale my first real smoke since New Year's Eve an odd fragment of the morning catches up with me.

"You're a good man, Guy. A good chap."

Victor would have been roughly the same age as my grandfather, had he survived the war. Late 80s. Perhaps even 90s.

And Victor had called me Guy.

Guy was my grandfather's name…

3

"No idea if he survived then?" asks Siobhan.

"Nah, they wouldn't tell me anything like that. Didn't hear anything else about it all day. He was breathing though, so I suppose that's good."

"Yes, I believe that's generally a good sign."

"Red again?" I ask, already unscrewing the top of the bottle.

"OK."

I fill half of my glass and down it in one go, then pour out another two. I hand one to Siobhan.

"Cheers."

"Thirsty?"

"It's the weekend, at last" I say.

I take another gulp.

"So, how was your day?"

"Ah, fine, almost ready for the big launch next week. In fact it was pretty quiet, a lot of people out of the office."

"So for once I've had a more exciting day than you - you'll be jacking in marketing and taking a menial gallery job too at this rate."

"Yeah, don't hold your breath love."

I don't. Siobhan's work days are almost always more exciting than mine, but that's to be expected when you spend your 9-5 doing marketing for Hollywood movies, rather than standing in the corner of a museum.

But today, for once, the drama had belonged to me.

I walk over to the window and gaze out at the darkened streets of Battersea as a parade of youngsters head past on their way to the pubs. I turn away and drink some more wine. I'm happy it's the weekend. The weekends are when life in London suddenly gets good - like I always thought it would be - when we're not working and stressing.

I head over to the sofa and flop down, flicking through the channels as Siobhan stirs the Thai curry. It's pretty rare for her to be home in time to cook for us both, so I intend to enjoy it.

At this point I hear the insistent vibrations of my phone from across the room.

"Oh bloody hell…"

"Who's that bothering you at 9 o clock on a Friday?" asks Siobhan.

I look at the display on my phone…

ABDUL

"Abdul," I say, "from work." Suddenly I'm taken back to the morning, and all I can think of is Victor.

This must be news about him...

And surely it won't be good.

"Hello mate," I say.

"Hello my friend, you having a good evening? On the wine yet?"

"Just started," I say, neglecting to mention the couple of beers I had in the pub after work.

"Good work mate. I've just finished my shift. Going for a Burger King. Lovely jubbly."

"Sounds good buddy,"

And it does, but I'm sure you haven't phoned to discuss food and drink, Abdul.

"Anyway, funny thing happened just before I left. Thought you might want to know."

"Oh yeah?"

"Yeah, you remember the old guy who collapsed in your room this morning?"

"Yeah, more or less..."

"Well, just before I knocked off, someone from his hospital phoned the gallery. Got through to Martin."

Martin - our supervisor. Surely it was to break the bad news...

"Oh right..?"

"Yeah, apparently he came round this evening. He's sitting up, talking."

"OK, and...?"

"And he's asking to see you."

4

Antwerp, Belgium, 1945

Before the war, the building on the corner of the market square had been a fine restaurant, but that was a long time ago. There are still echoes of its former grandeur in the heavy curtains and delicately carved tables, but everything is obscured by several layers of dust.

"Lot 243 - two pairs of silver-plated candlesticks."

The auctioneer - bald and flabby with a small moustache - glances around the room as his assistant places the candlesticks on the table in front of him.

"Starting at 75 francs. Do I have 75 francs?"

There isn't a huge amount of interest - a couple of hands are raised, almost out of politeness.

Towards the back of a room a man in a British Army uniform slips through the door and takes a seat at a table next to an elderly Belgian.

The auctioneer continues...

"I'm bid 85 francs, do I hear 90?"

"I say old chap, what's going on here then?" asks the British soldier. The Belgian man next to him stares back, blankly.

The soldier switches effortlessly to Dutch:

"What's all this about then?"

The elderly Belgian looks surprised to see this young Englishman speaking fluent Dutch. He looks him up and down - he's slim, wiry, with short, untamed blond hair, blue eyes and a clear, commanding voice. Impressed by his impeccable accent, the man replies in hushed tones...

"This is the first auction I've attended since the war began! I never thought such a thing would be possible, but now it is, thanks to you and your fellow soldiers."

He offers his hand and the soldier shakes it firmly.

"Are you bidding?" he asks.

"Oh, no, no, I'm just here to watch," says the old man.

"Very well... I say, where is all this stuff from?"

The auctioneer carries on his patter in the background: "95 francs - going once, going twice..."

The old man leans closer to the soldier, he whispers...

"The previous owners of this restaurant were a wealthy Jewish family, but they no longer live in Antwerp. They no longer live... anywhere."

The soldier nods...

"The new owners are selling off most of their assets, some of it from the restaurant, some from their home. Some of it is quite nice stuff."

"Sold. 95 francs to the gentleman by the piano."

"Oh really, you say?"

"Yes... they had quite a large collection of art. All of it out of my price range, sadly."

"A shame."

The soldier lights a cigarette as Lot 246 is carried out.

"Lot 246, then. A portrait of a young girl collecting straw - artist unknown; possibly a follower of Jan Vanderschoot."

The picture is settled in an easel and the assistant backs away from it. It's fairly compact; small enough for a man to carry easily, big enough for it to hide most of his body above the waist, and encased in a chipped wooden frame that's seen better days. Probably before the war. Despite this, the painting itself seems to leap from the canvas, outshining everything in the dusty room.

It depicts a young peasant girl in a simple blue and white dress, kneeling, gathering straw and placing it in a pile under her arm. Her task is dull, but her gaze is aimed somewhere far-away from the mundane rural setting - somewhere into an imagined distance behind the artist. Her eyes are blue, her skin clear, her beauty plain.

The auctioneer speaks…

"Recently rediscovered and restored, this work is a fine example of Flemish painting. Although unproven, it has been suggested that this painting - known as 'Straw Girl' - is in fact a missing work by the legendary seventeenth century Flemish artist Jan Vanderschoot."

"A bold claim…" says the old Belgian to his new English friend, who nods sagely.

"Starting at 1000 francs. Am I bid 1000 francs?"

A flurry of hands are raised.

The soldier looks on neutrally as the bids increase.

"My, my," mutters the Belgian, "you would have thought there was no money left in this town."

"People will always appreciate beauty, war or no war," says the Englishman.

"Very true, but for a work with no provenance…"

The Belgian shrugs. The bidding continues and the two strangers sit in silence for a while…

"2000 francs. Do I hear 2100?"

The flurry of hands have receded to a mere couple.

"Looks like it's between these two," says the Belgian.

"So it does," says the soldier, "still, there's always time…"

He extinguishes his cigarette and raises his khaki-clad arm towards the ceiling.

"2200,"

The whole room stares. The soldier winks at his neighbour and taps his round spectacles...

"Must be worth a shot!"

The Belgian raises his eyebrows, the auctioneer nods his head, "Going at 2200..."

The sharp smack of hammer on wood reverberates around the quiet room.

"Sold."

The Englishman grins...

Nobody in the room notices him, probably because he looks so unremarkable, but at the back of the restaurant a thin man in a long overcoat, with curly dark hair and a small moustache, watches on. He takes a notebook and pencil out of his pocket, looks at the painting, then at the Englishman, and slowly begins to write.

5

Siobhan looks at me, incredulous.

"Really? I mean, you're really going to spend your Saturday morning visiting some random old man in hospital?"

"Well, yeah. He did ask for me personally."

"He may well have done, but, well, I just don't see the point."

Neither do I, really. But something I can't quite pinpoint tells me I should go…

"I won't be there long, he probably just wants to say thanks."

"For what?"

"Well, I stayed with him… called the first-aider."

"Wow, you're virtually Florence Nightingale."

"Haha."

"I mean, I do think it's nice, but, we *were* going to the farmers' market..."

Oh yeah, the bloody farmers' market. I think on balance I'd rather visit a confused pensioner on his sickbed...

"I know. Sorry. But I'll meet you there afterwards. We'll get a coffee."

"OK, OK..."

So Siobhan heads off on a circuitous, shop-filled route to the farmers' market and I pull on a coat and scarf and head out to catch a Victoria-bound train from Clapham Junction, just like it's any other work day.

A short tube journey later and I'm crossing Westminster Bridge with St Thomas' Hospital looming in front of me, all grey and drab. The building matches the weather - austere and unwelcoming. A sharp wind whips up the Thames and cuts through my scarf and I trudge onwards, beginning to think that this might have been a mistake. I'm transported right back to the turn of the millennium, when I'd come here to visit my father after his first heart attack.

And his second...

I'd been a new graduate back then, with an upper second in English from Sussex University in my back pocket and my whole life ahead of me. The world should have been at my feet back then, but for several reasons it felt like it was resting on my shoulders instead.

I hear my father's voice in my head as I cross the river...

"So, what have you done since I died, boy? What have you actually achieved?"

It's like he's still here.

I begin to wish I was at the dreaded Saturday farmers' market with Siobhan; grimacing at the price of artisan bread rolls…

I make my way to the hospital reception.

"Hi. I'm here to visit, er, Mr Botham, apparently he's on Alexandra Ward…"

The receptionist smiles sympathetically at me. She probably thinks I'm a grandson, or favourite nephew, and I feel a bit guilty. I'm just a bloke he collapsed on one morning at work. Should I really be here?

She smiles again.

"First floor, then take a left turn and keep going. Alexandra Ward is on the right."

"Cheers, thanks."

When I'm alone on the staircase I take a few deep drags on my e-cigarette. It's probably against hospital policy, but nobody's looking. I find Alexandra Ward, and the feeling that I don't belong here returns.

Come on Charlie, the man asked for you…

I recognise Victor straight away. He's sitting up in bed, sipping what looks like orange juice, with a headphone attached to one ear. The headphone trails into an iPad. He beams at me.

A deathbed this isn't.

"Charlie, my dear old thing!"

"Um, Victor, hello."

"Just listening to the cricket. England are three down already. We never could play spin on the subcontinent. How are you?"

"I'm, er, I'm fine. Thanks."

At this point I notice his pyjamas. They are quite something... a bright yellow colour, they appear to be made of silk and above his left breast are the blue embroidered initials:

V.G.B

I'm no medical expert, but he looks like the healthiest octogenarian - possibly even nonagenarian - that I've ever seen.

"So, er, how are you?" I ask.

"A damn sight better than I was yesterday morning, old boy. Not perfect; I've got cancer, and that's not going anywhere, but I'm actually feeling pretty dashed chipper."

"OK, good."

"Have a seat, my good man."

"Er, thanks."

I lower myself into a hard plastic chair and drag it a respectable distance from his bed. I begin to wonder if I ought to have brought him something. Grapes, perhaps?

"So, how are you?"

"Me? Er, fine."

"Sorry to drag you into this infernal place on a Saturday morning."

"Oh, not a problem. I was only going to the farmers' market."

"A farmers' market? Goodness me," he elongates the words an old Etonian manner... "sounds a bit of a smelly business to me."

31

"It is, but my partner likes it. Apparently there's no point buying jam for a quid in a supermarket when you can pay a man in a wax jacket a tenner for it."

Victor laughs heartily.

"I say. So this partner - would that be a man or a woman? You can never be sure nowadays…"

"Haha, er, a woman. Siobhan."

"Not that it matters, but one likes to know where one stands. Siobhan. Nice name. Is she Irish?"

"No, no, English. From Sussex…"

"Ah, lovely place. What part?"

I'm wary as to how much information to give to this elderly stranger… he seems harmless and friendly, but I've known him roughly 24 hours. I err on the side of caution…

"West Sussex…"

"Ah, the best half!"

"You know it?"

"Spent my childhood in that neck of the woods. Just outside Horsham."

"Ah, I grew up in Shoreham, near Brighton."

"I know it well. So how did you end up working at the National Gallery?"

"Oh, well Siobhan and I moved to London last year. She got a new job, and I started doing this. It's only temporary… I'm really a writer."

I try to convince myself of this from time to time…

"Do you like art, Charlie?"

"Art? Well I don't know much about it really. But since working at the national I've definitely started to appreciate it more."

"That sounds like a yes, to me. You don't need to know about art to appreciate it. Sometimes too much knowledge can spoil things…"

"I suppose that's true…"

"No suppose about it. Think about the greatest artists; Da Vinci, Botticelli, Van Eyck, Turner. Who did they paint *for?* Themselves? The people? Or the experts?"

"Er, I don't know, a bit of each, I guess…"

"Quite possibly. But I imagine the 'experts' would be last on most of their lists."

"Yeah, I suppose you're right… I mean, I'm trying to get into writing film scripts, and I suppose the really successful ones aren't written with the critics in mind."

"Quite. See, I knew you were an artistically minded fellow."

"If you say so…"

"I do, you see, I remember just before I collapsed… on no, damnation!"

He breaks off from his sentence to gesticulate at his iPad, and I assume England have lost another wicket.

"Four down already?"

"I'm afraid so. Cook's out. Now we really are scuppered…"

I shake my head.

"Oh dear, oh dear."

"A cricket fan too, Charlie?"

"I follow it - played it at school..."

"Oh really?"

We embark on a cricketing discussion for the next ten minutes or so, until Victor glances at his gold wristwatch and tuts at the time.

"Well my good chap, one of the lovely nurses will be round soon to check up on me, forcibly remove some more blood, that sort of thing. I'd better let you get on to your... farming market."

"Yes, I suppose I should be going..."

Victor removes his earphones and places his iPad to one side.

"I'm glad you came today Charlie, because I did want to thank you. It's a scary business, collapsing in public. You never really get used to it. But you were jolly good to me."

"No problem," I say "it was a pleasure to meet you, and I'm glad you're doing better..."

Despite the cancer...

I bid him farewell and make my way out of the hospital, dragging on my e-cigarette as I descend the stairs.

I carry on puffing as I leave the building and walk through the hospital grounds towards the main road. As I cross the carpark I'm aware of a vehicle looming behind me. I turn and glance over my shoulder and see a people-carrier of some description; shiny, black and obscenely big. The driver is wearing dark glasses, a flat cap and a scarf, and waves me across with a leather-gloved hand.

I wave back and step out in front of him, but instead of slowing the driver speeds up, just enough to make me rush to get across his path. I don't quite make it with my dignity intact. Or my balance...

One foot hits the other and I stumble. The wing mirror clips my shoulder as the vehicle passes and I'm thrown spinning into a heap on the concrete. My e-cigarette spins away from me across the hard floor.

"For fuck's sake!" I yell at the 4x4, but the driver doesn't even look back. I watch as it turns onto the main road, speeding away without even indicating. I catch another glimpse of the driver; behind a cap, glasses and scarf he could be anyone. But something about the angle of the nose and chin nags at me, like I've seen him before, somewhere, sometime…

I drag myself to my feet, rescue my e-cig from the floor and head back across the river towards the tube. It's only when I'm finally sat on a Circle Line train that I look down at my leg…

There's a dark red stain seeping through my jeans, and blood is running down my leg from a gash on my knee.

6

So, I don't go to the farmers' market.

Instead I head back to the flat and scrape the dried blood off my leg. Then I wash the cut and cover it in a trio of sticking plasters, before making coffee and bacon as a peace offering for Siobhan.

She arrives home just after one.

"Where did you get to?" She asks.

"Sorry, but I was in the hospital longer than expected," I lie. "He was a confused old chap, so I hung around a bit to humour him."

"Well, aren't you good?"

"I thought the market would be winding down a bit, so I came home to make you lunch."

I gesture towards the frying bacon.

"Mmm, lovely."

She kisses me. The bacon has worked its magic…

"Well as luck would have it..." she continues, "there was a lovely selection of artisan olive rolls down there today. I picked up a few bags full."

"Great," I say, deciding not to enquire about the cost.

"So, did you see the email from Tim?" she says, heading back across the kitchen.

"Oh, no," I reply. I haven't checked my emails so far today. It's not a typical Saturday morning activity for me... unlike Siobhan, who seems surgically attached to her inbox, even on her days off.

"Well he's coming to London next weekend... wants to meet up for drinks on Sunday afternoon."

"Oh, cool," I say. Tim Anderson - or Major Tim - to give him his proper title, is an old university friend. His infrequent visits home are always good for the spirit, if not for the liver. Months of dusty abstinence in places like Afghanistan means he usually arrives back in England with a hell of a thirst on him and on the lookout for someone to quench it with. Still, he's a good laugh, and next weekend suddenly looks like it could be a lot more lively than usual...

"Well, I'm up for it, if you are?"

"Yes, I suppose, but it can't be a late one. Work on Monday."

Work for Siobhan means a half six alarm clock, but the National Gallery doesn't open till ten...

That's almost a lie-in.

"I'll email him back and say yes."

"OK. Great."

"Cool."

I take a sip of coffee and sit down at the kitchen table. As I lower myself into the chair my knee twinges and a sharp sensation shoots up my thigh. It feels as though I've re-opened the cut just by sitting down.

"Ah, shit!" I say, clutching my knee."

Siobhan frowns at me.

"You alright?"

"Er, yeah. Fine."

"Didn't sound it."

"No, it's OK, honest. I just fell up the stairs at the hospital, like a bloody moron. Luckily no-one saw. Think I've bruised my knee a bit."

It's not unusual for me to be accident prone, so she simply rolls her eyes and says no more. I sigh with silent relief. I really don't want to worry her with the story of the black 4X4, and anyway, it probably isn't anything worth worrying about anyway. Just another incident of micro-aggressive driving in a city that's full of hot-headed motorists.

But underneath this, there's a feeling I can't quite shake.

For some reason, I feel as if I've been given a warning....

7

(Nine days later…)

One minute there's nothing but oblivion. The next, the blackness is pierced by an insistent digital drone.

BEEP. BEEP. BEEEEEP.

I stir slowly to life. I'm splayed diagonally across an empty bed and the eight o'clock alarm is going off. It's Monday morning. My mouth feels like a cave in which something has died slowly of nicotine poisoning. My head feels like I've spent the previous evening being punched in the temples by a boxer of a far higher weight division. And my neck is worryingly stiff. I make the diagnosis immediately: this is a hangover.

A bad one…

I work out that I've got two hours in which to shower, dress and make my way to work. So what do I do?

Well of course, I sleep for another forty minutes.

Fragments of the previous evening flash through my mind as I lie in a semi-conscious stupor…

I remember Siobhan heading home at around 7pm, by which time Tim and I were onto at least our fifth pints. Maybe sixth.

I remember telling Tim that it might be a good idea to order some food, and him coming back from the bar with another bottle of red wine instead. I also remember buying a packet of fags from a shop on the way to yet another pub, and Tim suggesting we sit under a heater in the garden... so we could have a smoke.

Those fags are now a crumpled, empty packet on my bedroom floor...

I can also vaguely recall getting some food after all the pubs shut - a burger, from a greasy catering van - and gallons of tomato sauce oozing out all over one of my nicest shirts as I bit into it.

I don't remember anything else.

I glance at the clock again. It's too late to have a shower, so I get out of bed, stagger into the bathroom and splash cold water all over my face. Then I coat myself in toxic amounts of deodorant, dress quickly and head off towards the station.

Get through the day. Just get through the day, then you can sleep.

A walk and a nauseating train journey and I'm heading through the doors of the National Gallery. I look at my watch.

10:17

Almost twenty minutes late...

Hopefully no-one will notice.

*

Sometime later, I'm aware of my shoulders being gently shaken by someone who's standing in front of me. I have absolutely no idea where I am, but I appear to have just woken from a dream in which a fleet of tanks were advancing in my direction, firing jars of jam at me as I floundered helplessly from left to right.

I rub my eyes and squint in confusion at the scene in front of me. A man in a dark suit is peering at me with a look of unvarnished disgust on his blurry face. Behind him, a crowd of tourists are staring at me in amusement. Slowly, the man in the suit comes into focus. It's Martin, my supervisor; I recognise his blotchy face and collared jowls.

I'm at work, and I've no idea how long I've been asleep.

"Oh, er sorry Martin."

He stares at me.

"How long was I asleep?" I ask, straightening myself up.

"About five months," he says, and storms away.

*

It's not surprising, really, that I'm called into his office later in the afternoon. I trudge down the corridor slowly, resigned…

He is sitting behind his desk next to a woman whose name I can't recall, but I know she's something to do with human resources.

My heart sinks.

Martin has always been a bit red in the face, but right now he's puce.

"Sit down," he says.

"Er, thanks."

"I've asked Julie from Human Resources to be here for this…"

Oh Christ.

Julie gives me some HR spiel which goes straight over my hungover head. Instead I focus on Nelson on top of his column, which I can just make out through the high window. When she's finished, Martin begins:

"Can you explain why you fell asleep at your post this morning?"

"Er, I was very tired. I was up late, doing a writing job…"

"We've had several reports that you came in smelling very strongly of alcohol…" Martin cuts me off.

"Oh."

"Do you know how long you were asleep?"

"Not exactly."

"Over ten minutes. And, while you were incapacitated, a child smeared ice cream on a Hans Holbein."

"Oh no, which one?"

"For God's sake. Does it matter which painting, Charlie? They're all priceless."

"No," I reply, "which ice-cream?"

"Sorry?"

Martin glances at Julie then back at me. He genuinely looks as though he wants to kill me, but by now I'm pretty certain I'm going to be sacked anyway, so I decide to have some fun.

"I mean, if we're talking about The Ambassadors, a mint choc chip could quite easily blend into the background, but something like a vanilla 99 might be harder to disguise."

Martin fiddles with his collar and Julie writes something down.

"Is that supposed to be funny?" he says.

"Well, sort of pithy I suppose…"

"Well here's something else 'pithy'. Have you checked Twitter this afternoon?"

Twitter?

"Um, well no…"

"There's something on it you might be interested in, being a man au fait with social media. A link to a video, posted this morning…"

He takes out a smartphone.

"It shows you, Charlie, asleep in the corner of the room whilst tourists come and go, sniggering as you snore."

"Er, what?"

"All allowed to roam within touching distance of priceless works of art while the gallery assistant snores. Do you know how bloody ridiculous this makes us look?"

He glances at Julie, probably hoping she hasn't noted down his swear word…

"And so far this little video has been shared six hundred and twenty-seven times."

"Er, right," I say.

"Oh, no, my mistake, six hundred and twenty-eight."

I carefully examine my palm, then look back up at Nelson.

"Still, no such thing as bad publicity and all that."

"Enough, Charlie. This is simply unacceptable. Julie informs me that you have still not completed your six months' probationary period, and as a result we have no choice but to terminate your contract forthwith."

I nod slowly.

Can't really blame him, to be honest...

8

So I walk out of the National Gallery as an unemployed man. It's almost a relief. I was beginning to get tied down there anyway... this could be a new start. A chance to do some more work on the screenplay, and find a more rewarding job...

Yeah, it's a good thing.

The only thing that worries me is Siobhan. She's not going to be overjoyed about being the sole payer of the mortgage once again. Even though she can afford it...

I watch the twitter video on the train home. Well, why not? It's a moment of fame for Charlie Marks - albeit not for the kind of reason I'd like. It starts with a shaky camera panning around the gallery. Sniggers can be heard as it focuses on me in my chair, dead to the world, my head back on my shoulder, mouth gaping, producing snores that could impact upon the richter scale.

It's not entirely flattering, but I'm fairly certain I can't be identified.

I arrive back in Battersea about five and kill the time until Siobhan gets home in The Mason's Arms - soothing my hangover with ale and thinking of a way to break the news of my sacking. I walk in the door of the flat a few minutes before her and I still haven't come up with anything…

"Hello?"

"Evening love."

I'm sitting casually on the sofa now, like I've just got in from a hard day's work… she looks unusually excited for a Monday evening. She grins; it's a genuine grin, going from side to side of her straw-coloured bobbed hair. The smile I fell in love with…

I'm not sure how to tell her.

In the event, I don't have to… she tells me.

"I've just had some amazing news!"

"Eh?"

She throws her bag onto the floor, jumps next to me as I sit stunned on the sofa and gives me a big kiss.

"So, it's like this... I'm going to California!"

"You're, er, doing what?"

"I'm going to California."

"Yeah, I got that much."

"I'm going to Cali-bloody-fornia. Tomorrow!"

"Er, you're what?"

She tells me the full details in an outpouring of excited words. But to cut a long story short-ish, the new British movie she's been leading the marketing for is to get a big American premier, and she's been asked to go over to the states to help oversee the publicity campaign.

It's fab news, for her, and to be honest, quite timely news for me.

"Oh, my goodness, that's amazing!" I say.

"Are you sure it's amazing? I mean, I'm going to be away for two weeks…"

"Yes," I say, suddenly excited, "It's a brilliant opportunity for you - just think of all the contacts you could make out there. And a fortnight isn't long. I'll be fine here on my own. I'll cope… won't burn the place down!"

She grins and throws her arms around me, and I grin too, but for another reason. And as I hug her all I can think is…

Two weeks, Charlie. You've got two weeks to find another job and it'll all turn out fine.

It will all be fine…

9

My first day back in the world of unemployment begins with an unpleasantly early start. I accompany Siobhan on the train down to Gatwick airport, mainly for the reason of helping carry the large suitcase she packed hastily last night. I help her drag it into the terminal building and wait while she checks in. Then it's time to say goodbye.

"I'll miss you," she says.

It's nice to hear her say it. It's been a source of growing irritation to me over the last few months that Siobhan seems to be investing far more time and energy into work than in our relationship. But I haven't said anything to her yet. I've just moped and bitched inwardly. I suddenly get a pang of guilt.

"I'll miss you too."

"Love you."

"Love you too."

She throws her arms around me and I hug her back.

OK Charlie, you really need to find a job in the next two weeks.

"Have a good flight."

"I'll phone you when I land. If it's not too late for you."

I kiss her goodbye again and try to fight off mental images of her at pool parties with various Hollywood moguls as I sleep in cold Battersea. I shake off the thoughts and head in the direction of the nearest coffee shop. As I sit down with my latte I idly check my email inbox to see if any of the job sites I've signed up for have anything to offer. But the first message I see is from a name I don't recognise…

Mallender-Hussain Solicitors: Meeting Request

I tap to open it, half expecting it to be spam…

Dear Mr Marks

I trust you are well. Please let me know when it would be convenient for us to meet to discuss a matter which might be of interest to you. Do feel free to telephone me on the number below.

Yours sincerely,

Mr B. Hussain

Mallender-Hussain Solicitors

I check the email several times in a state of confusion, racking my sleep-deprived brain to come up with a reason why a solicitor might be demanding an audience with me. I'm not married, so divorce proceedings are out of the question. Siobhan takes care of most things relating to the mortgage. My parents are both dead, and I have no other elderly relatives that I know of who might have suddenly popped their clogs, leaving me a considerable windfall. I re-read the email, seriously considering that it might have been sent to me in error.

Then it hits me.

Lennie…

But… that was all sorted out legally, years ago, for good. Or so I thought…

In most other circumstances I would have deleted Mr B Hussain's email as some sort of phishing scam, but the thought that it might be somehow related to Lennie makes me read it again, and the fact that I am unemployed and at a loose-end makes me decide to follow it up.

After all, what have I got to lose?

I email him back, suggesting that this afternoon might be a good time…

Just minutes later I get a reply from a Miss Sunita Sharma, Mr Hussain's assistant.

Mr Hussain would be pleased to meet you today, would 3pm suit you?

10

Mallender-Hussain Solicitors' offices aren't quite as grand as the picture I've created in my head. You can't blame me, as the address I look up is in Marylebone and a quick Google maps check tells me that it's round the corner from Baker Street. In reality however Mr Hussain's offices appear to comprise a couple of rooms above a cafe in what must be one of central-London's quieter backstreets.

I press the buzzer next to the sober black door and am invited in. I make my way up a narrow staircase and find the entrance to Mallender-Hussain. The wooden door has a distinctly 1970s feel to it, right down to the wire grid on the window and the gold name-plate. It's all very smart and well-maintained, but a little bit old-school. I peer through the little window and see a serious, dark-haired young lady peering at a computer screen above her spectacles. Sunita Sharma, I presume.

My presumption is correct. She introduces herself as she lets me in and shakes my hand. Hers is small and smooth. She smiles and asks me to sit while she buzzes through to Mr Hussain.

"Benedict, I have Mr Marks here to see you."

"Super, send him through," comes the silky reply.

I enter Mr Hussain's office and am again struck by the 1970s vibe. Under my feet is a thick beige carpet and surrounding me is dark green wallpaper with orange trim. But the most well-preserved 70s artefact in the room is Mr Hussain himself. He is dressed in a smart blue suit coupled with a yellow kipper tie. His hair is swept-back and flecked with silver, as is his luxurious moustache. He greets me warmly with a strong handshake.

"Ah, nice to finally meet you Mr Marks!"

Finally? You only emailed me this morning…

"You too."

"Please, take a seat."

I settle into a soft leather chair.

"Now, let's get down to brass ticks. I expect you must be wondering why I asked to see you, yes?"

"Yes, you could say that…"

"It concerns a client of mine. A long-standing client, by the name of Botham."

I have to think for a minute. Botham? As in Victor? I've all but forgotten about the old man I met last Saturday, what with all the drama about losing my job and seeing Siobhan off on her visit to the states.

"Oh, Mr Botham?" I stammer, "I thought this might be about Lennie..."

"Who's Lennie, Mr Marks?"

"Oh, er, don't worry. Not important."

But Victor Botham is, what could he possibly want from me that would involve a solicitor?

Mr Hussain answers my question...

"If you haven't heard already, then I am sorry to be the bringer of bad news. But Mr Botham passed away on Sunday evening after a long battle with cancer."

"Bloody hell. He's died? But he looked so healthy when I saw him on Saturday."

A silly comment, to be honest.

"He was a proud man, Mr Marks, and as an old soldier, particularly adept at hiding any discomfort. But he was a very ill man, nonetheless."

"Oh dear, he just looked so... healthy," I repeat.

"Nevertheless, he is dead, and this is where you come in, Mr Marks."

"Me?"

"Yes," says Mr Hussain in a matter-of-fact way, opening up a blue folder and retrieving a single piece of paper.

He continues:

"My client's will was mostly straightforward. As one would expect, Mr Botham's assorted children were the main beneficiaries."

I nod. *Assorted children?* I get images of an entire cricket team.

"He also left a generous amount to some favoured charities. The Lord's Taverners, among others. But there was one particular bequest for you, Mr Marks."

"Me?"

"Yes you," says Hussain, peering up at me over the paper. "Surprised?"

"A bit, yeah. I only met the man last week."

"Well I can't speak for him, particularly now he is dead. All I can say is that this particular item is now your legal property. To do with as you please."

"OK, right. And, er, what is it?"

"A painting, Mr Marks."

"A painting?"

"Indeed."

"Well, er, thanks. So, is this painting here?"

Mr Hussain shakes his head.

"It is not. The painting is currently located in a safe deposit box in a facility in Marylebone. Sunita has all the details for you."

"Right, OK. So I just go and get it?"

"You can do as you wish, Mr Marks. The painting is yours."

"Great," I say, standing to leave. "So, like, is there anything else you can tell me about this painting?"

"Anything else? Well, let me see" says Hussain, looking back at the paper.

"No, well except for the name."

"The name?"

"Yes. Apparently the painting is called Straw Girl."

11

Antwerp, Belgium, 1945

Two men in British army uniforms sit at a chipped wooden table in the spartan kitchen of a house which has been requisitioned to accommodate allied officers. One man is wiry and lean with slightly longer than regulation blond hair and a neat pencil moustache. He wears thin round spectacles, above which he eyes the backgammon board...

The other man is taller, with dark hair and a thicker moustache. At first glance, he looks more like a British army officer would be expected to look, at least in comparison to his backgammon opponent. He sits upright.

"Your move."

The blond man grabs the dice and spins them out of the back of his hand with a theatrical flourish. They settle almost instantly. Two sixes.

The tall man rolls his eyes.

"I don't know how the hell you do it, Vic," he smiles.

"It's all in the wrist," smiles the blond man as he rearranges his pieces.

Behind the two men, propped against the mantle-piece, sits a painting of a young girl. She is collecting straw and is looking over her shoulder into some unseen distance as she works. Underneath her blond curls, two bright blue eyes seem to focus intently on the men's game.

'Thud, thud...'

An insistent beating on the door causes the game to stop. The blond man flicks ash into the fire and looks at his companion.

The beating gets louder, and is soon accompanied by the groaning and snapping of wood.

"What the hell?"

The tall Englishman grabs his gun. The blond one stubs out his cigarette and also goes for his weapon, but it's sitting on the sideboard, out of reach. Before he can grab it the door is smashed open and a trio of dark-clad figures swarm into the room. At the front is a thin man in a long leather overcoat with tight, curly hair. He holds a pistol in front of him and aims it at the unarmed blond Englishman.

"Get out of here," says the Englishman, but the thin man simply smiles, and cracks him around the jaw with the butt of his gun, sending him sprawling into the fireplace. Outnumbered, the tall Englishman lowers his gun.

"Take the painting," says the thin man in a German accent, and his two companions stride towards the painting and lift it up. The blond man stares up, blood running from his chin.

"For God's sake be careful with that" he says.

The thin German smiles.

"I shall be."

The blond man wipes some blood away and keeps his eyes trained on the German, who smiles back through narrow eyes.

"It's been a pleasure doing business with you."

"Who in hell are you?" asks the taller Englishman.

The tall German smiles again.

"Just think of me as 'the rightful owner'. Thank you, gentlemen. It's been a pleasure."

His accomplices wrap the painting in a plain brown sack and pass it to him. He tucks it under his arms, takes one last look around the room and walks away.

12

I've never been to a safe deposit facility in my life. I've never needed to. In fact, if it hadn't been for heist movies, I probably wouldn't have been aware of their existence. But there's a first time for everything.

I find Capital Safe Deposits fairly quickly thanks to Google maps. It's only a short walk from Mr Hussain's office, and within five minutes I'm staring at an unassuming front door, sandwiched between a Tesco Express store and a post office.

Somewhat hesitantly, I make my way inside…

It all goes weirdly smoothly. I show the man behind the desk my papers from Sunita along with some ID and am swiftly led down towards the vault by two other employees - a large middle-aged man and a younger woman. Apparently this is company policy. We pass through an almost comically thick metal door; like something out of a Bond film, and I'm surrounded by walls of shiny metal doors of varying sizes - some barely large enough to contain a wallet, and some quite bigger…

The man looks at his card.

"OK sir, number 2208, just over here."

I swallow and follow him. All of a sudden my mouth feels dry; I wonder exactly what I've stumbled into, and what riches might be contained in all the little metal boxes around me. Gold? Jewels? Cash?

The man opens one of the larger, wider boxes and stands to one side, then the woman speaks for the first time...

"Would you like some privacy sir? We have a room you can use."

"Er, no, you're alright thanks."

The man and woman step back and look away regardless, and I slowly pull the painting out of the box. It's heavy, but fairly easy to lift, and wrapped in brown paper and bubble wrap. Eager to see my new possession, I take my keys from my back pocket and start hacking at the bubble wrap. The male member of staff approaches.

"Please, sir, allow me."

He produces a box cutter and carefully makes an incision along the bubble wrap. I tear off the brown paper and colour slowly seeps from underneath.

Staring up at me is a wide-eyed blonde girl kneeling in a field with a bunch of straw under her arm. Her eyes shine out of the painting to meet mine and light surrounds me, almost as though someone has flicked a switch in the basement. I'm momentarily lost for words, thoughts… I run my hand gently along the bumpy canvas. The painting is beautiful, and I can't quite grasp what I have done to deserve being its new owner.

I look dumbly at the two staff.

"So, er, am I free to take this?"

"Sir, this is your property," says the woman. "Of course, we would advise you continue to store it here, however, the year's storage plan that the previous owner purchased is due to expire in a few days' time."

"OK, and, how much would it cost me to renew it?"

This is our largest box size sir, so it would be just over £2500 for the year.

I gulp and try not to look too shocked.

"It's OK, I'll take it with me. Thanks."

"As you wish, sir."

I fumble around with the ripped and crumpled paper and bubble wrap, trying to cover the painting back up. I think I notice the man glance at the woman. I don't think this is the kind of behaviour they usually witness in the vault…

"Sir, we may have something to help you wrap it in," says the woman. The man disappears and comes back with a black bin liner and some tape. With their help we re-attach the bubble wrap as neatly as possible and shuffle the package inside the bin liner. When we're done the man passes the painting back to me.

"Are you parked nearby, sir? Perhaps we could help carry it to your car?"

"Car? No thanks, I'm getting the Jubilee Line."

The two members of staff exchange another glance and show me up the stairs and out of the building. I walk off into what is now a sunny, cold winter morning with a newly-acquired canvas under my arm and head towards the nearest tube station.

13

For the first time in my life, I find myself carrying a painting wrapped in a bin liner home on public transport.

It hadn't seemed particularly heavy when I picked it up at the safe deposit, but, by the time I've changed at Green Park and Victoria Station and arrived back in Battersea, the thing's started to feel like it weighs a bloody ton.

I carry 'Straw Girl' up the stairs into the flat and plonk her next to the TV with a sigh of relief. Then I sit down and ponder what, exactly, has just happened, and wonder whether it's too early in the day to pour myself a scotch...

Instead I open my laptop and log onto my emails and remind myself of Mr Hussain's phone number. I've been given a gift, after all, and it's only polite to say thank-you. That's the way I was brought up...

But in this case I owe my thanks to a dead man...

I dial. A few seconds' ringing follows, then a click.

"Hello, Mallender-Hussain…"

Sunita…

"Oh, er, hi, is Mr Hussain there?"

"I'll try his line, who shall I say is calling?"

"Mr Marks. Charlie…"

There's a slight pause, and when Sunita speaks I detect the slightest hint of concern in her voice…

"Oh, Mr Marks, all OK?" she says quietly.

"Yes, fine thanks."

"Good. I'll put you through."

"Thanks."

"Hello Mr Marks" comes Hussain's.

"Oh hi,"

"Everything OK?"

"Yes, fine. I just, well, I meant to ask when I saw you earlier, but when is Mr Botham's funeral taking place? I'd like to go along and pay my respects."

There's a pause.

"Hello? Mr Hussain?"

Eventually he answers.

"The funeral? Well that has taken place already Mr Marks. A small family affair on Monday afternoon. It all went very well."

"Oh, I see."

That was quick…

"In that case, perhaps you could let me know where Mr Botham's been buried? I would like to pay my respects, and say thanks for my gift."

Hussain replies quickly.

"He was cremated Mr Marks, in the small village he grew up in. I believe that the family are in the process of deciding what to do with the ashes. I'm sorry I can't give you any more information, now if you'll excuse me, I have a client I need to see."

"OK, thanks anyway."

Mr Hussain clicks the phone down and I'm left staring at the bin-bag clad painting. I remove it from its packaging and admire it again. It really is beautiful. It's simple, on the surface at least; the only colours are the blue of the sky and the girl's dress and eyes, the green of the field, the gold of her hair and the straw and the white of the clouds, but each glance at the canvas reveals a new detail, like the tiny woolly sheep dotted on the horizon.

Still, pretty as it is, I'm fairly certain the painting is worthless. If there was any monetary value to it, Mr Botham would surely have left it to one of his 'assorted children', not to a man he barely knew... It must be a copy or something.

Still, copy or not, I make sure it's propped up safely before I put my coat back on and head out to the Mason's Arms for a pie and a couple of pints.

*

As it turns out, I enjoy more than a couple of pints in the pub, and by the time I order a pie I'm told the kitchen has shut, so I go for a woozy late-night walk to the nearest chip shop for a dubious burger.

It's after ten when I get back to the flat. I look at the painting of Straw Girl - still safely propped up against the wall, flick the TV on and, sit down and immediately fall into a fairly deep sleep.

I have no idea what time it is when the sound of the intercom pierces my subconscious brain. I wake with a start and walk woozily over to the entry buzzer - fully expecting it to be local youths making a nuisance of themselves.

It isn't...

I pick up the handset and speak gruffly into it.

"Who's there?"

The reply comes in a calm female voice that I vaguely recognise.

"Mr Marks, sorry to bother you so late. My name is Miss Sharma, I met you earlier, at Mallender-Hussain's offices."

"Sunita?"

"Yes. May I talk with you?"

"Er, yeah, sure, I'll buzz you in."

I glance around at the flat. There are two empty crisps bags and a half-drunk tin of lager on the coffee table and various items of clothing strewn across the leather sofas. Across the room the smart kitchen tops are littered with toast-crumbs and soiled plates. I wasn't really expecting guests, and I decide it's too late to tidy up.

I do, however, stuff the crisp bags into my jean pockets. Sunita knocks on the door and my sleepy brain racks back over the day, trying to make sense of what's happened and what she might want.

"Oh, hi, er, Miss Sharma" I mumble, "do come in."

She is standing in the doorway in a cream overcoat and dark suit. Away from her desk she seems even more petite, and she looks up at me with a serious expression in her dark brown eyes.

"Hello again, Mr Marks."

"Hi, how are you?"

"I'm well, thank you, but sorry to bother you at this time of night."

"No worries… would you like to come in?"

"Thank you."

Sunita follows me into the flat and glances around her. She stands very still, seemingly unsure where she should place herself.

"Er, would you like a drink?"

"No, thanks."

She is now looking directly at the Straw Girl painting. I see her hands trembling…

"Actually, yes, I will have a water. Thank you."

I head to the kitchen and find a clean glass which I fill. I am aware of Sunita moving closer to Straw Girl, inspecting it.

"All OK?"

I pass her the water. She takes the smallest sip and places it on the coffee table, still staring at the painting.

"Not really, Mr Marks."

"Oh, right."

"It's the painting, you see. It concerns me that you have it in your flat."

"It concerns you? Why?"

She closes her eyes and fiddles with a button on her coat.

"I can't say. I shouldn't be here, you know. This isn't part of my job role. But someone needs to say this to you."

"Say what?"

"Don't keep the painting in your flat, Mr Marks. Take it back to the safe deposit company. As soon as possible."

I stare at her, trying to make sense of what she's saying through a haze of beer and disturbed sleep.

"Why? Is it... is it worth something then?"

"I've already said too much. Just please, take my advice."

"But it must be worth something, if you think I should take it back to the safe place?"

"I'm not an art expert, Mr Marks."

"Then why are you saying this?"

"I don't know. I know someone has to, that's all."

"But, but I can't take it back to that place. They charge far too much."

"OK. Anywhere then. Please, just take my advice and get it out of your flat."

"OK, if you say so." I attempt to use some charm… "Are you sure you don't want to tell me why?" I ask, winking.

It's clearly far too late for charm... She fixes me with an icy stare.

"I can't."

"OK, well, er, thanks for the advice. You sure I can't make you a coffee?"

"No. I really must go. But before I do, take this…"

She produces a white envelope from her bag.

"I was going to post it tomorrow from work, but, seeing as I was coming here, you can have it now."

"Oh, cheers."

I take the envelope.

"Goodnight Mr Marks."

Sunita turns towards the door. I follow and open it for her.

"Please, call me Charlie."

"OK, goodnight, Charlie."

"Night..."

She walks briskly down the hallway and I slam the door after her, bolting it and sliding the chain in place. Then I slump down on the sofa and tear open the envelope...

The first thing that flutters out is a cheque. It hovers in the air and lands on my lap. I turn it up the right way…

The account holder is Mallender-Hussain Ltd. Written in block biro capitals are the words: *PAY MR CHARLES MARKS TWO THOUSAND POUNDS ONLY.*

I should be happy that people appear to keep giving me things like money and paintings, but in reality I just feel a rising sense of unease. This isn't helped by the document I fish out of the envelope next.

It's a letter…

14

Mr V. C Botham
Marylebone, London
January 2019

My Dearest Charlie,

I'm ever-so sorry if this all seems a bit cloak and dagger, like something out of a spy novel that one might pick up at the airport, but here goes: If you are reading this letter, it will mean I have finally succumbed to the darned cancer that has blighted my later years. It is a shame our acquaintance was ever-so brief.

My solicitor, Mr Hussain, will have been in touch to arrange the transfer of my bequest to you, and I expect that the painting known as Straw Girl will be now be in your possession.

You may think it a little odd that I should choose to leave the painting to you, but allow me to explain myself...

Straw Girl first came into my possession in the last days of World War Two, when I was serving in the British army in Antwerp. I have long believed it to be an original work by the Flemish painter Jan Vanderschoot, however I have never been able to prove this conclusively. Now, alas, I will never be able to do so.

I wanted to thank you for the way you treated me when I collapsed in the National Gallery. I thought Straw Girl would be an ideal way to express my gratitude. I have collected many works of art throughout my life - many worth considerable sums of money - and these have been divided between my children. But Straw Girl, without any proven provenance, is currently as good as worthless. I hoped that with your contacts at the National Gallery you might be able to succeed where I have failed and prove this painting to be a genuine old master. Should you achieve this, the financial rewards could be vast.

To aid you in your research and to cover your expenses I have included a cheque for a small amount.

Of course, your efforts may prove fruitless. Straw Girl might turn out to be a substandard copy, but something inside me has always told me the opposite. This is a very special painting, and it deserves a champion. I believe that person could be you. I hope I am right, but if not, I hope you enjoy her anyway.

Wishing you continued health and happiness.

Yours sincerely,

Victor.

I'm too tired to even process the letter properly, let alone get the painting out of my flat. But still, I decide I'd rather not let it out of my sight for too long. I slip the chain onto the front door lock and drag my blanket through to the sofa. I down the rest of my lager, crawl into the blanket and sleep fitfully, with one eye on the painting, which may or may not be worth a small fortune.

I wake up when the winter sun penetrates the thin curtains. It's early, and Straw Girl is still in its place next to the TV. I rub my eyes and open my laptop. Minutes later I've located a self-storage facility a few minutes away in Battersea. It's not the kind with an underground vault and 2-foot thick metal doors, but something tells me it's going to be a lot cheaper. I search for a quote against their smallest size and am pleased to see it come back as a more manageable 12.99 a week. I select the four-week option, which I guess should be long enough for me to sort out what I'm going to do with the painting, and close my laptop, before heading to the kitchen to make a strong coffee.

After a welcome caffeine hit I wrap Straw Girl up in the tattered remains of the bubble wrap and slip it back inside the bin liner. I cover the package with packing tape and stand back to look at my handiwork. It looks a bloody mess. I turn back to the laptop and google 'how to store paintings'. I am presented with a jumble of information about temperature, humidity control and other ways to avoid damage. It's all too much to process, but I decide another layer of protection isn't going to do any harm.

I head to the bedroom and rifle through my wardrobe. I have the grand total of two suits. One from the high street and a slightly more expensive one which mainly gets dusted off for weddings. This one is privileged enough to be kept in a suit bag, but not any longer. I slip it out of the bag, dump it on the bed and use the bag to wrap up my new most valuable possession. Straw Girl.

Is this for real? I ask the inanimate package. *Are you really going to make me my fortune?*

Probably not. I mean, things don't tend to happen like that. Not for me, at least. You don't suddenly become a *lucky person* after being the polar opposite for 38 years. Still, the optimist in me hasn't entirely given up… I quickly find myself thinking about a recent news story about the rediscovered da Vinci painting which sold at auction for over 400 million dollars. Jan Vanderschoot is not da Vinci, but I'm vaguely aware of the name, and wonder how much a newly discovered work of his could go for...

Even if it's only a tiny fraction of a da Vinci, that could still be a fortune...

Enough for big cars, foreign holidays, swimming pools, champagne and all the other clichés I can think of....

With this rather vulgar thought in mind I pick up the suit bag as carefully as I can, let myself out of the flat and start the walk to the storage facility.

As I walk through the South London streets I'm painfully aware that I'm carrying a cargo which - in my wildly over-excited mind - could be worth millions of pounds. But the weekday morning shoppers I pass have no idea about this. All they see is a slightly dishevelled man carrying a grey suit bag, emblazoned with the phrase 'Marks and Spencer Men'. I'm absolutely sure that not one of them gives it a second glance...

*

It all goes according to plan at the storage depot, but once the yellow door to Starw Girl's box closes I feel strangely reluctant to walk away from her. Despite Sunita's warnings, I'd probably prefer it if she was still propped up next to my telly. But I tell myself this is for the best, and a glance up at the myriad CCTV cameras in every corner makes me feel a bit better.

My thoughts immediately turn to food, and I arrive back at the flat after a stop for a greasy breakfast. Nothing seems unusual at first. The front door is closed, and I open it to access the shared staircase.

It's here that the first sign of something being wrong greets me; a smudged black handprint on the recently-painted clean white of the walls. I thank my lucky stars that Siobhan's in California, and hope that the maintenance company can sort it out before she returns.

I round the corner at the top of the stairs and reach for my keys to open the door, but there's no need. It's already ajar.

"Hello?" I call. "Siob?"

No answer.

I pull the door fully open. It takes a few seconds for me to fully comprehend the scene in front of me.

It's chaos…

Every drawer and cupboard is open. Everything that should be in a drawer or cupboard is strewn across the floor, hurled across the bed or thrown across upturned chairs and tables. The TV is on its back, pictures have been torn from the wall and the rug up-ended. And yet, amongst all this chaos, my eyes are drawn straight to our cream leather sofa; smeared on the back is another angry black handprint.

15

Devon Lamb descends the steps from the National Gallery onto Trafalgar Square and the cold wind sends her hair flying in every possible direction. She groans, digs a bobble hat out of her bag and stuffs it down over her curly mop. Raindrops speckle her glasses, so she takes them off, wipes them over and carries on towards the bus stop.

As she settles down in a seat on the top deck she retrieves a small piece of notepaper from her jacket pocket. It has the name 'Tom' scrawled on it in biro, alongside a phone number.

It had been given to her at lunchtime by a young man - Tom, apparently - who recently started working in the gift shop. He'd sat on the same table as her in the canteen over lunch; as he seemed to be doing a lot recently, and made the usual inane attempts at small talk, which she'd batted away politely but firmly. But this time he'd finished the conversation by asking if she fancied "getting a drink sometime."

Surprised, she'd said maybe, and he'd been quick to pass her his name and number...

But... the gift shop? Really?

No thanks, Tom...

It's not as if Devon doesn't want a partner. She does. But she wants it in an abstract, far-off way... in the same way she wants a little cottage by the sea, with a cat, and a room she can use as a library.

In the future.

There might be a man sharing that cottage with her, in the future, but he's not going to be someone like Tom, with a hipster beard and a part-time folk band. He'll be someone older than Tom and considerably more intelligent; like the historian Dan Snow, or the documentary-maker Louis Theroux.

She tries to imagine her life with someone like Tom. He'd be waiting for her in her tiny flat, strumming an acoustic guitar, making a mess in the kitchen, spilling craft lager all over her art books.

Eww, no. Devon is perfectly happy as she is right now. Maybe there'll be room for a Louis or a Dan in the future, but there certainly isn't room for a Tom in the present.

She tears the scrap of paper into four bits and pokes them out of the bus window, watching as they're blown violently across the wintry streets of south London.

She thinks no more about the note. Instead, she takes a book out of her bag. It's an art book, of course.

A history of Flemish painting.

Satisfied, she begins to read.

16

I've barely started to get the flat straight when a video call from Siobhan comes through. She's managed to choose the worst possible time. The TV is still on the floor, there are several pictures next to it which need to be put back on the wall, and there's still a bloody great handprint on the back of the sofa. That might take some explaining… So instead of answering the call, I place one of the cushions back onto the sofa and stick my phone underneath it. It carries on its muffled vibrating underneath.

As I tidy the flat it becomes quite clear that nothing is missing. My laptop is still there, and so is the TV, the stereo and anything else of value. Even the jewellery that Siobhan declined to take away with her is untouched. I keep tidying, but soon reach the conclusion that nothing has been stolen at all. Whoever was here - a man, going by the size of the black handprint - was looking for one thing only, and that thing wasn't here. I'd been busy lugging it across London at the time.

Thank goodness for Sunita's warning...

It takes me a good two hours to get the flat straight. Then I inspect the front door. There's no sign of a forced entry. The lock is still intact. It's simply been left ajar, as if Mr Black Hand was in a hurry to get away.

When everything is finally tidy, I pour a little scotch into a mug and sit on the sofa with my e-cigarette. I dig my phone out from under the cushion and look up the number of the local police on the internet.

Then I stop myself.

Nothing's actually been stolen, so what crime has been committed here? Breaking and entering, I guess...

I think about Straw Girl. It bothers me, of course, that someone's been inside the flat, rooting around in our things. But, perversely, it also excites me. If someone's prepared to go to these lengths to get hold of Straw Girl, then it must really be worth something. I think of Victor's letter... what did he say? Oh yes, if the painting proved to be genuine, "the financial rewards could be vast." My mind begins to boggle with the possibilities...

If I can just manage to sell it in the next fortnight, surely I'll get enough money to set me up properly as a writer. I won't even need to find a new job. I can pay the mortgage, work on screenplays, network with contacts, keep Siobhan happy...

No more tedious, 9-5 drudgery.

All I need to do is sell the painting. If I can prove it's worth something…

I make a snap decision. I put my phone down and pick up my laptop instead and go to my email. I still remember the format for email addresses at the National Gallery, and I type it in, with the prefix ***Devon.Lamb.***

I didn't have that much to do with Devon when I worked at the gallery, but I was always polite to her, especially as she had a reputation for being a little 'difficult' at times. I never thought that of her. I always saw her as young, intelligent and driven.

But more importantly, she was an expert on Flemish Art.

I bash out a quick email, run it through a spell-check, and hit send.

17

06.43.

Her alarm goes off as usual, and - also as usual - she allows herself a five-minute lie-in before heading to the shower. She's out of the shower by 06.55, reading at the kitchen table while she waits for her unruly hair to dry. Breakfast is an avocado, smashed onto sourdough toast, and by 07.19 she's dressed, pulled her hair into a hat, and started the journey into central London.

While on the bus, Devon continues to read about Flemish Art. She'd spent most of the evening engrossed in the book, reading it almost right up to the point that sleep overtook her. She's close to finishing when the bus reaches Trafalgar Square. She hops off, power-walks past Nelson's Column and reaches her desk just before 8am. She's the first there, of course. A few minutes later Bernard arrives.

"Morning Devon" he says. She doesn't reply.

"Morning" he says, louder.

"Oh, er hi." She says, eyes fixed on her emails.

Bernard shakes his head in amusement. You don't normally get both eye contact and a greeting from Devon. It's generally one or the other…

Devon continues to clear her email inbox - a tedious task that's long overdue. She's almost read through all her messages when she gets to one close to the top. She doesn't recognise the sender's name, but decides to open for a quick pre-deletion scan:

Sender: Marks, Charlie

Dear Devon,

I'm not sure if you'll remember me, but until recently I worked as a Gallery Assistant in the National Gallery.

I am writing to you because I remember that you are an expert in Flemish art and this is an area I also have a particular interest in. I would greatly appreciate it if we could meet sometime? I have some questions which I would like to get an expert's opinion on.

Perhaps you could email me back or alternatively give me a call on 07…

Devon doesn't read to the end of the email. Instead she hits 'delete' and moves onto the next one.

18

I wait almost 24 hours, but still Devon Lamb hasn't dignified my email with a response. I phone the National Gallery, but am palmed off with that old stand-by for unwanted callers: "she's in a meeting." I call again just before 4pm, and apparently 'the meeting' is still in progress. So I grab my coat and head for the station.

On the train I try again to work out who the black-handed intruder might have been, but every train of thought reaches a dead-end. The bottom line is that nobody knew I had the painting, except for Mr Hussain, Sunita and Victor Botham. Who's dead.

It's at this point I remember visiting Botham in hospital, and the man in the carpark afterwards who'd driven his 4x4 towards me and sent me sprawling on the tarmac. I'd passed him off as just another hot-headed London driver, but now the incident assumes a murky question mark. Perhaps the man had been waiting for me to leave Botham's bedside. Perhaps he meant to send me a message...

Like, back off...

I suppose I should be worried, but Siobhan's out of the country, and there's no chance anyone could get to Lennie... I've only really got my own safety to fret about. Haven't I?

No, there's no chance of Lennie being dragged into this. Definitely not...

I've convinced myself of this by the time the train enters the tunnel that leads into Victoria Station. If someone intends to scare me into giving up Straw Girl, they can bloody well go ahead.

The girl is mine.

19

Devon is almost ready to call it a day when she glimpses her in the corner of the office.

Venetia Jardine.

Instantly her afternoon gets a little worse.

Venetia is chatting to Richard at the other end of the office. Devon has no idea how long they've been in conversation for, because she's been so engrossed in her latest report that all the sounds around her have morphed into one continuous blur.

But now she sees her.

Venetia appears to finish her chat with Richard and heads over to Devon's end of the office with a flick of her hair. Even her appearance annoys Devon; the needlessly high heels, the dyed blonde hair (it must surely be grey underneath) and the far too-short skirts. She's coming over now, sliding her irritatingly slim frame past several desks.

"Afternoon Miss Lamb"

"Oh, hi" says Devon, still staring at her screen.

"How's the report on that Titian coming along?"

"Nearly done."

"It'll be in my inbox first thing Monday I assume?"

She says it more as a statement than a question.

"Yep." Says Devon, without even feigning enthusiasm. Venetia hates her. It's bloody obvious; although Devon's never really known why... it's not as though Devon hasn't made it abundantly clear that her specialism is Flemish Baroque, yet Venetia keeps giving her early-Renaissance religious stuff to concentrate on.

The cow.

"I'll look forward to seeing it then."

"Yep."

Devon glances at the time on her computer screen. 16:59. She'd hoped to get away early tonight. There's a documentary she wanted to catch...

Still, work comes first. Back to bloody Titian...

*

It's almost ten to six by the time Devon leaves the gallery, having emailed off her report to Venetia with a curt message. (Find report attached. D.)

She heads out through the Sainsbury Wing as usual, stopping in a darkening Trafalgar Square to pull her bobble hat on. Commuters and tourists rush past from both sides, braced against the January wind, and Devon searches for her headphones, hoping to cut out some of their noise.

As she fiddles with the wires she notices a man leaning against the wall opposite her, puffing on an electronic cigarette. She looks back down at her tangled headphones.

When she glances back up the man is still there, looking at her. He's quite big; about 6 foot, and scruffy. His hair could do with a cut, and, there are noticeable streaks of grey at the sides. He looks vaguely familiar.

He stuffs his e-cigarette back into the jacket of his dark-blue overcoat and starts walking towards her. Devon looks at her phone and begins walking away, but the man speaks.

"Excuse me, er, Devon…"

She pretends not to hear.

"Devon… um, Miss Lamb, could I have a quick word with you?"

Devon glances back, trying to gauge where she recognises him from, and he catches up with her.

"My name's Charlie, sorry to bother you, I used to work with you."

Devon stops and frowns back at him.

"Yep, so?"

20

I make it to the National Gallery just before five. I head into the Salisbury Wing and ask at the information desk. Not surprisingly, they can't get hold of her...

I go and wait outside on Trafalgar Square, watching as a line of floating Yodas compete for the tourists' money. People file in and out of the gallery, most are visitors, but a few I recognise as staff. There's no sign of Devon though...

I take out my e-cigarette and puff away, just to pass the time. The weak January sun begins to set, and as it nears half five the stream of visitors dwindles.

It's almost six when Devon finally emerges. I approach her as she pulls on her hat and fiddles with her phone.

"Could I have a quick word with you?"

She shoots me a look that I'd say was approaching a scowl.

"My name's Charlie, sorry to bother you, I used to work with you."

"Yep, so?"

"I sent you an email, not sure if you got it?"

She frowns.

"Oh, yes, yes I did. And?" She raises her eyebrows.

"Well, I er, I just wondered if we could have a quick chat? Perhaps we could find a pub, there one just down Whitehall."

Devon looks down at the pavement and appears to sigh. Then she looks back up at me and meets my eyes. Her dark hair is thick and unruly, and she's not wearing make-up, but there's something striking about her wide cheekbones and pensive brown eyes.

After a bit of a pause she speaks.

"Look, the thing is, I'm just concentrating on my work at the moment. I'm not looking for... dates or whatever."

Dates?

I manage to stutter a reply...

"No, no no. It's not like that. I really do just want to ask you about art. Flemish art. Honest."

She looks a bit relieved.

"Flemish art. OK then," she says with a nod. "I can spare half an hour."

We make our way down Whitehall and head into the first pub we find. I order a pint and Devon opts for a diet coke. We sit amidst office workers enjoying a post-work drink. It's loud, but not too loud to make conversation difficult.

What *does* make conversation difficult is Devon's attitude. She shifts her stool until she presumably feels comfortable, takes a small sip of coke and meets my attempts at small talk with monotonous, short answers, like an opening batsman fending off a spell of fast bowling…

"How was your day?"

"Good."

"Have you worked at the gallery long?"

"Eighteen months."

"You live nearby?"

"Brixton."

"Oh, that's cool."

"It's my home."

I sigh and take a long sip of my pint, deciding to abort my rapport-building tactic as the abject failure it clearly is, and go straight to the point. Luckily, she seems to prefer this.

"Your speciality is Flemish art, I seem to recall?"

"Yes, that's right."

I don't say anything, but nod as if expecting more information, which she eventually provides…

"I focused on Flemish art in general for my masters, and I'm currently doing my doctoral thesis on the Antwerp School."

"I see. That's interesting."

"I think so."

"The Antwerp school, wasn't Jan Vanderschoot part of that?"

"He was, yes, quite a prominent member in the latter part of the seventeenth century. Why do you ask?"

Devon looks almost *interested* for the first time in our acquaintance. I feel like high fiving her. I don't.

"Well, I, er…"

I take another sip of my pint, trying to work out how to say it.

"I own… well, I've recently come to own, a painting which I'm led to believe could be a lost work by Vanderschoot. But I have no idea whether it is or not. I don't know where to start. That's why I wanted to talk to you."

As I say the words I realise how utterly daft it all sounds. I picture myself; sitting in a pub, jobless, drink in hand, trying to convince myself that I own a priceless painting. I remind myself of a character in one of my own movie plots; a chancer, hanging onto reality by a thread.

My dad's words echo around my head. They usually tend to at moments like these...

Life isn't a film script, Charles. It's hard work, bloody hard, and even then you might not get any reward for it. You can't just lie around waiting for things to fall into your lap. You have to get out there...

It's then I notice what Devon's doing. She's gripping the base of her coke glass so firmly I'm worried it's about to shatter, and fixing me with a stare. It's the first time she's made eye contact for longer than a second. Instinctively I reach for her hand to guide it away from the straining glass. She pulls it away sharply.

"You… you say you have a lost Vanderschoot?"

"So I've been told."

"Do you know the name of this painting?"

"They call it Straw Girl."

Devon pushes her coke to one side.

"Who calls it that?"

"Well, the man who gave it to me."

"Who gave it to you?"

Suddenly, I'm the one being interrogated…

"I got it from an elderly… friend, through his solicitor."

Devon fixes her eyes on mine.

"Please, tell me more, Charlie, from the start."

So I do tell her, right from the start: Victor Botham collapsing in the gallery, the meeting with Mr Hussain, the safe deposit facility. I neglect to tell her about the break-in at the flat though. I don't want to scare her off…

She pauses when I've finished.

"Where is the painting now?"

"In a storage lock-up."

She frowns.

"Hmmm. Safe, I guess, but not ideal. God knows if they have the correct humidity levels for a work of art. How long has it been there?"

"Since yesterday."

"OK, well that's not long enough to do any damage."

"Um, Devon, look, do you think it might actually be worth something then?"

"Hard to say. But I've done some research into Vanderschoot and the name Straw Girl has come up - as one of a number of paintings that were sold in Antwerp in the early 1900s. But since the war there's been no trace of it anywhere."

"And you think this could be it?"

"Again, hard to say, without seeing it. Where did you say this storage unit was?"

"Battersea. I can show you it tomorrow, if you're interested..."

Devon glances at her phone.

"What about now?"

I'm surprised at her eagerness, but the storage company closes at six.

"We can't, they've shut."

Devon drains the last of her diet coke.

"When do they open?"

"Eight, I think."

"See you there, then?"

"OK sure, but, aren't you working?"

"I'll go in after. Besides, this *is* work."

"Sure, see you then, then."

Devon takes a pen from her pocket and writes her phone number on a beermat, which she pushes towards me.

"Here, text me the address. I'll meet you outside."

"You're keen. Think it might be the real thing?"

She stands up and pulls on her bobble hat.

"Hmm, it could easily be a cheap fake, or some inferior work that's been passed off as a Vanderschoot. Don't get excited."

"But there's a chance it's real…?"

"I need to see it. I just want to know if we have something I can work with or not."

"You'll be able to tell just by looking?"

"Oh yes. Right away. I'll be able to tell in seconds if we have a dud or something that might just be worth looking into further. So, see you tomorrow?"

I finish the final third of my pint in one go.

"See you then."

21

Straw Girl. The lost Vanderschoot…

One of the unaccounted-for paintings on the inventory of 1925. Sold to an anonymous buyer by a bankrupt hotelier and never heard of again…

It's unusual for Devon to find it hard to organise her thoughts, but as she settles into her seat on the top deck of the bus she realises that her usually rigid mind is flying in all directions.

Could it really be genuine? If so, it would be a massive discovery. The kind that reputations and careers are built on.

And Venetia Jardine would be extremely pissed off… which would be a nice bonus.

Devon allows herself to imagine what her supervisor's face might look like when she finds out she's been usurped by her 23-year-old graduate underling.

It's a picture.

Devon reminds herself not to get carried away. She digs a book out of her bag and starts reading as the bus creaks towards Brixton, but for the first time in ages, she's barely able to take in a word of it.

22

To be honest, I'm not exactly thrilled by Devon's suggestion that we visit the safe storage place at eight in the morning. I could do with a lie-in, but instead I haul myself out of bed at the ungodly hour of seven to shower and walk across Battersea to meet her.

The storage building is a large, ugly box on a grey industrial estate near the river. I approach it from the road and half-notice the familiar fluorescent yellow livery of a police car parked outside.

It barely registers at first...

A bus pulls in front of a shelter and obscures my view of the panda car. I stop and watch as a sole passenger steps off it and blinks in the bright morning sunshine.

It's Devon Lamb.

From a distance, she looks younger than she did yesterday. Her green bobble hat, big parka coat and long red scarf gives her the look of a lost student, unsure which way to go as she circles the bus stop in her Dr Martens boots. Then she catches my eye.

"Oh, hi."

"Hi Devon."

"Yeah, hi, so, shall we..?"

"Yeah, let's go see this painting of mine."

She nods.

"So, you alright?" I ask in a lame attempt at small talk. Devon merely nods.

A sizable pause follows before she asks:

"How are you?"

But I don't answer... We approach the doors to the office and I notice a second police car, parked just around the corner from the other. I start to put things together in my sleep-deprived head.

"Oh my God…"

Devon catches on and frowns at me. I push the door, but it's locked. I glance at my watch - six minutes past eight. They should be open by now…

Straw Girl.

I leave her in my flat - it gets ransacked. I put her in a storage facility - and the place is surrounded by police the next morning…

What's going on here?

"Bloody hell" I say helplessly, pulling at the locked doors. Devon joins me and starts banging her fists on the doors. After a while a woman in a yellow fleece appears and unlocks the doors with a harried manner.

"I'm sorry, but we're not open yet."

"Right," I say, "but..."

Devon takes over.

"But we have some property here we'd like to access."

"Yes, well, it's just that we've had to delay opening today. Sorry. If you wouldn't mind coming back in about..."

"Have you been burgled?" interrupts Devon.

The woman stutters...

"Er, we..."

Devon pulls an ID card on a red lanyard out of her pocket and waves it at the woman. Her voice is suddenly official...

"It's just that we're from the National Gallery, and we have some property stored here which we urgently need to check on."

The woman is taken aback by Devon's sudden assertiveness. She glances behind her.

"Well, I'll have to check with my manager. Come in."

We enter the reception.

"What exactly is the problem?" asks Devon, "it's just that we noticed the police cars outside..."

"I'll phone my manager" says the woman, whose badge identifies her as Liza. She picks up a phone.

"We're just a bit concerned about our painting" I chip in.

Liza pauses. There's clearly no answer from her manager.

"Has there been a break-in?" asks Devon.

"We had an, er, a minor incident in the early hours. But I can assure you that nothing has been stolen. The police arrived before that could happen. Now, I'm afraid I really need to speak to my manager."

She tries the number again.

"Please would you ask if we can access our property?" asks Devon.

"Of course. One minute."

Devon ushers me into a corner of the room, out of Liza's earshot.

"We need to get that painting out," she says.

"Yeah, I guess, but if the police got here that quickly, it shows their security systems work... isn't that a good thing?"

Devon shakes her head.

"Look at the computer."

I turn to Liza's desk and notice that her PC is wrapped in clear plastic. Attached is a blue sticker:

POLICE EVIDENCE - DO NOT TOUCH

"See?" asks Devon.

"What?"

"Whoever broke in wasn't looking to steal the painting. They were trying to hack into the computer system - probably to find out where the painting is, whose name it's in, the access code... that sort of thing. Then they could come back at a later date and check it out, easy as anything."

"Oh. Shit."

"Yep. So trust me, we need to get it out of here."

*

Liza finally gets through to her manager, and Devon goes outside to call the National Gallery and tell them she won't be in work today. I don't hear what her excuse is. Instead I sit in the corner of the reception and read the sports pages of the Daily Mail. Or pretend to.

Neil, the manager, is a tall, ginger, moustachioed man. He's equally impressed by Devon's National Gallery ID, and agrees to let us remove Straw Girl. We fill in some paperwork, I show my ID, and within minutes we're approaching my lock-up. As the metal door swings open I suddenly realise how much I'm sweating.

To my intense relief, Straw Girl is still there. I breathe deeply.

"I can't believe you put it in an M and S suit bag," says Devon as we walk away from the building.

"Why not?"

"Well, at least it was wrapped up. It's not how we'd do things at the gallery though."

"No, I guess not."

"Anyway" says Devon, "doesn't matter. What we need to do is work out where we're going to keep this thing now. Clearly the storage place isn't to be trusted."

"What about at the gallery?"

Devon shakes her head.

"No. Not yet. I'm not taking that painting into work until I can be sure it's a genuine Vanderschoot, and I haven't even seen it yet. Talking of which, can I have a look?"

"Er, yeah" I say, looking at the bus stop, "we could open it back at mine."

Devon glances over my head at some point in the distance. "How about there?" she asks.

I turn around to see what she's looking at.

"You serious?"

"Sure."

"Burger King?"

She nods.

23

I'm not sure whether a potential 17-century Flemish masterpiece has ever been brought into a Burger King before, but there's a first time for everything.

I order a large breakfast muffin and a coffee - Devon gets a diet coke - and we find a table in the corner of the quiet restaurant. Devon leaves her drink untouched and places the suit bag on the table, unzipping it with reverence. She pulls out the bubble-wrap and taped bin liner inside and raises an eyebrow in my direction.

"Not how you do things in the gallery?"

She shakes her head and delves into her bag, pulling out a box cutter and cutting through the wrap. She pulls it off neatly and the colours of Straw Girl begin to shine through the plastic, like the painting is lined with tiny lights. Every time I see it I'm taken-aback by how beautiful it is. I stop eating my muffin.

2

Devon holds the painting out in front of her and breathes in sharply. She looks over it, up and down, and turns it over, inspecting the back. Then she runs her fingers around the frames.

"Oh man…" she whispers under her breath.

"What do you think?" I ask.

"It's beautiful."

"Yeah. But is it genuine?"

"Wait," says Devon, and lays the painting carefully on the bin liner.

"Don't go touching it with your greasy muffin hands."

She walks over to the counter and returns with two pairs of plastic catering gloves.

"Put them on when you've finished eating."

"Er, OK."

She runs her gloved fingers up and down the canvas slowly, peering closely at the painting.

"So?" I ask, unable to bear the suspense any longer.

"I can't say" says Devon, still touching the canvas.

"I thought you said you'd know immediately?"

"I said I'd know if it was *potentially* genuine right away… whether it would be something worth investigating."

She's still looking at the painting.

"And? Is it?"

"Oh yes. Most definitely."

An intoxicating rush of blood surges into my head, the kind you get when you stand up after a lunchtime pint.

"How can you tell?"

"Well, for a start the detail and juxtaposition of colour is what you would expect from a Vanderschoot. But most importantly, this…"

She points at a clear section of white cloud.

"You see this… the craquelure?"

"Come again?"

"These tiny cracks in the surface of the paint, here, look closely…"

Devon turns her phone torch and shines it at the canvas. I look at the wispy clouds and see the white paint has fragmented into tiny lines of cracks. She aims the torch down at the girl's blonde hair and blue dress. The cracks are less obvious but still there.

"Oh, yeah."

"These cracks are caused by the drying of the original paint, and they are very, very hard to forge."

"Yeah?"

"Yeah. So this would suggest to me that it's pretty unlikely for it to be a modern copy."

"Well that's good…"

"It's reassuring, yes."

"But?"

"But it could easily be a contemporary copy. By someone inspired by, or even taught by Vanderschoot. Someone who learned how to mimic his techniques."

"But it's a promising sign?"

"Oh, most definitely."

"What else can you tell?"

"Hmmm" says Devon, shining her torch and peering closer, "not a whole lot at the moment."

"No?" I ask, mildly disappointed.

Devon glances around at the interior of Burger King. A harassed-looking couple come in with three noisy kids of varying sizes and inspect the menu.

"These aren't really the most conducive surroundings," she says as one of the children starts screaming. "I'd like to investigate it further, but I think the most important thing is that we find somewhere to store it safely. The break-in at the storage company doesn't exactly fill me with confidence."

"No, me neither. But I can't think of anywhere that *would* make me feel confident..."

"Why not?" Devon raises an eyebrow.

I decide to tell her the truth...

"Whoever broke into the storage firm turned my flat over the other day. Ransacked it. Luckily I was moving the painting at the time. But they seemed to know exactly where I took it. I wouldn't be surprised if they're watching us now..."

Devon glances out of the window.

"In that case, we need to think outside of the box."

"Eh?"

"Hide it where nobody's going to go looking for it. In plain sight, if you know what I mean?"

"Kind of. You got somewhere in mind?"

Devon sips her coke.

"Yeah. I think I might know just the place."

24

On Devon's suggestion we hail a taxi and climb into the back with the painting.

"Where to?" asks the driver.

"Pimlico Tube Station" says Devon.

"Why there?" I whisper.

"We need to get on the Victoria Line. I'll later."

The cab fights its way through the morning traffic and across the Thames in the shadow of Battersea Power Station. We reach the tube station and make our way through the gates. I keep glancing behind me, half looking for some shady figure following us...

It's half ten on Friday morning, so the tube station is pretty quiet. We head underground and make our way onto the southbound platform. There's a few other passengers on the platform. I glance around at them; a couple with two kids, a millennial with headphones in, an older man in a brown jacket. Nobody looks overly suspicious, but I guess they wouldn't…

After a few seconds a couple of other men join the others on the platform. One is middle-aged and clad in black lycra running gear, probably heading to the gym. The other one holds my attention a little more. He's also middle-aged, wearing a blue waterproof coat and a red baseball cap, which is pulled down to his eyes. I glance at him and he meets my eyes before looking away at the tracks. I turn to Devon.

"So, where are we going?" I ask.

"My neck of the woods. Brixton."

"So why did we head back to Pimlico? The cab could have gone straight there in 10 minutes…"

"Because we need to make sure we're not being followed."

"Right, and how do we do that?"

"I'll show you."

"OK…"

A Brixton-bound train pulls into the station.

"Right," says Devon as passengers spill onto the platform, "get on".

We step onto the train and wait by the doors. Devon pauses, her hand held in front of mine…

"Not yet…"

"What?"

The train's doors are still open, but the platform's empty. Devon times it to perfection. Just as the doors begin to close she jumps out onto the platform and drags me after her. The sliding doors hit me on the shoulder as I dart through. The train pulls away and I look around me…

Red-cap man is nowhere to be seen.

"Bloody hell" I say, rubbing my shoulder. "What was that for?"

"If anyone was following us, they're still on that train" she says, "If they'd followed us, they'd have given themselves up."

I'm quite impressed.

"OK. Cool. So, how did you know how to do that?"

Devon smiles.

"I only read two kinds of books; art history, and spy thrillers. I got that trick from the spy thrillers. The old ones are the best."

We repeat Devon's trick at Stockwell station, just to be on the safe side.

"I think we can safely say we've shaken them off" I say.

"Let's hope so," says Devon.

We turns carrying Straw Girl through the streets of Brixton. It doesn't take us long to reach our destination. We take a left turn down a narrow residential street, at the end of which is a dull 90s building which looks like a bog-standard block of flats surrounded by a small garden. On the surrounding wall is a name-plate reading Porterleigh House and a CCTV camera.

Devon presses a buzzer.

"Good morning, I'm here to see Mrs Lawrence."

"Who's Mrs Lawrence?" I ask as Devon pulls the entry door open.

"My Godmother. She lived in the flat next door when I was growing up. She and my mum were very close. She used to babysit me."

"OK, right, so what is this, an old folks' home?"

"Yep. Specialising in dementia care. Muriel's only in the early-stages though - she's still with it."

"Good for her."

I stop her as we walk through the little courtyard.

"Look, Devon, you can't be suggesting that we leave a potentially priceless work of art here, in some home for the confused? They'll end up raffling it or something."

She smiles and shakes her head.

"No they won't. Look around…" she points at the CCTV cameras and the high walls, "this place is designed to stop people coming in or wandering out. Besides, how will anyone know that the painting's here? We're not being followed, and Muriel's nothing to do with you…"

"She's linked to you though…"

"Yeah, but not by blood. Come on Charlie. Can you think of anywhere better?"

I think for a second, and have to admit that I can't.

We enter the main reception and are greeted by a stocky, cheerful man in a blue uniform.

"Good morning Miss Lamb."

"Hello Dinos, I'm so sorry it's short notice. This is my friend Charles."

Charles?

"Er, hello."

"Not a problem" says Dinos, "I've just served Mrs Lawrence her morning coffee, she'll be happy to have visitors."

He appears to spot the painting.

"A gift? It's not her birthday yet, is it?"

"No," says Devon, "the anniversary of my Christening - always nice to say thank you. She was like an aunt to me."

We head up some stairs, down a corridor and arrive at Muriel Lawrence's room.

"Mrs Lawrence?" says Dinos, "some visitors."

The room is small but cosy. There's a bed, a sink and a small sitting area with an armchair and TV. The room smells fresh, with flowers in a vase on a coffee table and pictures of family dotted around. The window at the end looks onto the small courtyard.

"Ah, Devon my darling, so nice to see you."

"Hello Muriel."

Muriel Lawrence is a small, black lady somewhere north of 70. She's sitting in her armchair with a mug of coffee in front of her wearing a blue jumper with a yellow shawl over it. She smiles brightly when she sees us and tries to stand.

"Please Muriel, don't get up."

She settles back down.

"Great to see you, and who is your handsome young friend?"

I smile, not sure if I'm more pleased with 'handsome' or 'young'.

"This is Charles, he works with me at the National Gallery."

I smile at Devon's subtle bending of the truth. Muriel extends a wiry arm and I move to shake her hand.

"I always knew this one would go on to great things" she says, nodding at Devon. "Her sisters and friends were all into music and boys and all the rest, but this one always had her head in a book. Either that or she'd be drawing in her sketchbook. I'm so proud of her, getting such a good job."

"Yes, she is certainly an asset to the gallery," I say, getting into the role. Devon smiles and looks down almost shyly; the first time I've seen her look remotely less than composed.

"I'm just having a coffee," says Muriel, "will you join me?"

"Thanks," says Devon, "but we've just had one."

"Have a choccy then" she persists, offering us a selection box; "these were a gift from Dennis downstairs. I think he's got a soft spot for me!"

She cackles loudly, and Devon smiles. We take a seat.

"So how is life at the gallery treating you?" asks Muriel.

"Good, good, they're keeping me very busy as usual" says Devon. I notice that he accent has slipped from her usual neutral tones into something approaching Muriel's Jamaican/cockney twang.

"Excellent. Soon as my hip's behaving I'm coming for another visit!"

"Great" says Devon. "I'm glad to see you're keeping well. I'm afraid we can't really stop long, got to be getting back to the gallery. But we did have a small favour to ask you."

"Anything for my favourite God-daughter!" smiles Muriel.

"I've got a painting that I'm doing a bit of research into at the moment, and I need to keep it somewhere near home. But there's barely any room in my little place, plus I've got a real problem with damp. Damp's no good for old paintings you see."

Muriel nods.

"I wondered if you'd be so kind as to keep it here. It'll only be for a couple of weeks."

"Oh, of course my dear. Anything for you."

Devon beams.

"Tell me dear, is this a painting from the national gallery?"

"Not at the moment, but it might be one day. Just think, it would have been on your wall first."

I frown, but Muriel grins like a toddler.

"Ah, dear, I'd be honoured to look after it for you."

Devon looks to me.

"Charles, perhaps we could show the painting to Mrs Lawrence?"

I nod and unwrap Straw Girl, holding her up to show Muriel.

"Oh my good Lord" she says, quietly. "She's beautiful."

*

"Are you sure this is a good idea?" I ask as we leave Porterleigh House, minus one expensive work of art.

"Course. What else are we going to do with it? Leave it in your flat so it can be nicked? Nobody has a clue it's here."

I nod.

"Just hope no nurses make off with it."

Devon gives me a look.

"This is one of the best-rated care homes in London. That sort of thing doesn't happen."

"I hope you're right."

"I am."

"OK, what happens now?"

"Well" says Devon, "First, we really need to have a proper look at the painting. I reckon we visit again tomorrow. I'll bring some of my forensic kit."

"Well count me out. I'm busy tomorrow."

"Busy? Doing what?"

"Going to a birthday party."

Devon stops and looks at me.

"A birthday party?"

"Yeah."

"Well, can't you make your excuses? Whose party is?"

I look back at her…

"My son's."

25

(*Antwerp, Belgium*, 1945)

Victor Botham enters the bar and few of the elderly patrons appear to notice the young Englishman through the cloud of tobacco smoke. He walks over to the counter and orders a beer.

Just past his 23rd birthday, Victor carries himself with the confidence of a man much older, in the way that Sandhurst usually do. He is slim but muscular, with sandy hair, small round glasses and a thin moustache.

He scans the bar and spies Guy sitting upright in a corner booth with a glass of red wine. An old friend from Sandhurst, Guy is tall, dashing, and to be honest, a far better prospect for promotion than Victor is. But Victor bears no jealousy towards his chum. Especially since he's vowed to help him...

Victor carries his beer over to Guy's table.

"Ah, good to see you, Vic," says Guy, standing. Victor approaches and slaps him firmly on the back.

"Likewise old boy," says Victor to Guy - a man a full year older than himself. Victor settles into a seat opposite and glances around at the bar's clientele. Nobody looks overly suspicious. Most are on the wrong side of sixty and appear more content on smoking, sipping beer and having muttered conversations.

It's another sunny late-winter day in Antwerp, but the only evidence of this inside the bar is a thin shaft of dusty light which cuts across the table between the two junior British officers.

"How are things going your end?" asks Guy.

"Pretty well, old man. Good news to report, I think I've found out who our bespectacled friend is."

"I say, that didn't take you long."

Victor grins and sips his beer.

"I did some digging around, waved a few francs under some noses, poked my own into a few places it probably wasn't welcome, but I've come up with a name."

"Go on?"

"Josef Strauss. Josef Strauss the Younger, to be more accurate. Son and heir of Josef Strauss, the German hotelier. Only, there was nothing left to inherit. Strauss senior lost everything he had in the depression of the 20s."

"So that's why he wanted your painting?" asks Guy.

"Yes, partly, but it goes deeper than that. Let me explain…"

Victor Botham lights a cigarette and takes a drag. Then he continues…

"Strauss senior, and his father before him - Albert - owned a string of hotels across the Low Countries, mainly in Germany, Belgium and the Netherlands. The busiest and most successful of the chain came to be the Antwerp Strauss Hotel, so this is where Josef Strauss ended up spending most of his time. Strauss junior was born here in 1890 and took over the running of the chain. Are you still with me old chap?"

"Still there," says Guy.

"Josef Strauss senior was a keen collector of art, as is his son."

"Ah, men after your own heart," smiles Guy.

"To a point, but not when it comes to politics. Both Strausses are known Nazi sympathisers."

"Ah."

"Anyway, the Strauss family were indeed once the owners of the painting we know as Straw Girl. Albert acquired it sometime in the late 1800s. However, when the chain went bust in the 20s they were forced to sell all their assets - including the painting."

"I see, which was sold to..."

"The Levy family. The restaurant owners. Of course, they were spirited away by the Nazis and the painting ended up in their hands, until the liberation, of course, when I acquired it."

"So Strauss Junior was taking back what he felt to be his family's property?"

"In his warped way, yes."

Victor stubs out his cigarette and catches the barman's eye.

"Same again when you have a minute, my good man."

"So what's your plan?" asks Guy, "I assume you're not going to let this lie..."

"Good Lord, no. Even if it turns out to be a worthless copy, there's a principle at stake. The painting is legally mine."

"Quite right."

Victor nods…

"Josef Strauss junior has spent the best part of his life trying to rebuild the family empire. He purchased a hotel here in Antwerp and renamed it The Hotel Strauss, and began his own art collection. Business was booming in the 30s, by all accounts, but then the war came."

"Familiar tale…" says Guy.

"Well, for Strauss the war began well. Everybody I've spoken to says he was an enthusiastic collaborator with the Nazi regime, even going so far as to let their officers have free accommodation at his hotel. It seems he fully expected Hitler to triumph and was setting himself up for a glorious future in third Reich Europe."

"How sad for him. I assume his hotel isn't doing so well now?"

"Not in the slightest. It's shut, but that doesn't stop it being vandalised on a regular basis. The word is that it's only a matter of time before Strauss is officially investigated for collaboration."

"So why is he still here?"

"He might not be for long. A good source, whose palms I had to cross with francs, tells me that he's in hiding with all he could salvage from the hotel, including my painting. He's made plans to *have his goods driven by van to the docks on Saturday night, where he'll be taking a boat to London."*

"I say. You're sure this is a reliable source?"

"A local politician, one who's terrified of being labelled a collaborator himself. Told him I'd put a word in with the powers that be."

Guy raises an eyebrow.

"So what's your plan?"

Victor looks around the bar. The bartender is out of earshot, and his wizened customers show no signs of interest in their chat. Victor leans closer across the table and whispers to Guy…

"When that van leaves for the docks on Saturday, I'll be waiting."

"In that case," says Guy, "I'll be right with you."

"I'd understand if you don't want to be involved," says Victor. "Could be a bugger where promotions are concerned if top brass get wind of this little enterprise…"

"Still, I'll be with you Victor. Can't let that Nazi rotter sail away with what's rightfully yours."

Victor finishes off his beer with a gulp and places the glass firmly on the table.

"You're a good man, Guy. A good chap."

26

Against all of my natural instincts I seem to have acquired a new habit for rising early; and Siobhan's not even here to shove me out of bed.

Saturday morning is no different, and by half nine I've showered, dressed and got myself to Clapham Junction, where I grab a coffee and catch the Brighton train. I find a window seat and watch the suburbs gradually merge into green countryside. Brighton was mine and Siobhan's hometown until recently, but heading back there doesn't fill me with a nostalgic glow. These 'family' occasions never do.

I begin to think about what I can buy Lennie for his birthday. As usual, I can't think of anything, which will no doubt lead to an hour spent dithering around the shops of Brighton before heading to Hove for the party.

I try to remember when I last saw Lennie…

I've definitely seen him since his last birthday. Not at Christmas though, because his mother had taken him bloody skiing. It might have been Easter…

My thoughts soon turn back to Straw Girl, and I decide to check in with Devon. I call her number.

"Hi," she says.

"Hi, all OK?"

"Yep."

"Good, are you still planning to have a look at the painting today?"

"Just on my way to Muriel's now."

"Oh, great. And you're not…"

"Not being followed, no. I've just changed buses to make sure."

"Great."

"So will you back from this family thing tonight?"

"Yeah, tonight, hopefully sooner," I say, with a sigh.

"I didn't know you had a son?"

"Oh, yeah…"

"But not with your girlfriend?"

"No" I say, "Lennie's 18. Well, 19 now. I was a student when he was born."

"Oh right."

There's a pause.

"Well, let me know what you find out…"

"Yes, will do."

"Speak later."

"OK."

Devon hangs up. *No have a nice day* or *wish your son a happy birthday* or anything. She's not one for pleasantries. I gaze out of the window for a while and when the novelty of green fields fades I close my eyes and try to grab some sleep. I jerk awake as the train pulls into Brighton station. With a good two hours until the party starts I plod around Brighton looking for possible gifts, eventually settling for a remote-control Star Wars figure.

Lennie was definitely into Star Wars, last time I saw him...

Shopping done, I stop for a quick pint in The Lanes before heading towards Hove along the seafront. I walk past the rotting husk of the West Pier and the gleaming steel of the new observation tower, turn right and trudge up Grand Avenue until I reach a large detached house with a trio of balloons tied to the gate. The sound of laughter and music emanates from within.

Here goes...

I ring the doorbell and take a long drag on my e-cigarette. The vapour clears as the door opens I see Richard behind it with a small child in a party dress at his feet.

"Oh, Charlie, hi!" he says, grinning and still looking annoyingly like his near-namesake Richard Gere. Richard Steel is not an actor though, but a dentist, and a pretty successful one; if the five-bedroom house, swimming pool, and needlessly big 4X4 BMW are anything to go by. Seems Vanessa was right for thinking she could do better than me all those years ago...

"Hi Richard" I say. Despite him marrying my university girlfriend and raising my son, I find it hard to *completely* dislike the guy.

Vanessa's family on the other hand...

"Come in, mate, join the fun" he says.

"Lennie's having a cake," says the small child, and I smile at her.

We walk into the hallway and then through into the kitchen/conservatory, where the epicentre of the party appears to be. It's in full swing, with adults standing around sipping drinks and youngsters spilling out into the large garden where they seem gloriously unconcerned by the January chill. I stand in the doorway and stare around me; I can't see Lennie, or indeed anyone I want to talk to...

"Hi Charlie, glad you could come," says a familiar voice. I turn around and see Vanessa, who, despite her words, doesn't sound thrilled to see me. I grin back.

"Wouldn't have missed it."

"Well, you did at Christmas."

"You took him skiing..."

"Not for the whole of the holidays," she says, gritting her teeth, "anyway, you're here now, I'm sure Lennie will be pleased to see you."

"Yes" I say, "where is he?"

"Having a break in his room... things were getting a bit much, but I'm sure he'll be ready to come down now. Get a drink. I'll go fetch him."

She gestures to a table laden with wine, beers and various fizzy drinks. I don't need any more invitation. I pour myself a glass of red and down it in one, then refill the glass to the top. It's going to be that kind of afternoon...

As if to prove my point, I notice Sheridan leaning against the kitchen unit, waving his glass around and braying loudly in the direction of two other men. Vanessa's brother is possibly my least favourite member of her family, despite stiff competition from his father. A bit older than me, Sheridan seems to have fully embraced middle-age spread in the year or so since I last saw him. He's developed a sizeable gut, which hangs over the belt of his chinos, and his round face is ruddy under his greying curly hair. I edge myself slowly to the opposite side of the room...

I find myself standing by several people I don't know, so take out my phone and have a quick look at it. No messages from Devon yet. I stuff it back in my pocket just as I hear a whirring noise coming from the stairs. It sounds familiar - like a human impression of a helicopter. I look over and see white-socked feet pounding their way down the stairs.

"Whirrrrrh whirrrrrrh..."

Lennie doesn't look that much different from when I last saw him. His curly hair is longer and he has a bit of downy fluff around his chin, and he's wearing his standard uniform of blue jogging bottoms and an oversize Marvel T-shirt.

"I tried to make him dress up but he was having none of it" says Vanessa.

Lennie bounds up to me and grins.

"Hello Lennie…" I say.

"Hello dad," he says, stiffly.

"Happy birthday."

He does his familiar, high-pitched laugh.

"So, are you enjoying the party?" I ask.

"Am I enjoying the party?" he repeats.

"This is for you," I say, proffering the Star Wars toy, which is still in its carrier bag. Lennie laughs again and jumps up and down on the spot, waving his arms. He does this when he's excited.

"Happy birthday, mate," I say again. Lennie pulls the box out of the bag and stares at it.

"Oh, Star Wars," says Vanessa. "We went to see that before Christmas…" says Vanessa.

"Yes," says Lennie. "It was called The Last Jedi, and it was the second in the sequel series but the eighth episode overall. One of the main characters was called Luke Skywalker and he was living on a sort of, rock, and there was a bad character called Kylo…"

Lennie isn't really looking at me, and I can tell he's about to go off on another of his rants unless someone stops him, which Vanessa does…

"Why don't you go and play with it, Lennie. Show Benji and Olivia. I'm sure Richard can find you some batteries…"

Lennie laughs and scampers off into the garden.

"I got him a card, too," I say, handing it to Vanessa. She smiles thinly. Annoyingly, she's still as pretty as she was at university. Back in the 90s, I used to think she looked like Winona Ryder. I don't see the resemblance anymore, but if anything the years have improved her looks.

"Thanks," she says. "He's a little overwhelmed at the moment, a bit of sensory overload - but I'm sure he'll want to spend some time with you later on. We're doing the cake about three."

"Cool. How is he, anyway?"

"Well," she says, annoyingly, elongating the word to show *just how long it's been…* "We've been to look at an agricultural college outside Brighton. They have a great learning support department."

"Agriculture?"

"Yep, well, he's interested in working with animals, isn't he?"

Is he?

"Oh yeah, course..."

"Yes," she says, looking over her shoulder. A tallish male figure brushes past us on his way to the drinks table.

"Ohn Arnie, have you met Charlie - Lennie's birth father?"

Somehow she makes the word *birth* sound like an insult. Like it's my genes that are to blame for producing an autistic son…

Richard would never produce a special needs child, oh no; just mini-Mozarts like 'Benji and Olivia'…

Vanessa knows full well that Arnie Russell and I have met. We played a tedious game of golf together with Richard, Sheridan and some other blokes on one of Lennie's previous birthday weekends, and I've bumped into him at several of these family gatherings over the years. Arnie looks down at me with his long, equine face.

"Yes, of course. Still playing golf, Charlie?"

I don't play golf. That's why I finished with a round of over 100...

"No, not much."

"Oh, keeping busy though?"

"Yes" I say, "still writing..."

"Oh yes, what is it you write again?"

"Screenplays - movie scripts..."

"Oh, anything interesting in the pipeline?"

"Yes, a few things here and there," I lie.

"That's interesting, I tell you what, Sheridan was telling me a story the other day and I thought it would make a good film, actually... it was about insider trading and that sort of thing. So, a chap working for, er, Coutts, I think..."

I zone out of the conversation, as I always do when Sheridan and his chums start banging on about the world of banks, investments and the City. It's a subject that bores me beyond tears. Even so, I'm aware that Arnie Russell's involvement in this world is pretty tenuous. He's nothing more than an IT drone for someone or other, and - I seem to recall - his main experience of investment has been with bookmakers rather than banks. An old university friend of

Sheridan's, he went into the army, nearly bankrupting himself through gambling debts, before Sheridan rescued him with the offer of a job.

I pretend to listen to him whilst sipping red wine and scanning the room... Lennie is laughing as his Star Wars figure scoots around the patio. I give myself a pat on the back for my choice of present, but realise that there are no kids his own age at the party. Most are far younger, and appear to belong to family or friends. Maybe this agricultural college thing is a good idea...

It's then I notice Leonard for the first time. Vanessa's father is all over Benji and Olivia like a rash. I sneer, remembering how proud he was when Lennie was born and named after him. How quickly he abandoned all interest when his 'problems' started to become obvious...

He's bent down over Olivia, admiring her party dress. Benji is next to them, showing off his rugby skills. The boy has inherited the family shock of curly hair, but while Benji's is brown his grandfather's is white and receding fast around a bald dome that catches the sun.

Old git.

Sheridan wanders up to his father and ruffles Benji's hair. He looks like a junior version of his dad; tall, curly hair, a body running to fat. The pair of them chuckle about something... probably how Benji's destined to grow up to work in the City, play golf and generally be an awful human being... I have a sudden desire to be a long way from the lot of them. I take my phone out of my pocket.

"Sorry, mate," I say to Arnie Russell, who's still droning on, "got to make an urgent call."

I nip through the house and out of the front door, and once in the driveway I start dragging on my e-cigarette and check my phone. I notice a text from Devon...

Have made a few interesting discoveries. Speak later, face-to-face. D.

I consider turning on my heels and heading straight back to the station. Lennie won't notice my absence, surely... but then I hear a window opening above me. I turn around and Vanessa leans out of it.

"Hope you're staying for the cake."

I nod.

*

I spend another few hours at the party, eat some cake and sink another few glasses of red wine. I make my excuses around half 4, say goodbye to Lennie with a high-five (he doesn't do hugs) and fall into a deep slumber on the train home.

I wake with a thick head sometime later, almost missing my change at Clapham Junction. I jump off the train in time and find the correct platform for Battersea. As I stand there waiting I notice something out of the corner of my eye. A red baseball cap...

I make eye contact with the man wearing it and he looks away. I realise where I recognise him from - it's the guy from yesterday, at Pimlico. He's still wearing the same blue waterproof coat. He looks down at something in his hands, looks back at me, and then wanders off up the platform and out of sight.

I get on the next train and see him again through the window. He's standing at the very end of the platform and looking down the tracks away from me. The train speeds past him, and I'm sure of one thing; if he had been following me, he isn't anymore...

27

(Antwerp, Belgium, 1945)

Under the cover of darkness, Victor pulls the van into the car park of a small cafe and locks the door. He's managed to borrow a rusty civilian van, the kind that won't arouse any attention. He is dressed in a long dark overcoat and flat cap, and as he walks across the carpark he notices a similarly dressed man emerging from the shadows.

"Ah, Archer, you're early. Good man."

The men shake hands and Victor lights a cigarette, offering one to Archer.

"Guy will be joining us soon," says Victor, and as if on cue a tall figure exits the cafe and strolls across the car park. He also lights up, and when the three men meet their conference is shrouded in a thick haze of smoke.

"Guy, this is Sid."

The two men shake hands.

"Gentlemen, we all know what we need to do. Now, there's no reason anything ought to go wrong, but if for any reason it does, we face our punishment alone. Not one of us is to mention the involvement of the others."

Guy and Archer nod.

"OK then, shall we begin?"

"Aye sir," says Archer. Guy nods at the fresh-faced young lance-corporal. The three men clamber into the van - Archer in the back - and Victor heads off up the long, straight road. After a while he pulls into a tree-lined clearing at the roadside and stops the engine. All is silent.

They. They wait some more. Guy passes round a flask of coffee, and the men drink silently, staring into the night and smoking.

When his watch ticks around to 3am, Victor turns to his two accomplices.

"OK, let's go."

The men walk around to the back of the van and Guy opens the doors. Each man takes out a shotgun. Guy and Sidney take rifles and Victor a small pistol, which he shoves into the pocket of his coat. Victor also pulls out a large brown sack, which he folds up and puts in his backpack.

They walk along the side of the road until the trees grow thicker and the light dimmer. There's hardly any traffic at this hour, but when a lone car passes the three men fall back into the trees and wait until silence returns.

After a longer silence a rumbling noise is heard in the distance. Victor holds a hand up to stop his men and peers along the road. Two bright headlights are just visible in the distance.

"OK," he whispers. Guy and Archer scurry into the trees on one side of the road, whilst Victor remains on the other. The lorry's headlights get bigger and bigger, illuminating the road ahead. When Victor can almost see the lorry's green paintwork he walks out into the middle of the road and flashes his torch. He sinks to his knees on the tarmac, then falls over onto his side. With one hand he clutches his leg, and with the other points his torch up the road.

The lorry blares its horn, but Victor doesn't move. Eventually the lorry begins to slow, grinding to a halt inches in front of Victor.

The two men in the lorry look at Victor in confusion. He's shed his dark overcoat and is wearing a threadbare brown suit. His hair is unkempt and his glasses cracked, and his face sports several days of beard growth. He looks for all the world like a lost, injured tramp.

The two men get down from the cab and walk up to him, speaking to each other in Dutch. Victor starts shouting in French:

"Aider! Cassé, cassé."

Thinking they have stumbled across some French vagrant with a broken leg, the driver and his mate bend down to help move Victor out of the way. At this point, Guy and Archer emerge from the trees on the other side of the road.

"Stop!"

They lower their rifles at the two men, who drop Victor and stand up straight, raising their hands high in the air.

"Don't move" says Guy. He aims his rifle at the driver's mate.

"Throw down your weapon!"

The stocky man retrieves a pistol from his pocket, holding gingerly it by the chamber, and placing it gently on the ground.

"Turn," says Victor, in English, standing up straight and abandoning all pretence of a broken leg. The two men turn towards the van and squint, startled by their own headlights. Victor takes off his backpack and paces around to the back of the lorry. He examines the padlock on the door, lifts his pistol and shoots it off. The metal splinters into the darkness with a screech. He steps into the van and shines a torch around it; illuminating various boxes and pieces of furniture. He roots around, chucking things left and right, until he finds what he is looking for: a locked trunk. Again, he shoots away the padlock and heaves the lid open. A stack of flat packages lie inside. All paintings, all priceless - but only one belonging to Victor…

With shaking hands he takes out a knife and makes a thin incision in the packing of the first one. He rips it open to reveal a rural landscape. Placing it painting carefully to one side, he repeats the process on the next painting, a still-life, and the next, until he finds Straw Girl. He doesn't waste time examining it, but wraps it in the sack and carries it to the front of the lorry.

"Sit!" he says to his two captives. They obey. "Now listen, there's a man in the trees with a gun. If either of you moves inside half an hour, you're dead. After that, well, enjoy the rest of your evening, gentlemen."

Guy and Victor back away, still training their guns on the men. The stocky man extends his foot slightly to the left. Guy looks down at the tarmac next to the man and notices his pistol, still lying there.

"Stop!" he yells, but before echo of the words has faded a gunshot rings out across the night. The man screams and grabs his thigh, blood oozing onto the road. Smoke is rising from Archer's rifle, and his hands start to shake as he lowers the weapon. He stares ahead.

"For God's sake, Archer," says Victor, "there was no need..."

Before he can finish, the driver dives behind his wounded comrade and reaches for the pistol. In one swift movement he raises it towards the Englishmen and fires. The bullet hits Guy just above his hip. He staggers sideways, collapsing in a heap on the ground. Archer fires again, killing the driver immediately. Victor swoops forward and grabs the pistol from the dead man's hand. He then runs over to Guy, who is lying on the tarmac, a dark pool of blood spreading around him.

"Hang in there old boy."

"Leave me, I'll be fine, leave me" says Guy.

"No chance" says Victor. He places the painting under his one and takes Guy's with his other. Archer helps lift him up.

"What do we do?" asks Archer.

"Get him to the van."

The drag Guy's bleeding body along the dark road and place him in the back of the van. Victor starts the engine and pulls away. Guy moans.

"What are we going to do with him?" asks Archer.

"We'll take him to the field hospital," says Victor.

"But... what do we say happened?"

"You're just going to say you found him like this..."

"But... they'll ask questions."

"I don't care. That's what I'm paying you for. Say nothing."

"But, but..." Archer stammers.

"Do it, man!"

From the back, Guy mutters something...

"Leave me here, leave me..."

Victor looks in the mirror; Guy's clothes are dark with blood.

"I'm not abandoning you, Guy Marks," says Victor. "Listen to me. You're going to be OK."

28

When I get back to the flat I down some black coffee and lie down on the sofa, hoping caffeine and a power-nap might alleviate the effects of all the red wine and put me in a clear enough frame of mind to talk to Devon. I've been asleep for about five minutes when my mobile jolts me awake. But it's not Devon; it's Siobhan.

"Hi" I say groggily.

"Bloody hell" she replies. "You sound half asleep, what is it, about 7pm there?"

"Yeah… what time is it there?"

"Mid morning."

"Cool, what's the weather like?"

"Sunny, of course. What's London like?"

"Grim," I sit upright. "You working today?"

"No. It's Saturday here too, you know. I've been invited to a pool party this afternoon."

A pool party?

My brain prepares to go into jealousy overdrive.

"Sounds fun."

"Yeah, probably quite dull really, just full of work people. What have you been up to today?"

"Oh, well it was Lennie's birthday party this afternoon, so I went down to Hove for a visit…"

"Oh God, yes. How was it?"

"Yeah, fine."

"And is work OK?"

I pause, hoping that my tone of voice isn't going to give me away.

"Yep. All good."

"Any news?"

I continue to give her a bland run-down on all I've been up to since she jetted off for the states. Obviously, I neglect to tell her a few things... like getting sacked, inheriting a painting, having the flat broken into and teaming up with an ex-colleague to go on some artistic treasure-trail…

After she's hung up and gone off to enjoy another day of California sun I inspect my phone and notice a text from Devon…

Want to meet for a chat then? D.

I text her back immediately.

Yep. Do you know the Mason's Arms by Battersea Park Station? In an hour? X

My phone buzzes again quickly.

OK. D.

Unsurprisingly, I'm down the Mason's within twenty minutes and am well into my second pint by the time Devon turns up. The pub's fine selection of ale is doing a great job of clearing my red wine hangover. Devon glances curiously at the boisterous Saturday evening crowd around the bar and joins me at my corner table. She's carrying a large portfolio case which she plonks down against the table.

"Hi," I say.

"Hi Charlie."

I finish the rest of my second pint.

"Would you like a drink?"

"I'll have a diet coke."

"Sure I can't tempt you into a proper drink?" I ask, largely because the act of ordering my third pint in an hour seems a bit more respectable if my companion is also drinking.

"No thanks."

"Go on, it is Saturday night," I smile.

"No, thanks. I've never drunk alcohol and I never will."

"OK, cool, a coke it is."

I return with the drink and notice Devon has started some papers out of the portfolio bag.

"So," I say, "fill me in."

"Well" says Devon, "I paid a visit to Muriel's today and took some photos of the painting," she pulls up some blown-up colour prints. "Seeing as we can't carry the real thing around with us, this'll give us something to refer back to."

"Great."

"I also spent a bit more time studying the painting."

"OK, and what did you find?"

"A few things caught my attention…" she takes a sip of coke and glances at the rowdy crowd at the bar. The tracksuit tops worn by some of their number tell me they're a rugby team enjoying a post-match drink or twelve, but at least their noise means our conversation can carry on in privacy.

"Like what?"

"I did some digging around in the archives last night. Did some reading…"

"Sounds like a wild Friday night!"

She frowns at me. I feel like I've had my wrist slapped.

"I've found out that Straw Girl, ie, the Vanderschoot painting, was painted in Antwerp, circa 1640. We know it spent some time in a private collection in the city."

"We?"

"Yes, us, art historians. The community."

"OK, I see..."

"Yeah. Well, by the 1840s it had made its way to Paris. We know this because it was exhibited there, in the Salon de Paris."

"The what?"

Devon puts down her coke, which was halfway to her lips, and looks at me.

"Are you sure you actually worked at the National Gallery?"

"Yes, technically, but I just stopped people touching the paintings. Art's not really my thing."

"Clearly not…" she sips her coke. "So, the Paris Salon was the most prestigious art exhibition in the world for over a century. And they published catalogues of all the works shown there. Straw Girl was on display in 1841. It's listed in the catalogue for that year."

"Blimey, and we took the thing into a Burger King…"

"No. We took something that might possibly be the same thing into a Burger King. That's what we're trying to find out. There's a slight discrepancy that came up when I looked at the catalogue though."

"Oh…"

"Yes. The dimensions are clearly stated in the catalogue. Their Straw Girl was 68 centimetres high and 46 centimetres wide. I've measured ours, and it's exactly 70 centimetres by 50. Now, that's not a lot at all, but it's enough to cause concern."

"Oh, right" I say, staring down at my pint, slightly deflated.

"Could the Salon people have got it wrong, I mean, it was way back in the day…"

"Hmm, possibly, but when you're building a case you want things like that to add up."

"So you think it's a copy?"

"No. Not necessarily. It's just something we have to look more closely at. Forensic analysis of the painting will tell us more."

"And you can do that?"

"A bit. But I know someone who's an expert. I'm going to ask them to have a look on Monday."

"Cool," I say, still thinking about the size issue. I take a glum swig of beer.

"I found something a bit more promising too" says Devon.

"Oh?"

"Yep..."

She takes an envelope out of her portfolio bag and slides out what looks like a small black and white photocopy of Straw Girl.

"This."

She passes it to me. I stare at it. It looks almost identical, except for the lack of colour.

"It's the same! What is it?"

"This turned up in a book on Flemish art. It's a copy of a later engraving by a British artist called Hubert Wilson-Neal. It was based on a painting by Vanderschoot."

"Wow. It's exactly the same."

"No, it's not, not if you look closely. It's very similar. The book states quite clearly that the original painting is missing. But there *was* an original painting he used as the basis. Now given the similarities with your painting..."

"It must be the one!" I say, loudly, before looking around me and lowering my tone, "but what about the size mismatch then?"

Devon finishes her coke.

"I don't know. We're just going to have to some more digging."

"Cool," I reply. "So what's next?"

"Well, tomorrow I'm heading to the National Gallery… going to have a closer look at some of the Vanderschoots in there and see if I can identify any similarities with ours. You can come with me, if you want."

Well, I don't have anything else to do…

"Sure."

"OK, so, meet you there at 10?"

"Cool."

"OK. Well, got to go..." she stands up.

"Do you want another drink?" I ask, if only to have someone to sit with me for my fourth beer. I don't really fancy heading back to an empty flat. But Devon shakes her head.

"No, thanks. Got to get back. I want to do some more reading tonight."

Wow, you really do know how to live…

"OK, no worries, see you tomorrow."

Devon shuffles the various pieces of paper back into her portfolio case and heads for the door of the pub. I consider my options; a solitary flat and Saturday night TV, or another drink.

I give it a couple of seconds' thought, then head to the bar.

29

Devon leaves the pub and a sharp gust of winter air hits her immediately. She pulls her woolly hat on and heads for the station. She plans to go straight back to her flat in Brixton, draw the curtains, turn down the lights, put on some music and disappear under a pile of books, to spend the evening chasing the mystery of Straw Girl.

Bliss...

She crosses the busy road and as she does she thinks about Charlie...

He worries her.

He's naïve, disorganised, has a flimsy knowledge of the art world, and also seems to be half drunk most of the time...

If she could have chosen a partner to pursue what could be a major artistic coup, Charlie would have been somewhere near the bottom of the list.

Still, some things you don't get to choose...

As she reaches the opposite pavement she remembers something she meant to ask Charlie... did he actually have any proof of ownership, or was he just given the painting itself? What if there's someone out there with a claim to ownership that trumps Charlie's?

And who the hell are these people, who seem to be following him...?

It all niggles at Devon a little bit, but the excitement of the painting's possible provenance outweighs her misgivings.

She reaches the entrance to the station, and as she delves into her parka pocket in search of her Oyster card she is half aware of a dark figure approaching over her left shoulder. She automatically moves to one side to allow the tall stranger through, but he doesn't walk past. Instead he collides forcefully with her – shoving an elbow in between her shoulder blades.

Shocked and winded, Devon starts to lose balance. She drops her portfolio case onto the pavement as she throws her hands in front of her and falls forward, scraping her palms along the concrete and ending up in a heap on her side.

As she lies there on the cold pavement, bruised and bleeding from her palms, and sees the tall figure in dark blue hurrying away from her. She closes her eyes, and when she opens them he's gone - vanished into the Saturday night crowds.

30

The crowd at the bar have broken into a chorus of 'Swing Low Sweet Chariot' by the time I sit back down at my table with a fresh pint, confirming my suspicion that they're a bunch of rugby boys on a night out. I take a swig of my beer and look up the football scores on my phone, pondering how quickly my normal weekend routines have become skewed. Chelsea were at home to Spurs today, and normally I would have been following updates all afternoon.

Instead, I have no idea what the score was.

I learn that the match finished in an unsatisfactory 0-2 defeat for Chelsea, which doesn't do anything for my mood. I take a bigger sip of beer and look idly back at the rugby team. The door behind them swings open and I'm hit by a cold draught. An excited-looking bespectacled man runs in and shouts at nobody in particular…

"Help, quick, a girl's just been mugged outside the station!"

The rugger boys sense an opportunity to assert their beer-stoked masculinity, and make a bee-line for the door. I put down my pint, pocket my phone and stand up to follow them. I cross the road and see a small crowd gathered around the entrance to the station. Some people shift as the rugby players cross the road, and I see that the figure on the pavement is wearing a green parka and a bobble hat…

Devon.

I pick up my speed to a run, weaving in and out of cars, which have slowed to rubberneck the scene.

"Which way did he go?" shouts a rugby boy. A woman points up the road in the direction of the railway bridge.

"That way" says the woman.

"C'mon fellas," he says. His mates follow him and the crowd around Devon thins out - some onlookers are clearly more interested in the prospect of a fight further up the road.

Devon is now sitting up and rubbing her bloody palms against her tights, leaving dark red smears on them.

"I'll phone an ambulance," says the woman.

"Please, there's no need…" says Devon, straightening her bobble hat.

"Well, the police ought to be informed," says the bespectacled man from the pub.

"No, I'm fine honestly," says Devon, inspecting her palms, "It's just a scratch."

"Hi, I'm her friend" I announce, "I'll take her to the police station myself, it's only round the corner."

"There's no need…" says Devon again.

"You're probably in shock dear," says the woman.

"No I'm bloody not" says Devon, sharply. It's the first time I've heard her raise her voice.

"Come on Devon," I say, helping her to her feet "I'll walk with you." I turn to the man and woman, "thanks for your help."

"She really ought to get those cuts looked at…" says the woman.

I smile and lead Devon away. She walks unsteadily at first, and glances up at me; a scowl on her face, but no sign of fear…

"He took my bloody portfolio case…" she says.

"Shit," I say, "did you get a look at him?"

"No," she says.

"So," I say as I lead her up the road, "are we going to the police station?"

She raises an eyebrow...

"What do you think?"

*

I take Devon round the corner to the flat and she uses my bathroom to wash her cuts and dab the blood off her tights. She comes into the front room and I give her some antiseptic cream and plasters, which she applies gingerly.

"So," I say, "I'd offer you a brandy, but I know you don't drink…"

"Nope, well remembered," she nods. "It killed my father."

"Coffee then?"

"Yeah, awesome."

I walk over to the kitchen area and put the kettle on.

"So, you didn't see this man at all? Assuming it was a fella, of course?"

"I'm fairly sure it was a man," says Devon. "He was quite tall, like, over six foot. He had dark blue clothes on - a tracksuit or something - and he had the hood up."

"Did he say anything?"

"Nah, just pushed me over, grabbed the case and ran."

"What would he want with the case?"

"Well, now he's got high-res copies of the painting, and the print of the engraving. This all stuff I was going to use to build a case for it being a Vanderschoot. But at least it's all replaceable."

"Yeah, guess so."

"Ouch," says Devon, touching her head.

"Hurts?"

"A little."

"Did you hit it?"

"I think it grazed the pavement."

I hand her a coffee.

"You really should get it checked out at the hospital. Head injuries can be dodgy…"

"I know. But I'm not going to hospital now. I just want to go home and rest."

"Well, OK, but maybe you should get someone to keep an eye on you, in case it gets worse. Is there a friend you could call?"

Devon groans and sips her coffee.

"Well, there's my sister, I suppose…"

Devon calls her sister, somewhat reluctantly, and arranges for a lift back to Brixton. I listen as she concocts a story about falling over after a meal out with some work colleagues…

"Yeah Soph, I'm back at one of their flats now. No, of course I wasn't bloody drinking, I just tripped on a kerb. Yeah. OK, see you in ten."

Devon's sister, Sophia, arrives in around twenty minutes. I am alerted to her presence by the pounding of drum and bass music coming from outside on the street. It sounds like a pop-up nightclub's just opened.

"Sounds like she's here" says Devon, rolling her eyes.

I get up and peer out of the window to see a white BMW, from which the music appears to be emanating. A young woman gets out, slams the door and the music stops. All I can see are high heels, tight white jeans and long dark hair. She rings the intercom and I let her into the flat.

"Hi, Sophia is it?"

"Yeah, so you're my sister's mate? I don't get to meet many of them."

The difference between her and Devon is even starker close-up. Sophia is tall and sleek-haired, with an abundance of make-up and angular, shaped eyebrows. She clutches a leather handbag in one hand and a gold mobile phone in the other. She looks like a long-lost Kardashian sister, and speaks like an Eastenders extra...

"Shit, mate, look at the state of you! What happened?" she says, noticing Devon on the sofa.

"Tripped, didn't? Told you that on the phone..." says Devon, and I notice her voice becoming less neutral and slightly more south-London as she speaks to Sophia.

"She thinks she's hit her head," I say, "someone really ought to stay with her and make sure she's OK."

I look from sister to sister, despite the differences in fashion, there is a likeness there. Sophia rolls her eyes.

"OK, I suppose I can do it," she says. "I was planning to go out tonight though. You owe me one, sis."

"I owe you?" says Devon, "how many times have I paid off your phone bill?"

Sophia rolls her eyes again.

"Please. Come on then, we'd better go, don't want to spoil your mate's Saturday night too," she says.

Devon gets to her feet.

"Thanks Charles, speak on Monday" she says. Then, when Sophia's back is turned, she makes a phone gesture to me and mouths the word "tomorrow." I nod.

The sisters leave my flat and another blast of drum and bass tells me they're driving away. I consider going back to the Mason's Arms to resume my evening, but the thought of the tall man in dark clothing puts me off a bit. Instead I pour myself the brandy that Devon declined and flop down on the sofa, deciding that stupefaction by Saturday night TV is a better option.

Within minutes I fall asleep.

31

A phone call from Devon wakes me at half eight on Sunday morning, and I begin to despair of ever getting my longed-for lie-in. I'm sprawled on the sofa, the TV is still on, and my neck aches from the odd position it's assumed on the armrest.

Oh, and I'm fully dressed...

I shower and meet Devon at the National Gallery at ten, as arranged.

"How's your head?" I ask.

"Absolutely fine" she replies, "and yours?"

I grin sheepishly. Devon looks far sprightlier than I do, even with a head injury...

We head inside and make our way to a place I've been several times before.

Room 44...

The Execution of Lady Jane Grey is still there, of course, bearing down on the spot where Victor Botham collapsed. People are milling about in front of it as if nothing had happened. We make our way into an adjacent room. Devon stops by a smaller painting than Lady Jane Grey. It's more the size of Straw Girl, actually…

She stops.

"There aren't too many Vanderschoots in the gallery, but this is one of the best known. It's his self-portrait, done when he was 35."

"Blimey" I say.

I never knew it was there; so close to where I worked. I look at it closely, trying to connect the face in front of me and the painting I now own…

He's a funny looking chap, to be honest. Despite being only three years younger than me, he looks to be in his mid-40s, at best. His messy hair is a gingery red colour and he has a patchy beard, almost like one a teenager might attempt to grow. His eyes are small, blue and set a little bit too close together and his skin is blotchy and pockmarked. Few of his clothes are visible, but those that are look scruffy and dull.

I picture him sitting down in front of an empty canvas and somehow coming up with Straw Girl, and find it hard to imagine. Straw Girl is a thing of beauty, whereas this self-portrait is, well, I'm not sure of the correct term…

"It's very honest, don't you think?" says Devon.

"Yeah."

"If you compare it to, say, Rembrandt's self-portrait at a similar age, you'll see that whereas Rembrandt depicts himself as richly-dressed and self-secure, Vanderschoot looks, well…"

"Like a vagrant?"

"If you say so."

Devon moves us along to another painting.

"Is this also his?"

"Yep."

"Wow."

This is a bit more like a painting I'd expect the artist behind Straw Girl to have come up with. It shows a similar, rural scene in which two children - a boy and a girl - are pulling a small handcart along some sort of country lane. I notice two things; firstly, the sky is a similar shade of bright blue to that of my painting, and secondly, the cart is full of straw...

I look more closely... the children are maybe six or seven, whereas Straw Girl looks to be in her mid or late teens, but the sky and straw are very similar. I begin to think that this painting could almost be a sequel to mine; that the kids are carrying on the work that Straw Girl started...

Devon speaks.

"Vanderschoot lived in and around Antwerp all of his life, but at this stage of his career he took to travelling around rural Flanders depicting the life of the local peasants, much like Bruegel the Elder had done in the preceding century. Much of his finest work stems from this period."

"Devon," I say.

She looks at me.

"Why are you talking like a tour guide? I'm not a tourist, I'm an ex-employee..."

She frowns.

"Oh, sorry. It's just that I used to do a few talks when I was a student. I still remember most of the spiel..."

"So, in plain English, this looks bloody similar to mine, don't you agree?"

I nod at the painting, which is labelled: '*Two village children pulling a handcart, circa 1640.*'

"Well, on the surface, yes," she says.

"On the surface?"

"Yeah. Ostensibly, your painting and this painting have a lot of similarities that point to them being by the same hand. *Signature strokes,* we call them. Every artist has a way of painting that's unique to them. Look at the way the children have been drawn - their eyes, hair... and look at the detail in the background, the fluffy white clouds, the sheep..."

"Oh yeah, the sheep!"

I look closer. A tiny sheep on a hill in the middle distance leaps out at me, so to speak. It looks identical to the sheep in the background of Straw Girl; almost as if the artist had used a cut and paste tool on a modern computer.

"The colour used is also very, very similar," says Devon.

"Yeah?"

"Mmm. I'd say that your painting bears all the hallmarks of a genuine Vanderschoot. On the surface…"

"On the surface. You keep saying that," I tell Devon.

She looks away from the painting and towards me.

"That's because art has *layers*. There's the layer you see on top, and the many layers hidden underneath."

"OK…"

"This painting here is 378 years old, Charlie. So, we think, is Straw Girl. In that time a typical painting might have been damaged and repaired, or painted over by another hand… this might have happened time and time again. How would you look after almost four centuries, Charlie? I'm sure you'd need a few running repairs."

I smile.

"I guess…"

"And remember, Vanderschoot was working at a time when it was perfectly normal for several copies of a painting to be made… these could be done by students, or other artists in the same circle. One thing I need to look into is whether any copies were made of Straw Girl. If it turns out there were, we need to be sure that what you have isn't one of them."

"Right, and how can you tell?"

"Forensics. And research."

"So, what's next?" I say, "are there any other Vanderschoots here?"

"A couple," says Devon. "We can go and have a look. Then I'm going to go and book annual leave for the next two weeks."

"Eh?"

"It'll be fine, I've got a lot to use."

"You off on holiday or something?"

"No. I want to dedicate some time to proving this is real, Charlie. Because, despite all these possible misgivings, I really believe it is..."

"Bloody hell, you do?"

"Yeah" says Devon. "I mean, if it was a fake, why would someone break into your flat? Or do this to me...?"

She lifts up her sleeve and shows me a livid bruise on her forearm.

"Shit."

"Yeah, shit indeed."

It's the first time I've heard her swear....

32

Devon goes off to arrange her annual leave and re-print the documents that were stolen yesterday, leaving me with an idle Sunday afternoon ahead of me. I think of all the productive things I could be doing and then decide to spurn all of them in favour of an afternoon in the pub with Tim Anderson. At least I don't have a job to lose this time...

I meet Tim in the Mason's Arms just as it starts raining, which is handy. Tim seems to have been there some time, judging by the number of empty glasses on his table, and has set up camp directly opposite a TV which is showing a Six Nations game. I'm not a big rugger fan, but Tim explains that he's hoping the French can beat the Welsh, as this is in some way beneficial to the English.

"I'm not usually one to cheer for the Frenchies, but needs must," he says, making inroads on another pint of Guinness. I have to wait until full-time and a Welsh victory before Tim and I can have a proper conversation, one that he begins with the words:

"Useless bloody frogs!"

He takes another slurp of Guinness.

"So, Charlie boy, been busy?"

"Yeah, you could say that…"

I sip my lager.

"Oh?" Tim raises his eyebrows, "care to fill me in?"

"Well. I'm not sure where to start, but perhaps I should kick off with the fact that I'm now unemployed."

"Goodness, how so?"

"Well, that little drink we had last Sunday ended up having some unforseen consequences."

"Oh really?"

"Yep. Overslept. Went in late, hungover, and fell asleep at my post."

Tim grins.

"Some bloody tourist took a video of it and I ended up going viral."

Tim puts down his Guinness and lets out a hearty guffaw. I smile sheepishly. To be honest, my inglorious sacking seems so long ago now that I'm past feeling bad about it…

Tim finishes laughing.

"Sorry, mate, but that's priceless. Can I still see the video?"

"Guess so… be my guest."

Tim scrolls about on his phone, and I reluctantly give him some advice to find the link to the video.

"Try the Metro website - they did an online story about it."

He taps the info into Google and finds it. He watches it and laughs. Loudly. Some people across the pub turn to look at him.

"Hahaha! Oh, shit, sorry to laugh Charlie. Could have happened to anyone! So, what are you doing now? Found employment elsewhere?"

"Well, as a matter of fact, I'm doing a bit of private research."

"Sounds intriguing. Research in what field?"

"Art."

"Never had you down as a beard-stroker, mate."

"No. Well, I'm not. But I was given an interesting lead…"

"Oh yeah?"

"Yeah."

Perhaps I've been looking for someone to offload to, in Siobhan's absence, but for whatever reason, I proceed to tell him everything - from Victor Botham collapsing, to the painting being given to me, right through to the mysterious individual who seems hell-bent on sabotaging things. I also tell him that Straw Girl is currently in Muriel Lawrence's care home bedroom. I wonder if I should be saying all this, but I know I can trust Tim. After all, he's told me things about his campaigns in the Middle East that were never intended to go further than the pub table we shared. And they never did.

He sips his pint...

"My oh my. What have you got yourself into, Charlie boy?"

"I don't quite know."

"Mmm, seems that way."

He puts his drink down and stares at the table.

"Well, it seems clear that you've been given some hot property. And this fella who's been tailing you, well, he strikes me as a professional."

"Yeah?"

"Oh yes. He's always there. Knows what you're up to. Keeps a low profile. In fact, I'd say it sounds like he's got a military background. Some kind of training in surveillance, at least. In my opinion, of course."

"So what would you advise we do?"

"Well, sounds like you're doing the right thing, mainly. But personally I'd take the painting out of that home for the confused and get the hell out of London. Go somewhere nobody knows you. Lie low and do what you can to prove the thing is genuine."

"Do you think the retirement home is unsafe then? Devon thought it was a good idea…"

"Bloody hell man. You're asking if I think leaving a potentially priceless painting in an old folks' home full of menial workers on the minimum wage is a good idea? Those nurses don't have any loyalty. If they get a sniff of a valuable it'll be spirited away in no time. No, I'd get it out of there, sharpish."

"I guess you're right."

"Of course I'm bloody right! Another beer?"

I nod, and Tim makes his way to the bar. I wonder through the haze of an early afternoon beer pint whether it was a good idea telling Tim everything, but, well, it's a bit late now… I stare out of the pub window and look towards the station, where Devon was knocked over only last night.

If whoever's after us really does have a military background, then it's probably a good thing to have Major Tim on our side….

As I gaze out over the street, I notice a slight, dark-haired figure in a cream mac. It's Sunita Sharma. I haven't seen her since she came around last week and told me not to keep Straw Girl in the flat. I'd almost forgotten about that…

She's holding her mobile to her ear with one hand and waving the other one about. When she talked to me, she'd been quiet and composed. She looks quite the opposite now. Her face is creased in anger and she's clearly shouting at whoever is on the other end of the phone. She clenches her fist as she speaks and shakes it up and down in the air to emphasise her point. I watch for a while in surprise.

Eventually, Sunita cuts off he call and jabs her phone angrily back into her coat. She looks around with gritted teeth and marches through the main doors into the station.

At this point my phone starts vibrating…

DEVON CALLING.

I answer.

"Hello?"

"Hi."

She sounds odd. Shaky…

"All OK?"

"No, it's not. It's… it's Muriel."

"Muriel? Muriel Lawrence?"

"Yes."

"She hasn't lost the painting has she?" I ask.

"No," Devon replies. "She's dead."

33

I bid a hasty farewell to Tim, meet up with Devon, and we race to the care home in a taxi. We barely say a word - but, then again, there's little to say. Our eyes occasionally meet and it's clear we're both thinking the same thing…

Is Straw Girl still going to be there?

For some reason, all I can think about is the tall, thin man on the platform at Clapham Junction, the one with the red cap and blue mac, who had been there when I returned from Brighton. The same man who had been on the underground when Devon and I headed to Brixton. The idea that he might be our military-trained stalker crystallises in my mind.

Had he managed to track us to the care home? Had he been there last night to assault Devon? Had he now killed Muriel Lawrence and made off with my painting?

Was I foolish to let Straw Girl out of my sight?

I look at Devon - she's staring out of the window and her face is as impenetrable as ever. She traces a rectangular outline in the condensation on the taxi window.

The taxi driver drops us outside of Porterleigh House and we rush inside, where we're ushered into a small office and asked to wait for the manager. He turns up - fairly young and dressed in a smart grey suit - and introduces himself as Jas Akram. He is courteous and seems sincere when he looks at Devon and says:

"Miss Lamb, I'm sorry for your loss."

"Thanks" says Devon, "it's certainly a shock. How did it happen?"

"Mrs Lawrence collapsed in her room, around 10am this morning. She was rushed to hospital but died very shortly afterwards, as far as I understand. Once again, I am sorry for your loss. We all are."

"Thank you, Mr Akram. My aunt always said how much she loved it here."

She was Devon's 'aunt' now? I thought she was just a friend...

"We were very fond of her," says Jas Akram, "everyone was."

Devon smiles.

"Have you got idea what might have caused it? How did Muriel seem this weekend?"

Akram looks thoughtful...

"Well, she seemed her old self. She came down for breakfast as usual. It was only after her visitor left that she seemed a little bit...

upset."

I look up.

"Er, sorry, visitor?"

"Sorry, yes," says Devon, "we weren't aware she had any visitors. Was it someone she knew?"

"Well, not to my knowledge," says Akram, "I certainly hadn't seen this gentleman before."

"Gentleman? What did he look like?" asks Devon.

"Well, he was an older guy, maybe in his 60s, and he was wearing a hat, sort of a baggy cap, which he didn't take off."

"Do you remember anything else about him?"

Akram looks upwards…

"Not really sir, sorry, I only glimpsed him. I just remember that afterwards Mrs Lawrence seemed sort of upset…"

"Upset in what way?" I ask.

"Well, she refused a cup of tea, which she usually always has about 11, and said she wanted to go back to her room. She seemed kind of… distracted. That was the last we saw of her. A member of staff checked on her half an hour later and she'd collapsed."

I shoot a look at Devon.

"Could you possibly describe this man in any more detail?"

Akram sighs…

"I couldn't really say… well, white, medium height, I guess. A bit on the flabby side."

"What about his hair?" I ask.

Akram shrugs.

"Hidden under his hat. I'm sorry, I really wasn't paying much attention at the time."

"No worries, Mr Akram" I say.

There's a pause, then Devon speaks…

"Sir, I recently left Muriel a painting, as a loan. It belongs to Mr Marks here…" she nods at me. "We wondered if we could take it back, today?"

Mr Akram fiddles with the knot on his purple tie.

"I'm sorry, but it's not possible at the moment. Only Mrs Lawrence's next of kin can access her possessions at the moment, and they will need to contact her solicitor to arrange what's going to happen to them, according to her will, of course…"

Devon shoots me a concerned look. I return it.

As we leave Akram's office I notice the door which leads from the communal lounge area to the bedrooms. It's locked shut. A nurse taps a code on the keypad and enters, shutting the door firmly behind her.

"So, what now?" I ask Devon.

She shrugs.

"If Straw Girl is still on Muriel's wall, and it's very much an if at this point, we're going to have to go through a lot of bother just to get it back. And time's not on our side. I've only got so much annual leave left…"

And I've only got two weeks until Siobhan's back...

"Unless we can think of some other way to get it…"

It has to be said, nothing springs to mind.

34

Devon heads back to Brixton to speak to her mother and try to find out who Muriel Lawrence's next of kin might be. Also, as we currently have no access to the painting, she calls her forensics specialist contact and cancels the appointment she'd booked for tomorrow.

It all feels very much like we've taken two very large steps back and a very small one forwards.

With nothing else to do, I head back to Mason's Arms, which is fast becoming my second home. Or first home, come to that. Tim seems to have gone home, so I buy a pint, take a seat in the corner and stare at the final minutes of the football game showing on the TV. Brighton and Hove scrape a draw with Everton, but I barely take in what's happening. Instead I rack my brains, trying to work out who could have been into Porterleigh House this morning, spooking Muriel Lawrence...

Had he been there to demand the painting? And was it the same guy who's been following me?

Mr Akram's description of a chubby, older white man in a cap doesn't exactly match with the tall man at the tube station who may also have pushed Devon over. It doesn't make sense. Nothing makes any sense, and all of it seems to be giving me a headache. I sip my beer and look back at the TV.

*

Devon gets off the tube at Brixton. Her flat is to the left, down a side street and above a laundrette, but she doesn't head that way. Instead she makes a right turn and starts walking a route that, in a way, is even more familiar. The route to the flat she grew up in.

After a while she passes the cemetery. She glances at it but doesn't stop to linger. However, she knows that somewhere among the clustered headstones is the one belonging to Julian Paul Lamb.

Her father.

The dates inscribed under his name read 1955 - 1999. He died when Devon was four years old.

It was the drink that killed him. That's what everyone in the family always says. As the story goes, his life was always one big balancing act between art and booze, and eventually the booze won.

Julian was from a middle-class, white family, but he never fancied the traditional route into university and respectability, instead choosing art college and the vibrant streets of Brixton. It was in a Brixton pub sometime in the 1980s that he met the young daughter of a couple of Jamaican immigrants, a bright, funny young girl named Doreen.

Doreen Walsh and Julian Lamb were married in 1985 and went on to have four children together over the next ten years - all of them girls. Amanda and Cheryl arrived in close proximity and were followed, after a slight gap, by Sophia in 1993 and finally - in the summer of '95 - by Devon.

Devon had always been different; perhaps even since birth, when she arrived with little fanfare. She even screamed less than her sisters. She was always a composed, quiet child who seemed quite content in her own company. The council flat she shared with her three siblings and parents was a constantly noisy home, but Devon usually managed to find a quiet place to read; often she could be found lying under her mum's bed with a book and a torch. And usually the book in question was one of her father's art books.

Julian Lamb was often away from the family home. When he wasn't working in one low-paid job or another he was locked in the small garage he used as a studio, often painting until the early hours of the morning. He would frequently go days without eating, spending what little didn't go on food for his kids on paints, canvases and tobacco. But as his artistic prospects declined, and the cost of raising a family increased, he was often more likely to be found in one of south London's many pubs, frittering away his meagre wages and limited talent on Irish whisky and questionable company.

One day, Julian didn't return home at all. He collapsed on the way home from the pub; his body ravaged by years of neglect. Unlike her sisters, Devon barely knew her father well enough to miss him, so she didn't. Instead she adopted his art library as her own, and swore to never succumb to the same temptations that he had...

Devon looks ahead. She's almost past the cemetery now, and she can see Lusaka House looming ahead of her. It looks like somewhere the hero of a TV detective series would go to apprehend some cliched gang member; all exposed concrete and boxy angles with multi-coloured front doors running along the length of its stacked balconies.

Devon enters the stairwell and steps over a windswept pile of rubbish that has gathered in a corner; beer cans, fag packets and crisp wrappers. She breathes in the familiar smell of damp and urine and makes her way up the stairs.

She sees the outline of her mum in the frosted glass window, moving towards the door as she holds down the bell. She hears the chain being removed and the door being opened.

"Oh, darling, hello!"

"Hi mum."

Doreen beckons Devon into the flat and its familiar smell hits her, the indefinable aroma which always takes her straight back to childhood.

Devon's mum doesn't seem her usual, sparkly self. There's a sadness in her eyes which even the pleasure of the sight of her youngest daughter can't disguise. She heads into the kitchen and Devon follows, kicking her shoes off as she goes.

By the time Devon is sat at the kitchen table and the kettle is on, her mum mentions Muriel for the first time...

"Lord, it's such a shame about Muriel... I keep thinking about the poor woman."

Devon nods.

"I know, I'm sorry mum, but she had a good innings."

Her mum looks at her.

"A what?"

Devon chides herself for using such a middle-class phrase. This one especially must have been picked up at the gallery rather than on the streets of Brixton.

"I mean, she had a good life."

"Yes darling, but what a way for it to end."

She shakes her head and starts making the tea.

"At least she wasn't alone at the end," says Devon.

"Not alone? How do you mean, love?"

"Well, I went to Porterleigh House earlier, to try and find out what happened, and apparently she had a visitor, just before she died."

"A visitor, really? Well, it might have been Maureen from church... she often goes to see her, not usually on Sundays though."

"No, it wasn't Maureen. The manager said it was a man."

"A man?" says Doreen, eyes widening, "could have been her brother, although I didn't think he'd been down recently..."

"No, it wasn't her brother either, this man was white."

Doreen stares into her mug of tea.

"Well, Lord knows who that could have been. Muriel didn't have many gentlemen callers, not that I knew about anyway. And I've known her for years, darling. She was like a mother to me when I first moved into this flat... and she often looked after you when you were little..."

"I know," says Devon, but her mum seems to have disappeared into reminiscence...

"And after her Bobby died she never had any interest in men at all. That's the kind of lady she was - God fearing. I don't know who this man might have been..."

Devon stares at the kitchen table. She traces her fingers around the outline of a cat. She'd carved it into the table herself, sometime in the late 90s, in a rare moment of naughtiness, and her house-proud mum had hit the roof. Her father hadn't been bothered at all.

Devon raises her voice to snap her mum out of her reverie.

"Mum... mum! Look, I'm a bit concerned about who this man might have been. Muriel had a lot of stuff in her room, some of it

179

was quite valuable. Do you know what's going to happen to it all? I mean, who would her next of kin be?"

Doreen wipes a tear from her eye.

"That would be her brother, Colin. He's the only family she's got left."

"OK, and do you have a phone number for this Colin? I think someone should check when he's coming to sort things out."

"No, I don't love. All I know is he lives in Birmingham somewhere. But he'll be down soon enough I'm sure. He was always on at her to auction off some of her stuff..."

Devon drains her mug of tea and traces her fingers around her childhood cat engraving and thinks. Birmingham. That's only a couple of hours' drive from London. Colin could be at the care home already, pound signs in his eyes, ready to auction off all his late sister's belongings for a knock down price.

Including Straw Girl.

She takes her mug to the sink and rinses it as her mother continues to tell Muriel anecdotes, but Devon isn't interested in stories from the past. She knows that she and Charlie have to act. And fast...

35

When the football's over I head to the bar to buy another pint, thinking about two related things:

a) How I seem to be spending more time in the Mason's Arms than my own flat.

b) How quite a large proportion of Victor Botham's cheque seems to have been invested in beer...

At the bar I notice a stocky, olive-skinned man with dark, curly hair. He's sitting on a bar stool with his head in his hands and a half-drunk pint in front of him. I look at him again. He seems vaguely familiar, although I can't quite put my finger on where I know him from.

As I pay for my drink, I hear a buzzing sound on the bar. The man's phone, placed next to his pint, lights up. He turns to glance at it then turns away, but when I see his face I realise where I know him from. It's Dinos - the care home worker who first took us to see Muriel Lawrence.

"Hello mate," I say, "don't I know you?"

He looks up, blankly.

"Don't think so."

He stares back at his beer.

"Yeah, I do, Porterleigh House… you were working there when my colleague and I went to visit Muriel Lawrence."

He looks up at the mention of her name.

"Yeah, that's right."

"I suppose you've heard the sad news?"

"I have mate. Made a shitty day even bloody worse!"

He downs a mouth-full of beer. I gesture to his pint glass.

"Can I get you another?"

"Nah, I can't… have to be on shift in half an hour. Fucking nightshift man, bloody hell."

To be honest, judging by the beery aroma surrounding Dinos, it's a little late for him to be worrying about sobering up for work. But I smell an opportunity…

"Let me get you a coffee then?"

Dinos looks up groggily and meets my eyes for the first time.

"Coffee? Yeah, OK, cheers. Black. Three sugars."

I order him a sufficiently sweet americano, which he starts as soon as he's finished his beer. I join him in a coffee, suddenly feeling like a clear head is a better idea. I pull up a stool.

"So, long shift coming up then?" I ask.

"Yeah man," he says, wearily, "12 bloody hours. Third one this weekend. I'm knackered. I'd call in sick, but I need the money too bad. Not that it's going to help me…" he rubs his hands over his face again, sighing as he does.

"How do you mean?" I ask, hoping that Dinos has drunk enough to offload his problems to a virtual stranger. Luckily for me, it seems he has…

"I've got debts man. Serious debts. Don't know how I'm going to sort this shit out. I'm going to end up on the streets man!"

"I'm sure it won't come to that," I say.

Dinos looks up at me, his eyes now red.

"You got kids?" he asks.

"Er, yeah, just the one. A boy."

"How old?"

"19."

He squints at me.

"You don't look old enough, mate."

"Thanks. I was quite young. How about you?"

"I've got a daughter. Larissa. She's two."

"Oh, a nice age."

Dinos looks down at the bar and breathes in deeply, then his shoulders start shaking.

"It was her first proper Christmas, man, and I just wanted to make it good for her. Shit. I took out one of them payday loan things, then I had to take out another to cover the rent for January."

"Oh, shit."

"Now I owe both companies more than I can afford, and I ain't got enough to pay this month's rent. We're going to be out on the streets man. They'll take my little girl into care."

He starts sobbing. Loudly. I look around us…

Can't your wife… or girlfriend help?"

"No man. She doesn't have a job, and she doesn't know anything about all this. Fuck me mate, what am I going to do?"

I take a deep breath and a swig of coffee.

"How much do you need? Overall? Like, to pay off your debts and your rent."

"Why?"

"Just out of interest...?"

He sniffs…

"Um, well, two grand would cover it."

I drain my coffee.

"Look, buddy, there might be a way out of this. I might have a one-off job for you."

He looks up through his teary eyes.

"Yeah?

"Possibly. Look, wait there. I'm going to the gents. Then I'll buy you another coffee and explain."

Dinos nods shakily and I head off to the toilets. When I'm out of his sight I take my phone out of my pocket.

*

Devon hugs her mum goodbye and is just leaving Kinshasa House when her phone rings:

CHARLIE CALLING

She stops on the balcony and answers.

"Hi Charlie."

"Hi. You alright?"

"Yeah, OK. Except it turns out that Muriel's brother is her next of kin. He lives in Birmingham but could be down to take possession of her estate any minute..."

"OK, OK, listen, I think there might be a way we can get Straw Girl back. Tonight."

Devon pauses.

"Tonight?"

"Yeah..."

"How Charlie? I mean, what's the catch?"

"Well, it's going to cost us two grand..."

36

As planned, Devon reaches my flat just after midnight and I greet her with a strong coffee.

"You got the money?"

"Yep, you?"

I point to a stack of notes on the coffee table. I'd just withdrawn £500, the daily maximum, from my local cashpoint, waited until just past midnight, then removed another £500. Devon had done the same on the way over.

Victor Botham's cheque is almost gone... Devon puts her cash down on the table.

"This is getting expensive," she says. "You sure it's going to work?"

"No," I say, "but what else are we going to do?"

She nods.

"Is Dinos clear about his part?"

"I hope so. I managed to sober him up enough to drill the plan into him."

"So what time are we getting there?"

"Three."

"Three?!"

"Yep. According to him, that's the quietest time. There's just him and one other bloke on duty, and the other guy is doing the rounds upstairs then. That's when we arrive."

"OK, so what do we do now?"

"Well, I don't know about you, but I'm going to set my alarm for an hour's time, lie on the sofa and try to sleep. You're welcome to lie down on my bed..."

Devon frowns at the idea and takes a book out of her bag.

"No thanks. I'll read."

*

02:50.

Devon and I are crouched in shadow of the wall surrounding Porterleigh House. We're both dressed in dark clothing, and the Brixton back street is mercifully quiet.

It's also bloody freezing.

In my coat pocket is a brown envelope containing two thousand pounds in cash. I drag on my e-cigarette and wonder, not for the first time, how I ended up here...

We wait in as much darkness as we can find away from the streetlights. A man in a hoodie saunters past us on the other side of the street and we both stare at the wall until he's passed.

I check the time on my phone.

02:59

I look at Devon.

"OK?"

"Yep."

I unlock my phone and dial the last number on my history. It belongs to Dinos. After three rings I hang up. Just as planned, the buzzer sounds, and I pull open the main gate. Devon waits on the street and tightens her backpack. I wander through the doorway into the small courtyard. Leaves brush against my hands, wet with dew, and my breath makes clouds in front of me. The main entrance lobby is just ahead. I look up at the building. All seems quiet, although I can see a couple of lights behind the first-floor windows. I hope Dinos' colleague is busy up there.

The lobby doors open slowly. Beyond them is darkness. I shift to one side and realise just how fast my heart is beating. A stocky figure emerges in the pale light cast by the upstairs windows.

Dinos...

He's dressed in his blue uniform and carries a large, rectangular shape wrapped in a blanket. He props it in the doorway.

"You got the money?" he asks. He looks edgy too, and I imagine his heart is going at a similar rate to mine...

"Yeah," I say, taking the envelope out of my pocket and holding it up with shaking hands. He nods.

"OK, bring me the painting. Carefully."

"Nah, not yet" he says, shuffling protectively in front of it.

"What?"

"There's been a change of plan," he whispers. "I'm going to need four grand."

"What?" I repeat, staring through the gloom at his face, trying to work if he's serious.

"You're asking me to risk my job man," he hisses. "You have to double it."

Shit. He has to be kidding me...

"Dinos, I don't have four grand. I've got two thousand, right here. Just hand over the painting and it's yours."

"Nah, man. You want it too bad. It's gotta be worth more. Four grand. Meet me here, same time tomorrow."

"I told you, I don't have four grand..." I say, my voice rising.

"You'll find it."

He backs away from me. I start to follow him, but he holds his hand up, showing me some sort of red panic button. He backs towards the doors and bends down to pick up Straw Girl. As he does, I notice that he slips the panic button back into his pocket in order to lift the painting.

I consider rushing him, but I can't seem to make myself move. I stand there, staring, as a dark blur rushes past me from the darkness of the courtyard. All I see is a flash of green bobble hat and dark hair.

Devon...

She runs straight at Dinos and in one smooth action pulls something out of her coat. Something dark. He turns, letting the painting fall, and throws his arms out in front of him. Devon swings her arm backwards and then smacks something forcefully into Dinos's leg. He falls to the ground, clutching his kneecap and swearing.

Loudly...

"Grab it!" she says, nodding at Straw Girl. I see what she's holding. It looks like a small baseball bat. She brings it down again, hitting Dinos right between his legs. I wince.

Unsurprisingly, so does he.

I rush over and grab the painting, as Dinos whimpers, curled up on the ground. Devon puts the bat back into her coat and looks at me.

"Give him the cash."

"Eh?"

"Give it to him!"

She glares at me, and I chuck the brown envelope at Dinos' prone body. It hits his midriff with a thud.

"Quick. Let's get out of here," hisses Devon.

I look up as a light snaps on in a first-floor room and a man's face appears at the window. Dinos lets rip an animal's roar. I grip Straw Girl tightly and follow Devon towards the road.

37

We stop running and Devon guides me around a corner and into an area of wasteland and rusty garages. She pulls the Marks and Spencer suit bag out of her rucksack and unfurls it.

"Put it in," she says, nodding at Straw Girl.

"You brought a bloody baseball bat?" I say, breathlessly.

"A mini rounders bat," she says, like it makes a difference…

"But, why?"

"I thought he might cut up rough."

"Yeah?"

"Yeah. Come on Charlie, don't be naive. The guy's desperate, and you've let him know that you're willing to pay at least two grand for the painting. Were you really surprised he held out for more?"

"Yeah, actually."

"Well anyway, he shouldn't be bothering us again. He's got his cash."

"He's got a bit more than that… it'll probably be summer before he can walk properly again…"

"Serves him right," says Devon, and I'm struck by how focused she is, while my hands are shaking and I'm desperate for a proper cigarette. Devon zips the suit bag up around the painting and passes it to me. I hoist it over my shoulders.

"Come on," she says, "let's keep moving." She paces away and I follow, obediently.

*

It's just gone 4am when we arrive at Devon's flat. She opens a peeling-paint door next to a laundrette and we pace up a threadbare staircase lit by a single lightbulb.

Inside, Devon's flat is far more welcoming than the stairway suggests. It is small but cosy, with dark walls, wooden floors and retro furniture. Prints of various works of art line the walls. Devon props Straw Girl against an armchair and sits down next to it. I pull a chair away from the kitchen table and sit opposite her. She looks at me.

"Right, Charlie, think. We need a new plan."

"OK," I say, but it's either too late or too early to think, and my brain can't help replaying everything that's just happened. "I'm starting to think that painting's more trouble than it's worth," I say.

"Then leave it with me. I'll take on the case alone."

"But... it's mine."

"I know, and it'll still be yours when this is over, but if you're worried, I'm prepared to go it alone."

"No," I say, "I can't let you do that. Not with that man after it... whoever the hell he is."

"I can handle it. But I'm glad you're still on board," she says. "OK, first, we need a new base. This flat's out of the question, and so is yours."

I look around me...

"OK, but we do appear to be in this flat now. Is that not dodgy?"

"Probably," says Devon, "which is why I'm booking a taxi into town and checking us into a hotel."

"Us?"

"Yep." She shoots me her trademark *look*... "Separate rooms."

"Obviously. Then what?"

"Then I'm going to get the thing forensically examined, and you're going back to your solicitor."

"Hussain? Why?"

"You say this painting is yours, but how do you know? Were you given any formal documentation, or just the painting?"

I think back to Monday, which seems an age ago...

"Well, just the painting, and a letter to say I was entitled to open the safe deposit box. But nothing about the contents..."

"OK, so you need to go and see Hussain and demand some official proof of ownership. He must have something. It's important, Charlie."

Judging by the stare Devon fixes me with, I don't doubt it.

38

Devon decides that the best hotels are likely to be the most secure, and decides to book us into the Langham. I have a minor seizure when I see the price and suggest somewhere more modest…

"How are you affording this anyway?"

"Charlie, if the painting's a genuine Vanderschoot you'll be a rich man."

"Yeah, *if*…"

Devon rolls her eyes.

"I've got savings. I'll pay. It's only for a night or two…"

Devon relents on her 'separate rooms' policy and books us into a twin, but only when I threaten to stay at a budget place around the corner. We take a taxi into an eerily quiet central London and check into our room at just gone five in the morning. I lie on my single bed and attempt to get some rest until Monday begins, and at some point I drift off into a light, restless sleep. I wake up with a start about an hour later in a confused and drowsy state. I stare at my unfamiliar ceiling and try to remember where the hell I am. Then the image of Devon whacking Dinos in his nether regions bursts into my mind, and I'm reminded starkly of just where I am and what I'm doing.

My alarm goes off at half eight, but I feel like I haven't slept at all. I get up, and a glance at Devon's empty bed tells me that she's already left. I wash my face in the opulent marble sink, comb my hair, and head out in the direction of Mallender-Hussain's offices.

I reach the quiet Marylebone street with the little cafe and soon I'm staring at a familiar wooden door with its gold nameplate. I'm buzzed into the reception and see Sunita Sharma, sitting behind her computer, looking far more composed than she had yesterday afternoon, when I'd seen her arguing on her phone.

She looks up from her screen and raises an eyebrow.

"Oh, hello Mr Marks."

If she looked surprised to see me, she certainly doesn't sound it.

"Please, call me Charlie..."

"Fine, how can I help you, Charlie?"

"Er, I was just wondering if I could have a word with Mr Hussain?"

"I'm sorry Charlie, but Ben... I mean, Mr Hussain, is out of the country at present - visiting relatives."

Out of the country. Great...

"Is there anyone else I could talk to? What about Mr Mallender? Or is it Mrs Mallender?"

"I'm afraid Geoffrey Mallender died some years ago, Charlie. Mr Hussain is the only living partner. It's just me and him. I can leave a message if you'd like?"

"Perhaps you can help?" I say, with a smile which she doesn't return.

"I doubt I can..."

I sit down on the leather seat opposite her.

"Can I call you Sunita?"

She nods, her face neutral.

"Sunita, I'm worried about this painting I've been given. Since you visited my home and told me not to keep it there, there have been several attempts to steal it..."

A flicker of concern touches Sunita's face. Her thick black spectacles rise and fall almost imperceptibly. Not for the first time, I wonder if there was any connection between her phone argument yesterday and Muriel's sudden death...

"I hope it's still safe?" she asks.

"Yeah, for now. But when I received the painting, there were no papers to say it was legally mine. I've had a letter from Mr Botham, but nothing else. Shouldn't there be, like, a formal statement of ownership?"

Sunita checks something on her screen and looks back at me.

"I'm sorry, Charlie, you really would need to ask Mr Hussain about such a thing. I'm only his assistant. He supplied me only with the information he thought necessary."

"OK. But there's one thing I don't quite get… if you're *only* Mr Hussain's assistant, how did you know that I shouldn't keep the painting in my home? You must have known there was some history there… that someone was prepared to break in to steal it back?"

"Someone broke in?" Sunita asks, frowning.

"Yes," I reply tersely. Perhaps it's because I haven't slept properly, but I'm finding her evasiveness irritating. I raise my voice...

"Come on, you must know more than you're letting on. What solicitor's assistant comes to a client's house at night, for Christ's sake?"

She stares at me, still impassive, but I see she's fiddling with her wristwatch.

"Look, Charlie, I'm sorry, I really can't help you any further. I suggest you come back when Mr Hussain's here.

"OK… fine."

I get up to leave, slightly regretting my outburst and stifling a yawn, and turn back before I reach the door.

"Look, sorry I raised my voice. This all just seems a bit of a mystery to me."

"To me too, Charlie," she says, quietly.

39

After my unsatisfactory meeting with Sunita I decide to head back to Battersea, just to pick up some belongings. I'm throwing stuff into a bag, unsure about how long I should be packing for, when my phone rings.

I pull it out of my pocket, expecting it to be Devon, but it isn't… It's Siobhan.

I'm tempted to stuff it back into my pocket and pretend I'm busy, but I haven't spoken to her for a few days, and I feel a pang of guilt when I contemplate avoiding her…

I answer.

"Hi love."

"Hi Charlie," she says, "how's everything?"

"Ah, OK, all pretty normal," I lie.

"Not burnt the flat down yet then?" she asks.

"No, not quite..." I say.

"Well, that's something."

"Yep" I say lightly, with a guilty look at the hold-all full of clothes across the room.

We share some small talk for a few minutes, and I try not to sound edgy and stressed, which is hard because, well, I'm edgy and stressed. In contrast, Siobhan sounds relaxed, telling me about the weather (hot) the food and drink (plentiful) and the people (nice, insufferably so, I assume). All her news seems reasonably mundane, until then she says the word 'anywaaaay' in a drawn-out manner and pauses. I know what this means... something's coming.

"Anywaaaay... I've got some good news. Well, I hope it's good news to you."

"Oh, go on..."

"Well, last night I had dinner with my boss over here, Joshua, he's a nice guy."

"Great." I say, bristling.

"Yeah, well, he wants me to stay on for another week. Right up to the American premier of the movie. I'll get to go to that, by the way. Apparently they've been really impressed with my work..."

I don't doubt it... Siobhan is the most organised and efficient person I know. Her skills in that area have always made up for my complete lack of them, which is probably why I'm in the mess I find myself in right now.

"Of course, that's great news," I say, and to be honest, it is. It buys me some extra time to sort things out here, for a start. I now have another fortnight to play with.

Siobhan continues…

"So, the marketing department over here are really pleased with everything, and, well, last night Joshua kind of gave me the impression that they'd like to take me on full-time. They handle a lot of British movies and actors and they're really keen on the knowledge I can bring…"

I'm jolted out of my own thoughts.

"Sorry, what? Like a full-time job?"

"It's just the impression I got from Joshua. He said that new openings were happening all the time. He hinted that something might come up soon..."

I decide I don't like Joshua.

There's a pause. It seems like I'm expected to say something.
"OK."

"OK?" asks Siobhan, "is that it? Did you hear what I said?"

"Yeah, there might be a job going."

"In Los Angeles."

"Yeah, in LA. So, what are you going to do, move?"

"*We*. We could move here Charlie. After all, you're not exactly tied to a career in the UK, are you?"

"Well, no..."

"And LA is the home of the movie industry. What better place to be a screenwriter?"

True…

"I do have a son here though," I say.

Now Siobhan pauses.

"Of course. I know. Look, it's all hypothetical at the moment. Just an idea. It might come to nothing. We can talk about it when I'm home."

"Sure," I say, "we'll talk about it later. But I'm pleased for you. Really. Well done, love."

I attempt to sound genuine, but I'm not sure I mean it. A relocation to LA would have been an exciting prospect a few weeks ago, but right now all of my interests are very UK-based. I listen to her talking about the film for a few more minutes, throwing in a few 'yeahs' and 'rights', and finish with a bare-faced lie about having to get off to work.

"Oh yeah," she says, "I didn't realise what time it was over there. Bye, love. Speak soon."

"Bye, love you."

I hang up and throw a few more things into my hold-all (a toothbrush, a phone charger, a half-drunk bottle of brandy) before letting myself out of the flat and locking the door behind me.

I'm not sure when I'll be back…

40

I make my way moodily back to the station and attempt to cheer myself up by reminding myself that I might just be in possession of a painting that's worth a fortune.

For some reason, it doesn't quite work… all I can think of is Siobhan and Joshua (who, in my head, is tall, handsome and has very white teeth) discussing exciting opportunities in the land of films, sunshine and botox.

I make my way onto the platform and look for the next available train to Victoria, but out of the corner of my eye I catch a glimpse of a familiar figure… he's standing at the end of the platform, just before the point that passengers aren't supposed to pass. He's wearing the same clothes as last time; a blue waterproof and a red baseball cap, pulled down close to his eyes.

I wander over to him and although I can't quite see his eyes, he moves his head in my direction and seems to clock me. At this point he looks down, furtively. Something inside me snaps. I stomp up the platform towards him, and when I'm within earshot I shout...

"Oi!"

"He looks up at me and I see under the peak of his cap. He's in his 40s, probably, and has a thin, gaunt face and a little goatee beard. He looks shocked, and I see that he has a notebook of some kind in his hands.

"Who *are* you?" I yell, walking closer.

"Who, me?" he asks.

"Yes, you… who the fuck do you think I'm talking to?"

I'm aware that I'm shouting now... but it doesn't sound like my voice.

He backs away, putting some distance between us, and holds his hands up.

"Look, I don't want any trouble..."

"Then why are you following me?"

"Me?" he says.

"Yes!"

I'm close up to him now; I can almost smell him. I don't think he's showered this morning... I grab his thin shoulders and shake him. I think of my flat being ransacked, and of Devon being barged to the ground, and I want to punish him.

I want to hurt him…

However, I'm not very good at this sort of thing. I usually dread confrontation. I feel light-headed and everything seems slightly unreal.

"Stop following me!" I shout. My voice sounds weird and high pitched.

Then I push him... hard, right in the chest, with both hands. He's surprisingly light, and falls backwards easily, ending up sprawled out on the concrete. His notebook falls from his hands and flaps open, facing upwards.

"Help!" he shouts. People on the opposite platform look over at us. I consider kicking him in the side while he's down, but fortunately the temptation is fleeting. Instead I kneel down and pick up his notebook. It's full of spidery handwriting in cheap blue biro. There are lines and lines of six-digit numbers broken up into dates... I stare at the page.

Monday:

537 761

544 569

477 617

598 113

I throw the book back down, just as a train pulls into the station. I look at its engine as it rolls past me. Printed on the front of the cab is a similar, six-digit number.

534 385

"Help me! Someone help!" cries the man in the red cap...

The man I now know to be innocent train spotter.

I look at him again, I see real fear in his eyes. He looks weak and scared. How I ever mistook him for a trained stalker is beyond me. I'm horrified at what I've done.

What I've become...

A sleep-deprived, violent, paranoid mess...

I see someone on the opposite platform, they're holding a phone to their ear.

Oh shit, they're calling the police...

I turn and run along the platform, through the ticket hall and out onto the street, my heart pounding, my mind racing.

I don't stop running for some time.

Part Two

<u>'Posie'</u>

1

Posie isn't my real name. It's just the name my father liked to call me, possibly because my real name was always a concession to my mother's family...

When I think of my father, I think of several things:

I think of art and cricket. I think of colourful clothes; particularly an MCC tie. I think of the smell of whisky and aftershave. I think of heated conversation and laughter.

I think of my mother.

And when I think of my mother, I think about how she died.

She, my mother that is, was born 1960. She came over to England in the 80s to study art and soon fell in with a group of artistic types based around North London. Among this group of aesthetes were a painter named Clara Swann (who would become my Godmother), her future husband Geoffrey Mallender, and an art dealer named Victor Botham.

My father...

When my mother met Victor she was in her mid-20s and he was in his early 60s. It seems outrageous now, but if the near 40-year age gap was enough to raise the eyebrows of wider society, it certainly didn't seem to bother the circles they moved in. Besides, my father never looked his age, and my mother was always wise beyond her years. I can't imagine either of them being with anybody else.

I was born in London in 1993. For the first four years of my life I lived in my parents' townhouse in Marylebone. When I reached school age, my parents decided to move to the suburbs in search of a quieter place to bring up a child. They chose Chorleywood; a leafy commuter-belt village in Hertfordshire. Chorleywood could boast good schools, a low crime rate and much greenery, and was still only 30 minutes from Marylebone Station, near which my father still had a share in an art gallery.

I can barely remember living in central London now. Fragments of memories still surface; riding on grimy tube trains, staring from a window at smoky traffic, being led by my mother around busy markets. It all exists like a fading, fraying dream.

I have better memories of Chorleywood. Until I was eight, my childhood in Chorleywood was idyllic in so many ways. We lived in a large, detached, red-brick house which backed onto open fields. My mother was young, and my father semi-retired and wealthy. It was a time full of days out, sunny picnics and trips abroad. I had no siblings, but I never felt deprived of company. I had plenty of friends at school and an abundance of interesting adults to entertain me.

One of the most interesting was my Godmother, Clara Swann. She always struck me as a child trapped in an adult's body, or even an adult trapped in a child's body, for she was barely five-foot tall and built like a little, flame-haired bird. It was only when you saw her eyes and the lines around them that you realised that she was actually a grown-up.

Clara was Scottish by birth and accent but had moved to London as an 18-year-old art student in 1980 and remained in the south of England ever since. Despite being something of a free spirit, I think Clara always equally yearned for security, and she found this when she met a young lawyer named Geoffrey Mallender. 10 years her senior, Geoffrey offered a good deal more stability than the hand-to-mouth existence promised by the flighty art students she was used to dating.

It was at Saint Martin's School of Art on Charing Cross Road that Clara and my mother first became good friends. They were both outsiders to London in their own ways; Clara hailed from a small Scottish town and my mother from even further afield. They shared a flat after university - where they both struggled to combine their art with dull office jobs - and when my mother fell pregnant to Victor, Clara was the obvious choice as my Godmother.

Clara and Geoffrey married in Marylebone Town Hall shortly after I was born, and when my parents decided to relocate to the suburbs, the Mallender-Swanns followed suit. That way, Geoffrey could commute into his office in London and Clara could use their conservatory as a studio.

Geoffrey Mallender couldn't afford to buy quite as impressive a house as my father could, but in a way, I preferred Clara's home to my own. It lacked the spaciousness, the swimming pool and the green fields to the back, but the cottage she shared with Geoffrey was cosier and chock-full of curiosities and crooked corners for a curious child to explore. There was a musty basement filled with canvases and paints; a spare bedroom-turned-study lined with old books and a telescope, and a tiny winding passageway that led up to a dingy loft. There was also a small and overgrown back garden which seemed to be permanently in the shade of a gnarled, twisted old tree.

I loved it there. I spent many happy hours being cared for by 'Auntie Clara' while my mother helped my father with the running of his art dealership. When I think back to my childhood, it's impossible to picture it without thinking of Clara.

Eventually, my father grew too old for the daily commute into London, and my mother began to take more of an active role in the art dealership. Which involved making trips abroad to talk to prospective buyers. She proved to be a natural at this, just like my father had been. If anything, she was even better at meeting businessfolk, as she was more to-the-point, without my father's tendency to waffle.

I remember my mother being very excited about her first trip to the United States. She was due to be away for two weeks, visiting clients in New York City before flying west to San Francisco. I was eight years old, and felt as uncertain about her upcoming absence as she was enthusiastic. I had never spent so long a time apart from her.

I remember my father driving us to Heathrow to wave her off. We watched through the terminal windows as the British Airways jumbo climbed slowly into the sky. A fortnight without my mother seemed like it was going to be an eternity.

My father did his best to keep me entertained, as did Clara, and most of the time I was able to suppress the thought of my mother being thousands of miles away. But when I was left alone, I would often creep into her bedroom and sit silently on her bed, staring at her favourite painting, which took pride of place on the wall.

The painting called Straw Girl.

According to my father, he had acquired the painting in Belgium during the war. Although he'd never been able to prove it, he always believed it to be a work by the Flemish master Jan Vanderschoot, and I knew my mother thought this too.

I could see why it was her favourite painting…

It was remarkably skilful, wonderfully colourful, and perfectly captured the innocence of the peasant girl it featured; whose beauty seemed to transcend her dull task. I would stare at it, and imagine my mother staring at it, and when I did, I felt a little bit closer to her.

Since taking more of an active role in the art business, my mother had grown interested in the provenance of Straw Girl. Whereas my father had become frustrated after several fruitless attempts to prove its veracity in the 50s and 60s, my mother approached the subject with a new vigour, and was planning to undertake more research on her return from the States.

That, of course, never happened...

My mother spent a week in New York City, meeting clients and beginning to grow a series of contacts across the Atlantic. The last time I talked to her was on the Monday night. She was in her hotel in New York, and I remember her telling me how – in-between business meetings - she'd managed to take in some of the sights; the view from the top of the Empire State Building, a stroll around Central Park and a ride in a yellow taxi. I was enthralled. It sounded like being in a film. I told my mother this, and she laughed...

"Well, next time I'll bring you with me. We can be film stars together!"

I can still hear her saying the words.

I went to bed happy, dreaming of one day going to New York City myself.

The next day, my mother took a taxi to Newark Airport and boarded an early morning flight to San Francisco.

It was Tuesday, September the 11th, 2001.

The plane never reached its destination.

2

It was a beautifully sunny, autumnal Tuesday afternoon when the news of the terrorist attacks in America first came through. I was playing happily in my little primary school playground. Under clear blue skies and lined with tall trees, it seemed like the most peaceful place on Earth. But when I made my way out of the school gates my father was waiting for me. I can still see him now - impeccably dressed as usual in salmon chinos and a linen blazer - but instead of his usual wayward smile he wore an expression I'd never seen before...

He looked worried.

Once we were in the car, he told me that my mother had been in one of the aeroplanes that was hijacked, and that she was missing.

A dark shadow fell across my childhood.

From that moment on, I've tended to divide my youth into two parts; pre and post 9/11. Afterwards, things began to get more serious. The carefree, sunny days of adventures and picnics were over. We still had fun, from time to time, but things were never quite the same.

My father was a man who'd been through a war and seen friends die, and he managed to adapt to life without my mother fairly well, on the surface at least. But I quickly became a far more cautious child than I had been before. Everything seemed to frighten me. I found it impossible to sleep without a light on, and stopped playing outside in the fields, preferring to find solace in stories instead. I devoured the books my mother had left behind, finding it far safer to remain inside the walls of our house. Outside, the word seemed a big, scary place, with death or tragedy lurking around every corner.

As if to prove me right, Geoffrey Mallender also died - two years after my mother, almost to the day.

He and Clara had visited a village pub for a meal with my father and some other friends. Afterwards, Geoffrey and my father stepped outside for a cigar. It was late on an autumn evening, and the sun was beginning to set. Out of nowhere a car, probably stolen - we never found out - raced past the pub at high speed. It veered towards the roadside where my father and Geoffrey were standing. My father was able to move out of the way, but the car clipped Geoffrey and sent him flying head first into a stone wall.

Geoffrey never recovered, and the driver was never caught.

After this, Clara moved back to her native Scotland, and my childhood became even more lonely.

*

From then on it was just my father and I, rattling around in our large house. I started secondary school and devoted most of my energies into being a model student. I particularly excelled at English, which I think would have pleased my mother.

My father entered his eighties soon after my mother died, and soon began to wind down his business. He sold the art dealership, and began sorting out his own private collection of art. Some of it he sold, some he gave away to friends, and the rest he brought home, to display or store around the house. But during all this time, Straw Girl remained on his bedroom wall, untouched and unmoved by the passing years; a permanent reminder of my mother.

She had planned to investigate the painting more on her return from the states, but this of course never happened, and after her death, my father seemed to lose interest in the painting's provenance. Perhaps it reminded him too much of her…

In fact, for the next decade years he never mentioned Straw Girl once. Not until one hot Friday night in July, 2012…

I remember it well. It was the night of the London Olympics opening ceremony. I watched the event on TV with my father in our living room with the summer night air bathing over us through the open windows. I'm not sure whether it was the result of some patriotic fervour stirred by the celebration of Great Britain we were watching, or the bottle of port he was making inroads into, but that evening my father started talking about Straw Girl again.

And all I had to do was listen…

3

Bring me my bow of burning gold...

My father had sung along with Jerusalem, after which the opening ceremony shifted into an Industrial Revolution segment. Where there had once been green fields and maypole dancers came burning furnaces and looming black towers. My father sipped his port, rose from his chair and left the room.

I wondered why.

Three minutes later he returned. And he was carrying Straw Girl.

"Dad, are you OK with that?" I said, as his octogenarian body struggled underneath the gilded frame.

"I'm no invalid," he replied, placing the painting against the living room wall and sitting back down to admire it.

"So, is there a reason you've brought that down here?" I asked after a few minutes spent feigning uninterest.

"It just reminded me of it."

"What did?"

He gestured towards the TV.

"The Industrial Revolution. The changing landscape. A lost way of life. This girl belongs to that long-forgotten world; when people lived and worked their lives on the land."

"Oh," I said. "It was a favourite of mum's, wasn't it?"

"Very much so. But it has a much longer history than that."

"Really?" I asked.

"Yes."

He pushed up his glasses and sipped some more port, then looked into my eyes.

"I bought it in 1945, at an auction in Antwerp. The entire possessions of a Jewish family were being sold off, as there was none of their family left alive to claim any of it. I was stationed over there, you see, and had got wind of this auction. I went to have a look at it beforehand, and I heard the story about it being an original by Vanderschoot. If I'm being honest, I didn't believe it. I thought it was just a bit of patter, embellished to bump the price up a bit. But then I saw it. And I knew then there must be more to it..."

I nodded.

"It didn't fetch too high a price, unsurprising really, given we were in the middle of a war-torn continent, but it was still a steep sum for me. But I won it, regardless. Little did I know though, but someone else was watching the auction. Somebody who couldn't afford the painting, but who wanted it just as much as I did. A man called Strauss."

"Strauss?"

"Yes. Josef Strauss. A hotel owner, Nazi collaborator and aspiring art collector with the morals of a rodent. A true 'rattus rattus', to use the Latin. Long dead now, of course. But he was the one who stole the painting from me."

"He stole it? So, how come you still have it?"

"I took back what was mine. But it came at a great cost. I lost a dear friend of mine in the process. A man named Guy Marks. I've never forgiven Strauss for what his men did that night."

"Who was Guy Marks?" I asked.

"An army pal. A great man... a brave man. I can still see his face, you know. He was very tall and handsome. Popular with the ladies too, of course, but he wasn't interested in any of that business. He was a married man. Jane was his wife's name... he showed me a picture once. Very pretty girl."

My father gazed down into his glass of port, as if staring into a deep sea of memories. When he looked up he did so slowly, and spoke with a quiver in his voice....

"She was expecting a child. Their second. Guy was so excited at the prospect of becoming a father again... but he never did."

I looked on quietly as he wiped away a tear. On the TV, the scenes had segued from industrial to modern Britain; a group of teenagers were dancing around in a modern street setting. My father continued talking ...

"I went to visit Guy's wife, his widow, after the war. They lived in a little cottage just outside Shoreham-by-Sea, in Sussex..."

"That's near where you were born, isn't it?"

"Same county, yes. We went to the same school too, Christ's Hospital, just outside Horsham, although I was a year or two older. Our background was what initially bonded us together in Belgium, but Guy's bravery was what drew me to him. When one was around Guy, it felt like anything was possible... even getting my painting back from that Nazi Strauss. Anyway, I visited his widow Jane and met his newborn son, William; a good-looking child, just like his old man. I offered them money, of course, but Jane wouldn't hear of it. She was too proud."

The music and dancing on the TV continued, but my father was oblivious to it by now. He carried on talking...

"Of course, I didn't expect her to take the money. I just wanted to do something for Guy."

He stared across the room; towards Straw Girl...

"He gave his life for that painting, and I'm forever indebted to him. I still intend to repay him someday. Maybe, that time is near..."

"Are his wife and son still alive?" I asked.

"Sadly, no. Jane died in the late 80s and William at the turn of the century. But William had a son of his own, and he's alive and well. Charles is his name."

"So," I said, "you intend to repay this Charles for what his grandfather did for you? By giving him the painting?"

"The idea had occurred to me."

"But?"

He finished the last of his port.

"There's a problem…"

"Oh?"

"Yes. After the war, Strauss fled to London. Married an English girl and had a son with her. Leonard, they called him. His family are still here."

"Right," I said, "so that's the problem, Strauss's ancestors are living in England?"

"My darling, that's just the start. You see, this Charles, or Charlie, is *involved* with the Strauss family.

I raise an eyebrow, quizzically.

"Involved?"

"Yes. In fact, you could say, he's quite *closely* involved…"

Part Three

'Glory and the Gutter'

1

London, January 2018

It's just gone 11 on Monday morning and I'm slumped on my bed in the Langham Hotel, scrolling through Twitter on my laptop. Among the accounts I look up is the British Transport Police's. It's full of grainy, CCTV images of various thuggish types wanted for assaults on the railways, but fortunately, I'm not among them. Yet...

I also do a quick search for 'Battersea Park Railway Station' to see if there's been any mention of the incident, but fortunately there isn't anything on there. No outrage. No appeal for witnesses...

I try to convince myself that the poor, innocent train spotter I'd pushed to the ground had simply got up, dusted himself down and decided against making a formal complaint. My palms are sweating… I don't think I've pushed anybody since school, if even then. I've always been one to steer clear of trouble… until now.

I close my laptop and make myself a strong coffee using the room's complimentary facilities. I take the half-empty brandy bottle from my bag and splash a good shot of it into my cup. I sit back down on the bed and stare through the window at the cold January sunshine. Devon has gone, and so has Straw Girl. She's left me a message on a piece of hotel notepaper.

Back this afternoon. Keep out of trouble. D.

So I do. I slump back on the bed, flick through some trashy daytime TV and sip my boozy coffee, wondering if I've ever felt so useless in my adult life.

I decide that I haven't, and that's saying something…

After I've finished my coffee I decide to go for a walk, mainly just for *something to do…* anything to feel mildly less impotent. I reach for my phone, and almost as soon as I touch it, it vibrates.

Vanessa calling

As usual, the sight of her name takes me right back to Sussex University in the late 1990s, when I was a long-haired English Literature student hanging around in dingy Brighton pubs. Back then, I'd always been delighted when I got a message or a call from Vanessa Strauss on my brick-like Nokia phone. I remember analysing her texts over a pint, wondering if this raven-haired

History student - the one who looked a bit like Winona Ryder - was really *interested* in me…

Turns out she was… for a while anyway. Then things went sour, obviously.

I answer.

"Hello."

"Hi, Charlie, how are you?"

"Oh, you know, fine, you?"

"Good thanks." She sounds, as always, like she'd rather get the pleasantries out of the way... "are you busy?"

"Not hugely," I lie.

"I just wanted to talk about this agricultural college thing…"

What?

For a moment my mind is completely blank. I've been so fixated on Straw Girl that my son has almost completely slipped my mind. But then I remember… *Lennie, the agricultural college, that's right...*

"Yes." I say, "well if that's what he wants to do, I think it sounds good."

"Great. Well, he's been asked to go in for an interview. Tomorrow afternoon. Trouble is, Richard's overseas on business, and I've got the other two to look after, and I'm struggling to find a sitter."

"OK."

"So, I was wondering if you wanted to go with him? I mean, I'm sure he'd like that."

"Oh, er, right" I say, taken aback by the request.

"It'll only be for an hour or so. You can borrow my car..."

"Sure, it's just, tomorrow could be difficult..."

It's bloody typical really. I'm hardly ever asked to be involved in my son's life, and when I am, it's in the middle of all this...

"OK, well, if you can't I can always ask Sheridan to take him..."

Oh God no, not Sheridan. The thought of her slimy, arrogant brother anywhere near my son fills me with disgust.

"Well, hang on," I say, "let me see if I can move some stuff around. What time is it tomorrow?"

"Half one. Can you let me know later today Charlie? Sheridan's pretty busy at the moment too..."

I bet he is...

"OK, will do."

"OK, thank you, Charlie."

I end the call and make my way down to the hotel lobby, deciding to continue with my idea of a walk. I make my way past reception and remember that I don't have a key card to get back into the room; Devon has taken the only one.

I make my way over to the desk.

"Hello sir," says the girl on the desk in an eastern European accent.

"Hi, can I get a key for my room? My friend's taken mine."

"Certainly sir, which room?"

"Er, room 328, I think."

"And the name?"

"Mr Marks."

"OK sir. One minute."

She does something on her computer.

"Here you go," she says, handing me a key card, before looking back at the computer. "Oh, there's a letter here for you, Mr Marks."

"A letter? OK…"

But nobody knows we're here…

She goes to fetch the letter. I take it to a corner of the lobby and tear it open.

It's another message from beyond the grave…

Dear Charlie,

I hope your mission is going well. In my unfortunate absence, the only assistance I am able to offer you is the financial kind.

I hope this helps.

Yours,

Vic

Folded behind the letter is another cheque for £2000.

2

Devon carries the suit bag containing Straw Girl out of the hotel and walks south along Regent Street. If she's honest, she's relieved to be away from Charlie for a few hours. She's beginning to find his company trying - a bit like babysitting an overgrown child.

It's a cold but sunny January day, and she pulls her green bobble hat further down over her ears. In spite of a lack of sleep last night, Devon feels alive and energised. She knows that the heavy package on her shoulder could be the making of her, professionally. If Straw Girl is, as she believes it to be, a genuine Vanderschoot, it will certainly trump anything Venetia Jardine has discovered in her measly little career...

But, as ever, there's always the possibility that it's just another very clever fake. Art forgers are everywhere nowadays - talented painters making a quick profit from mimicking far more famous artists. A quick trawl of the internet would uncover many examples of such dubious works. But there's something about Straw Girl that's just... different. Something in it speaks to someplace deep inside Devon - to the little girl in the council flat who would lie under her parents' bed for hours reading her father's books. The instinct for true art that had been stirred inside her as a lonely child, eager for knowledge, is the same part of her that Straw Girl touches.

She is sure...

And nothing is going to stop her from proving it. Not the booze-fuelled celebration of chaos that Charlie seems to call life. And certainly not some common criminal in a baseball cap, even if he is doing the bidding of some more sinister figure, as Devon is starting to suspect. To her, the fact that someone else is out there after the painting only adds to the likelihood of its veracity...

Someone else knows, and they seem determined - very determined - to claim it for themselves...

Well, not if Devon has got anything to do with it.

*

She reaches Piccadilly Circus and diverts around Leicester Square in the direction of the Strand. She continues eastwards until she reaches the imposing entrance to the prestigious Cowdrey Institute School of Art.

Dr Agnew's office is based on the second floor of the Cowdrey Institute. Devon remembers this part of the building well, having been a Masters student at the Cowdrey only a few years ago. She's been to visit Phil Agnew on a few occasions since graduating, mainly for work, because Dr Agnew happens to be one of the world's leading experts on the scientific study of paintings. He also happens to be an authority on Flemish art, who tutored Devon during her time at the Cowdrey.

Which, for Devon, is rather fortunate.

Without wanting to be too big-headed about it, Devon always thought that Dr Agnew had a bit of a soft spot for her. Perhaps, she sometimes wondered, it was because Devon wasn't your typical Cowdrey student... she hadn't been to some posh private school. She didn't come from a rich or well-educated family. She was from Brixton. Her mother was black. Her father was dead. She'd only been able to afford the course fees thanks to a scholarship.

Whatever it was, Dr Agnew always seemed to have time for Devon. Always seemed friendly and eager to help. Other students used to talk of him being brusque and unapproachable, but this was never Devon's experience.

She knocks on the door to Dr Agnew's office.

"Devon, lovely to see you!"

"Hi, Phil... thanks so much for agreeing to meet me, again" says Devon, hoping that he isn't too disgruntled by the fact that

Devon's already cancelled the meeting once. Thankfully, Dr Agnew doesn't seem bothered.

"No problem at all, come in."

His office is small and dustily academic; full of shelves heaving with old books. Devon shuffles in and stands still, holding the suit bag in front of her. Agnew perches on the side of his desk. In his late 50s, he's several inches shorter than Devon, stick thin, with a mop of dark hair scattered with streaks of grey.

"So, coffee? Then you can tell me what's so urgent. I assume it has something to do with that?" He nods at the suit bag and starts playing around with a mini coffee machine, inserting cartridges and flicking switches. Devon smiles, remembering his no-nonsense, hive-of-activity demeanour from tutorial meetings in the same office. She doesn't say yes or no to the coffee. She knows she's going to get one anyway...

"So, what's in the bag?" asks Dr Agnew once he's handed Devon a grimy mug of strong coffee and motored through a few pleasantries.

"I'll show you," says Devon, unzipping it.

"Please do," says Agnew, resting back against his desk as Devon removes Straw Girl; slowly and wordlessly. Dr Agnew puts his hand over his mouth.

"My goodness!"

"I know…"

Devon passes it to Dr Agnew, who accepts it carefully, like it's a new-born baby.

"She's gorgeous."

"Isn't she?"

"Yeah-huh. So, what can you tell me about her?"

"Well," says Devon, taking a breath and launching into a potted history of the painting. Dr Agnew listens, wide-eyed.

"OK, let's take a closer look," he says as Devon finally finishes, and opens another door at the side of his office.

"Shall we?"

Devon nods, takes the painting and follows into hallowed territory – Dr Agnew's private studio. It was in here that he famously proved a Rubens acquired by the Cowdrey Gallery was in fact a copy by a 20th Century Dutch forger. The discovery had made international headlines at the time.

Dr Agnew's studio is a long but surprisingly cramped space, with white walls and long strip-lights overhead. A scattering of easels, some carrying paintings, jostle for space with more technical-looking contraptions. Agnew sits down on a battered office chair and wheels himself over to a table. He lays Straw Girl down on it and carefully turns her over.

"You said there was a query about the size?" asks Dr Agnew.

"Yes," says Devon. "The painting was exhibited at the Paris Salon in 1841, and I've managed to track down the catalogue for that year…"

"OK," says Dr Agnew, looking up at Devon…

"The dimensions for the painting listed were 68 by 46 centimetres, when converted to metric, of course. This one has slightly different dimensions. 70 by 50 centimetres."

"I see," says Dr Agnew, putting on a pair of round glasses.

"It's one of my main misgivings about this being the genuine original," continues Devon.

Dr Agnew nods and focuses on the back of the painting. He takes a screwdriver and slowly removes the painting from its frame with great care. He lifts the original canvas from its wooden casing and specks of dust dance around him. He lays it flat on the table and extends a tape measure over it.

He mutters to himself...

"Hmmm..."

"You see," says Devon, "this discrepancy is one of my main worries. Surely, if this is the original Vanderschoot Straw Girl, its dimensions would be exactly the same as those in the Paris Salon catalogue..."

Dr Agnew continues measuring.

"You would think so, yes."

Devon feels something inside her stomach sink. The dream seems to be slipping away... she fiddles with her watch.

"So, the chances are that this is a fake?"

Dr Agnew peers up at Devon over his glasses.

"Not necessarily..."

3

I turn the cheque over in my hands and inspect the writing on it. It's the same hand as the last one. The account holder's name is *Mallender-Hussain Ltd.* The words: PAY MR CHARLES MARKS - TWO THOUSAND POUNDS ONLY are written in in block biro capitals.

I make my way over to reception, turning things over in my head. Victor Botham keeps sending me money via Mallender-Hussain; yet Botham and Mallender are dead and Hussain has disappeared abroad. The only member of staff left is Sunita. A lowly assistant.

What the hell is going on? Who is behind all this?

I summon the girl on the desk.

"Yes, sir?"

I hold up the envelope.

"I just wondered, who brought this in?"

The receptionist looks a little unsure how to respond.

"Well, it was a young woman. You just missed her, actually. She only came in a few minutes ago."

"Thanks" I say, and run out of the front doors, narrowly colliding with a uniformed porter.

"Sorry mate!" I shout.

I run down Regent Street, squinting in the winter sun. I barge past tourists and strolling shoppers as politely as I can, and all the time keep my eyes focused forwards, trying to get a sight of Sunita Sharma.

She must have been the one to deliver the cheque.

I have to ask her who's behind this... who's giving her the money.

I look for a long cream-coloured mac somewhere in the crowds. Nothing stands out. I look behind me... the traffic appears to be held at some red lights, leaving me with a window of clear road. I jump onto Regent Street itself and sprint down the bus lane, aware that quite a few people are staring at me in concern. I reach Oxford Circus, where a great mass of people are crossing the road or disappearing into the tube. The traffic catches up with me again and I re-join the slow-moving throng, edging my way through. Another red traffic light stops a herd of obedient shoppers from crossing the road and I'm boxed in behind them. I stop, stare ahead of me, and then I see her...

As I expected, she's dressed in her cream mac, with her dark hair tied back, but it's definitely Sunita Sharma. She glances backwards as she descends the steps into the tube station and I get a sight of her face. She looks anxious…

I push my way through the scrum of people. A string of cars and black cabs stream around the corner. I wait for a tiny gap and dart out onto the road, narrowly avoiding a fast-moving bus. The driver slams on his brakes and beeps at me, but I hurry across the road and follow Sunita down into the station. I lose track of her as I enter the ticket hall and jostle with some more tourists, but then I see her again, making her way through the ticket barriers and heading for the Bakerloo Line.

I reach for my pocket, trying to find my debit card. I look down, then look up to keep an eye on Sunita. My card is stubbornly caught in my coat pocket. I look down again and run straight into what feels like a brick wall. For a second everything goes dark.

I slump forwards and fall to my knees, shocked and winded. I glance up to see the 'brick wall' is a man – about my height and almost as wide – with huge tattooed arms bursting out of a blue polo shirt. He is bald, red-faced and squints down at me with narrow eyes.

I cough violently, then manage to half-speak.

"Urgh… sorry."

"No worries mate."

The man mountain offers me a hand and pulls me to my feet, placing his other hand on my shoulder. I stand up slowly, and he pats some dust off my coat with surprising gentleness.

"You alright fella?"

"Yeah, fine, sorry... didn't see you," I say, coughing again slightly.

"Don't worry about it," he says, patting my shoulder a bit more firmly this time. I nod and head towards the gates, but Sunita is nowhere to be seen. I press my card against the gates and head down the escalator to the Bakerloo Line, but the platform is empty. A distant rumbling tells me that a train has just left.

I consider following Sunita to Marylebone on the tube and confronting her at Mallender-Hussain's offices, but the moment's kind of gone, and she'll probably be just as evasive as she was last time. Instead I turn and make my way back up to street level and take the exit onto Regent Street.

The sun is bright, and I reach into my back pocket for my phone, intending to check the time, but something's wrong... I pat my pocket again. It's empty. I check my front pockets, and those on my coat, but they're all empty. It's not there.

My phone has vanished...

4

Devon watches intently as Phil Agnew examines the canvas.

"You see here," he says, "these edges are unpainted."

Devon looks closer. Dr Agnew is right. It's more obvious now the frame has been removed, but the very edges of the painting are blank. The beige canvas underneath can clearly be seen.

He turns the painting over, examines the back again, and continues...

"And, yes, this painting has been relined at some point over the years. Attached to a new canvas, probably to strengthen it."

Devon nods.

"So, it's been stretched onto the new canvas, and the original painted edges have been moved further in. Basically, there are parts of the painting which used to be folded over, but are now part of the front..."

"So that could explain the slightly larger dimensions?" says Devon.

"Yes. It could..."

Dr Agnew puts his tape measure against the painting again.

"So, allowing for the relining, if I measure from the original painted edges, the dimensions are..."

He runs the tape across the canvas... Devon holds her breath.

"46 centimetres across..."

Dr Agnew does the same thing down the length of the painting, and Devon watches with clenched fists as he moves his bony finger along the tape measure.

"And the height is... exactly 68 centimetres."

Devon slams a clenched fist into her thigh in silent celebration.

"Exactly the same as the Paris listing!" she says.

Dr Agnew smiles.

"Exactly, indeed. Which is a very good sign."

Devon grins back. She doesn't need to be told just how good a sign this is.

5

I make my way back to the Langham and let myself into my. I'm sure I'd taken my phone out with me, but I decide to double check... I turn everything in the bedroom upside down. I empty drawers, strip the bed and shake the contents out of my bag. But the phone is nowhere to be seen.

I think back to my tangle with the huge man in the tube station... the way he patted me. That must have been it.

Who was he... and why would he want my phone?

Maybe he was just a common pickpocket, targeting me at random...

A coincidence.

I'm busy rooting through the wardrobe when it occurs to me that I could try to phone my mobile from the room phone... So I do.

To my surprise, it rings, but not in the room. It carries on ringing. I've never bothered setting up a voicemail, so I know my phone will just carry on ringing until I hang up, or someone answers it. I sit on the bed and prise the room phone against my ear, listening to the incessant bleeping. I'm just about to give up, when I hear a click. And then a voice…

"Hello Charlie."

It's a gruff male voice with a cockney tinge. Like someone doing a Ray Winstone impression. It's a voice I've heard before. Recently…

"Er, hi."

"How's your cough? Didn't sound too good back at the station…"

Christ. It is him. The man mountain.

"It's OK. Er, who are you?"

"Doesn't really matter mate. But you can call me Grant."

"OK, and… why did you take my phone?"

"Because I could, mainly. I can take anything I want from you, Charlie boy. Anything."

"OK..."

I get the impression I'm being threatened now. I'm not sure how to react.

"You can have your phone back though," says Grant.

"Yeah?"

"Yeah."

"When?"

"Whenever you want. You can have your phone back, along with a promise that I'll never take anything from you again Charlie. There's just one thing you need to do in return."

I think I know what's coming...

"Yeah? What's that then?"

"I want something from you. I think you know what it is."

"I do?"

"The painting, Charlie. Give me the painting and nobody will ever bother you or your mate Devon again."

I decide to play dumb, after all, 'Grant' may not have any proof that we have the painting at all. He might just be fishing...

"What painting?

"Don't play silly buggers, Charlie. Have a think about it, and when you decide it's the right thing to do, give me a call. After all, you know the number."

There's a click, and then silence. I realise that my hands are sweating.

6

Dr Phil Agnew and Devon are now in a darkened room just adjacent to his studio. The atmosphere is quiet and cool, with the hum of machinery the only sound. In her hand, Devon has the monochrome print of Straw Girl – the one made from the later engraving.

Dr Agnew takes another glance at it and then looks back in front of him... he's sitting at a large flat-screen monitor attached to a hefty-looking computer, busily pressing various keys. Devon lays the print of the engraving next to Straw Girl and examines the differences again. These few minor details have bugged her ever since she found the engraving, and she's hoping that Dr Agnew can shed some light on them... literally.

Ultraviolet light.

The room is bathed in a cool blue colour as Dr Agnew brings up an ultraviolet image of Straw Girl on his screen.

"This should give us an idea where later layers of paint have been added," he says.

"Great," says Devon. She looks at the screen. The familiar image of Straw Girl is there, but across the picture are several angry black marks, like scrawls, drawn across seemingly at random.

"I assume that's some sort of damage?" says Devon.

"Quite right," smiles Dr Agnew, proud of his former pupil. "From this, it's quite clear to me that the painting has been torn and repainted in several places. It looks like there might have been several restoration campaigns over the years."

This comes as a relief to Devon. She's aware that the more efforts there have been to touch up a painting point to its authenticity – and help explain the differences to the later engraving.

"So, which specific areas were you most concerned about?"

Devon looks back at the print and painting lying next to each other.

"Well, firstly, here," she points to the top of the girl's white blouse, the part visible above her blue dress. "There's a definite difference between the two – see, on the print, the pattern is much more detailed, whereas on the painting it's a much plainer white."

Dr Agnew zooms in on the girl's blouse. On the ultraviolet image, it appears as though a large dark cloud is covering the whole blouse area.

"Yes, as I thought," says Dr Agnew, "it appears as though this area has had the most substantial amount of overpainting out of the whole canvas. See, whatever was underneath has been almost completely covered up."

"By someone retouching it at a later date?"

"Absolutely, yes."

"OK, so the other bit that worried me was the girl's basket... again, on the engraving there seems to be much more detail in the way that it's weaved, whereas on the painting it's just a bit, well... not so detailed."

"Let's see," says Dr Agnew, scrolling across the zoomed-in ultraviolet image and settling on the girl's basket. Once again, the whole area is covered in a large dark smear.

Devon smiles.

"Overpainting again?"

Dr Agnew nods. Devon looks back at the painting through the strange blue light, and her smile grows even wider.

7

It's just gone midday when Devon arrives back. I've already spent the first bit of my latest dead man's cheque on a cheese baguette from room service. It was so pricey, it's a wonder I've got any of the two grand left. It sits half-eaten on its plate while I drag on my e-cigarette and drink another strong black coffee. Brandy-free, this time... I feel like I need a clear head.

Devon enters the door and frowns at the vapour clouding the room.

"Careful you don't set off the smoke alarm."

"It's not smoke, it's vapour..."

"Whatever, you're paying the fine if you set it off."

"Shouldn't be a problem," I say, fluttering the cheque in front of her.

She places the suit-bag down on the bed and takes the cheque from my hand.

"What the hell?"

"It was left at reception today."

She looks at it closely.

"By whom?"

"Sunita."

"Who?"

"Sunita. She's the assistant at the solicitor's office, you know, the ones who gave me the painting in the first place."

"Oh yes. So why is she giving you money?"

"Well, it's been left to me by Victor Botham, to help me prove…"

"Yes, I know… to prove the painting's by Vanderschoot, but why is it coming in stages? Like, instalments, from a dead man?"

"No idea."

"It's a bit weird, don't you think?"

"Devon, this whole thing is weird."

She looks at me and nods slowly.

"You're not wrong" I say. "Oh, by the way, in other news, I've haven't got a mobile phone anymore."

"Eh?"

I tell Devon about my encounter with 'Grant' on the tube, and his subsequent menacing phone call. She doesn't look too concerned, which doesn't exactly surprise me…

"Well, you'll need to get a new one. Pay as you go, that'll be cheaper."

"Yeah, I guess so."

"You're going to need a phone. And this…"

She sits down on the bed next to the painting and picks up the cheque, passing it back to me.

"Oh. Why's that?"

"Cause we need to make a little trip."

"Eh? Where to?"

"Antwerp?"

"Antwerp?"

"Yes."

"When?"

"Today. Like, now…"

I stare back at her…

"So, hang on a minute, you're saying we have to go to Holland? This afternoon?"

She rolls her eyes.

"No Charlie. I'm saying we have to go to *Belgium*. This afternoon."

8

So, after sorting out the minor geographical confusion, Devon attempts to explain things in greater detail. I make another strong coffee from the little room kettle, sit on the bed and listen as she talks about her visit to the Cowdrey Institute.

"Dr Agnew was able to put my mind at ease about several issues that were puzzling me. Like the size of the canvas… remember I said it was slightly bigger than the listing in the Paris Salon catalogue?"

"Er, yeah."

"Well that was explained by a relining that took place at some point in the past."

I nod sagely.

"Have you got a clue what I'm talking about?"

"No."

"Well, in layman's terms, it was stretched onto a fresh canvas, and new parts were brought into the surface, altering the dimensions."

I nod as if I understand, but I'm not sure that I do…

"And remember this?" she asks, slipping the black and white print out of the suit bag…

"Oh yeah, isn't that the engraving?"

"Yes. The engraving was based on a Vanderschoot painting, but there were several differences that worried me. Look here…" she points at the print… "The girl's blouse is very ornate, very intricate here… but on the painting it's just a plain white."

"Is it?"

Devon nods. I try to remember what the painting looks like, but I can't visualise it in any great detail, apart from the basics; the girl in a blue and white dress, the straw, the green fields… I wonder how she's able to recall such detail. It's her job, I suppose…

"Have a look…"

I unzip the suit bag and gently free the painting. Devon's quite right. Straw Girl's blouse is a much plainer white than the print of the engraving.

"Yeah," I say, "so, what does this mean for the painting?"

Devon continues.

"It could mean that it's a copy of the original Straw Girl. Made by a painter inspired by, but not as talented as Vanderschoot."

"Oh."

"Or the plain white paint could have been added later. Painted over the original."

"Right. And why would someone do that?"

"As part of a previous restoration campaign…"

"A campaign?"

Devon sighs.

"Look, let's imagine you've bought a painting, but it's damaged in some way. Let's say there's a hole in a bit of sky. So, you repair the hole, or tear, or whatever it is, but the mark still stands out. So you need to cover it up. You've got two choices; spend ages mixing pigments until you get exactly the same colour as the artist used, or just paint over the whole sky in a different shade of blue. That's overpainting."

"Ah, I see. So, which one was it?"

"Well, Dr Agnew was able to establish that the top of the blouse on our painting… *your painting*… has been significantly overpainted."

"Wow, that's good. How could he tell though?"

"He looked at an ultraviolet image of the painting, which allowed him to identify where exactly newer paint had been added..."

I'm about to ask how this works, but then it dawns on me that I'm not particularly interested. Dr Agnew could have used magic X-ray specs for all I care, as long as it means Straw Girl is more likely to be genuine.

Devon continues…

STEVEN F. GALLOWAY

"There was a similar issue with a part of the girl's basket. The weave was far more intricate on the engraving than the painting. Dr Agnew studied that under ultraviolet light too."

I mentally cross my fingers.

"Overpainting again?"

Devon nods.

"Yuh."

I punch the bed in celebration.

"Get in! This doctor chap thinks it's genuine then?"

Devon smiles…

"He was fairly well convinced."

I stand up from the bed, feeling more energetic than I have at any time in the last few days.

"So, so what do we do now? Can I put it up for sale?"

"Whoa, hang on," says Devon, "Dr Agnew's by no means an authority on Vanderschoot. He's an expert on technology and forensics, but his opinion doesn't automatically make this a genuine Vanderschoot painting."

"Oh, right. Well, whose opinion does?"

"That's where Antwerp comes into it."

"Antwerp… how?"

"Have you heard of the De Boer Institute?"

"No, should I have?"

"Really? You never heard it mentioned once, all the time you worked at the gallery?"

258

"No, can't say I did… what is it?"

"The De Boer Institute is in Antwerp. Belgium," she emphasises the word *Belgium*… "It's an art institute and school. They publish the Vanderschoot catalogue raisonnè."

OK, I'm completely lost now…

"Sorry, what? Catalogue of raisins?"

Devon rolls her eyes and repeats it…

"Catalogue raisonnè. It's an official published list of all the known works by a particular artist."

Oh right, like a discography, I think.

I decide not to say this to Devon. Instead I nod.

"So, they get to decide what makes the Jan Vanderschoot list?"

Devon nods.

"Yes, indeed they do. The De Boer committee examines all potential Vanderschoot works and decides if they are viable for inclusion in the catalogue."

"OK, and if they don't, what happens then?"

Devon pulls off her green bobble hat and lets her unruly hair fall down. She runs a hand through it.

"If they say no, that's it. Game over."

"Really? But what about all the evidence?"

"It's meaningless without their approval. Inclusion in a catalogue raisonnè makes all the difference." She perches down on the other end of the bed to me. Her eyes look tired, but despite this, there seems to be an energy flowing through her. She continues…

"Inclusion in a catalogue is everything. The difference between glory and the gutter. Here's an example for you... a few years ago an art dealer bought a painting off Ebay. The auction website..."

"Yeah, I know..."

"Well, it turned out to be an original Pissarro. The publishers of the Pissarro catalogue raisonnè accepted it, and it sold at auction for over five hundred thousand pounds. Now, if the committee hadn't decided to include it in their catalogue, the very best the owner could have hoped for was two grand. Less than one percent of what it finally went for..."

"Blimey. So, these De Boer people will look at Straw Girl?"

Devon nods cautiously.

"I think so. Dr Agnew thought so too. He's written them a letter with his thoughts, recommending that they evaluate it. I'm expecting a formal reply, but I reckon the best thing to do is just to go over there and ask if they'll see it. Especially seeing as it's not exactly safe here in London..."

"And you suggest we leave now?"

"Yeah. The sooner the better, Charlie."

I nod. All I can think of is the five hundred grand that the Pissarro went for. I stand up from the bed; excited thoughts circle my head like helicopters...

This is it. This could really be it... a simple yes or no from the De Boer people, and I'll be rich... And we could get an answer tomorrow...

A propeller hits me.

Tomorrow. Lennie. The college interview…

I slump back down on the bed.

"Oh shit!"

Devon frowns.

"What's wrong?"

"Tomorrow… there's a problem…"

9

"So, he's not your child with your current partner? Siobhan…"

It's the first time I've ever discussed anything vaguely personal with Devon. It feels slightly weird…

"No. His mother's Vanessa - my university girlfriend. We split up soon after he was born."

"Oh. Why?" says Devon, matter-of-factly.

"Er, well, I suppose we were just a bit young… I mean, I was only 20 when Lennie was born…"

I think back to the turn of the century; a time of anxiety all round, but while most people fretted about the millennium bug confusing computers and planes plummeting from the skies, I'd been worried something else…

Fatherhood. Responsibility.

Scary words, especially as I was barely out of my teens myself…

I'd always been quiet child; happy in my own company. I loved books and stories, and spent many happy hours on the beach or in the fields around my little hometown of Shoreham-by-Sea, playing the starring role in my own personal fantasies. But then secondary school came along, and my dreamer tendencies didn't exactly fit with the quasi-military austerity of a 1990s comprehensive school... The uniforms, the timetables, the sadistic PE teachers, the suppression of individuality... it all made me retreat further into my shell, and I spent the best part of my early teens doing little else but trying not to stand out.

I managed to get reasonable A Levels, but I didn't go far to university... the nearest city in fact - Brighton, which was just down the road from me. Once I'd started my English Literature degree and found my feet around campus, I began to realise I was finally among like-minded people, and slowly emerged from my shell. I embraced all the student clichés... I grew my hair long, started smoking and joined the film society.

Film society, as the name suggests, mainly involved a bunch of students sitting around smoking, watching indie films and talking about how our own screenplays were going (slowly, mostly, although we never admitted that). It was at the film society that I first laid eyes on the dark haired, brown eyed, Winona Ryder-resembling Vanessa Strauss.

University would never be quite the same again...

I'm still not entirely sure how it happened, but a few months later Vanessa became my first girlfriend, a state of affairs that never seemed quite real, even to this day. I spent most of the relationship in a weird state of ecstatic euphoria mixed with crippling anxiety that the whole thing would fall apart… that she would wake up one day and realise that I wasn't a deep-thinking, creative rebel but a lazy idiot with greasy hair.

In the event, the whole thing did fall apart, but for a reason I hadn't anticipated…

I'm jolted back the present and look back at Devon, who seems to be waiting for me to continue talking…

"Vanessa moved back home to live with her parents after the birth, they were very… protective… and they didn't particularly like me. Plus, Lennie had… *has* difficulties."

"What kind of difficulties?"

"He's autistic."

"Oh," says Devon, "so am I."

"Wh… what?"

"Yeah, I was diagnosed when I was 12."

"Oh, right. I didn't realise…"

I'm not sure what to say. Devon seems so different to Lennie that the thought had never even crossed my mind…

"Sorry."

"What are you sorry for? It's never bothered me. If anything, it's helped my career. Art's always been my special interest. I'm lucky I can do it as a job."

I'm amazed. Devon may seem blunt at times, and she doesn't really do small talk, but I've never considered the possibility of her being anywhere on the same spectrum as Lennie. She has a career, a flat, her own life... whereas I've never expected Lennie to have any of those things...

"Um... yeah, that's cool."

I struggle to find the right thing to say, and there's a moment of silence.

"So, your son?" asks Devon.

"Right... well he's got his interview at a college tomorrow... he wants to study animal care, and I'm supposed to be taking him."

"Can't anyone else go with him?"

"No, his mother has her other children to look after, and her husband, Richard, is away on business or something. I don't want to let him down... it's just, I'm never allowed to be as involved in his life as I want to be."

Devon nods. I carry on...

"Vanessa got full custody at the time... it seemed like the best thing to do. My father was ill, and mum had her hands full caring for him. Vanessa's family were far wealthier, and much better placed to provide for Lennie. The downside is that I've never had much influence in his life. He's a Strauss, not a Marks."

I stand up, trying to think of a way round it...

"What if we flew out to Antwerp tomorrow evening, after the interview with the college?"

Devon shakes her head.

"Hmm, I really think we need to go straight away, I mean, we could only have a small window of time to see the De Boer people. They won't just see anyone, but I'm hoping Dr Agnew's letter will have some sway."   —

"OK, right..."

This is your big chance, Charlie. There's only one thing for it. You're going to have to let your son down... again. He'll understand. Maybe...

"Can I borrow your phone?" I ask Devon, "I'm going to have to call Vanessa and cancel. His uncle will have to take him."

The idea of smarmy Sheridan Strauss standing in for me is unpleasant, but there really is no other option. Devon takes out her phone, and is just about to hand it to me when she stops.

"There is another way, Charlie..."

"Yeah?"

"It's just that, perhaps you don't need to be in Antwerp anyway..."

"OK..."

"I mean, I'm the art expert, and although as the painting's owner you would be expected to be there, I could always act as your representative. It's not as though there'll be anything you can say which I can't..."

None taken...

"No, I suppose not."

"Look, fly out after the interview, by all means. But, why don't I go ahead to Antwerp this afternoon, with the painting, so I can try and get an early appointment at the De Boer Institute. That way the painting will be safely out of the country and you can take your son to the interview."

She smiles at me, and, I have to admit, her plan makes sense.

10

A few hours later I check out of the Langham, feeling more grateful at the prospect of leaving a five-star hotel than I would have thought possible. But during my short stay there I'd felt helpless, and now things feel like they're moving again. A clear plan of action opens up ahead of me; head down to Brighton, take Lennie to the interview, fly to Antwerp and finally uncover the truth about Straw Girl.

Finally, then, I'll be able to move on… either back towards the status quo; finding another job, working on another screenplay, and facing rejection and disappointment all over again. Or to something else. *Something life changing…*

It frightens me how much is riding on Straw Girl – which Devon is currently hauling overseas. If genuine, it could change my life beyond all expectation. But if it's fake, I'll be exactly where I was before. And having had such dizzying prospects opened up to me, the idea of going back suddenly seems all too grim.

I try to console myself by remembering how confident Devon seemed before she set off.

"Charlie, I'm convinced by this. Fly out as soon as you can, but leave it up to me till then."

She's the expert, after all.

I carry my bag down Regent Street and turn onto Oxford Street, heading into the first phone shop I see. Inside, I'm surprisingly excited to find you can buy a pay-as-you-go mobile for a fiver. It's small, lightweight and doesn't have all the needless distractions of a regular smartphone; just the ability to call and text. It also promises me a huge amount of battery life. I vow never to buy another smartphone in my life.

Once outside I text my new number to Siobhan:

Hi love, managed to lose my phone, so this is my new number. Speak later. Xx

I fully expect her to jump to some conclusion involving me, a large quantity of beer and my phone being left in the corner of some pub, but I decide it's better than the truth.

I then text Devon:

This is my new number. Let me know when you've landed. Charlie.

I know now why Devon doesn't exactly go in for small talk and pleasantries, so I decide it makes sense to communicate in the same way...

Next on my afternoon chore list is a visit to the bank, where I deposit Victor Botham's latest posthumous cheque into my account. After that, I make my way back to Oxford Circus tube station and catch the tube to Victoria station. Throughout my journey, I keep a look out for a red-faced, bald gentleman with arms the size of Christmas hams lurking in amongst the commuters, but fortunately Grant is nowhere to be seen.

Within half an hour, I'm on another train, heading through the suburbs of London towards Brighton. A vista of Victorian terraces and concrete tower blocks soon gives way to the green Sussex countryside, and I realise how relieved I am to be heading out of from London with Straw Girl safely out of the country. It feels like a huge weight has been lifted off my shoulders. I slump back in my seat and drift off into a gentle sleep, accompanied by the repetitive rhythm of rail travel.

*

By the time I arrive in Shoreham it's already getting dark. The cold January sun sets and streetlights illuminate the little streets. I fasten my coat and head out of the station, turning right into the wind. The air feels different here; like I can taste the salt from the sea.

Suddenly I'm 21 again... heading home from university, with a degree in English Literature in one hand and a baby son in the other.

Not literally, of course...

Vanessa had also moved home to allow her parents, Leonard and Caroline, to help her care for Lennie. We were still in a relationship then, technically, but unsurprisingly that broke down a few months later. Shortly after that, my father died.

It's with these bleak memories in my mind that I turn into the street I grew up in and as if to greet me a steady patter of rain begins to fall. Eventually, I reach number 144.

After a while, my mum opens the door.

11

Devon boards the plane, turns right, and finds her seats – next to the window, just as she selected. She takes one for herself and props Straw Girl in the other, adjusting the seat belt so it covers the suit bag.

There was never any chance of her trusting this piece of luggage to the baggage handlers…

Feeling hot, she takes off her bobble hat and ties her hair back. She fans herself with the in-flight magazine and gazes out of the window. Devon hates flying. She hates the feeling of being enclosed, and the loss of control. She hates the enforced proximity with other people, and the unsettling noises of the engines. She hates not knowing what's going on…

But she's looking forward to this particular flight…

She's still looking forward to the flight when the large man comes and takes up the empty seat next to Straw Girl. His broad shoulders and muscular arms force Devon to shift the painting over towards her slightly, making her seat a little less comfortable. The man nods a wordless thank you and Devon manages a smile in return. The bald, red-faced man doesn't return it.

Devon turns back to the in-flight magazine. Despite the cramped conditions, Devon is eager for take-off, and she silently watches the landscape outside her window shift as the plane begins taxiing.

Antwerp can't come soon enough...

12

It seems as though mum is keeping herself busy, as ever. She welcomes me over the fresh hold with a hug, offers an uninvited appraisal of my appearance (tired, apparently) and disappears into the kitchen to make me a sandwich and a cup of tea. The house is neat, the furnishings unchanged and Moby the cat still in her favourite position by the electric fire. Everything is as it should be. I slump into an armchair.

Mum returns with a cheese and ham sandwich, mug of tea and a scone; she's apparently been baking the latter on an industrial scale for a church event. I take bites in-between fielding off the obligatory barrage of questions…

"How's Siobhan?"

"Good," I say, telling her about the work trip to LA. She seems impressed.

"I always knew that girl would be a high-flyer."

I nod.

"How's work?"

"Fine," I lie. "Just on a few days' leave."

She doesn't press the subject. My employment, or occasional lack thereof, has always been a bone of contention between us. The subject moves on to Lennie, and I tell her about the college interview – ostensibly the reason for my visit.

The conversation soon shifts onto a rundown on family friends, bridge club and her watercolour classes. I'm pleased to hear she's maintaining her busy schedule, particularly as this evening it involves a meeting at the church, which allows me some much-needed peace and quiet.

After she heads off to the Church Hall I take a soak in the avocado bath tub, which reminds me of preparations for youthful nights down the local pub. On this occasion though, I decide to stay in. After wrapping myself in a large towel, I head to the kitchen and locate the corner of the larder where the spirits are kept. Mum isn't a big drinker, and most look like they haven't been touched since my Dad's days, but fortunately there's a bottle of brandy which she probably uses for cooking. I pour myself a very generous glassful and retreat to my old bedroom, where I wait for the sweet oblivion of sleep to envelop me.

13

Another hotel in another city beckons, but this one is nowhere near as grand as the Langham. The taxi drops Devon and the suit bag outside the front entrance to the Hotel Schubert, which is an ordinary four-storey building just around the corner from the city's Grote Markt town square. What it lacks in marble floors and concierges it makes up for in location; being less than a five minute walk from the De Boer Institute.

Devon checks into her room, places the suit bag containing Straw Girl carefully on the bed and retrieves her laptop. Her email inbox contains the usual amount of junk and offers, but to her annoyance there is no email from the De Boer Institute.

Devon closes the laptop firmly.

They must have received Dr Agnew's email by now, Devon reckons... and it clearly said to copy any reply to her email address...

Devon checks the time and sees that it's just gone 7pm. The Institute will be shut now. She decides to go for a walk instead, to see if she can find something to eat before trying the Institute again in the morning. She puts her parka and bobble hat on and heads out into the cold city. She moves quickly through scattered tourists in winter coats and backpacks; little groups taking selfies by the Brabo Fountain or wandering around the cobbled town square. She feels completely cut-off from all of them. She has one mission on her mind, and nothing is going to distract her from it...

Not even the bald, red-faced man who cuts across her path as she passes the fountain; causing her to stop and change course.

Devon ignores him, just like everyone else, and walks on.

14

Surprisingly, I sleep rather well in my childhood bedroom. I wake up sometime after eight when the sun begins to penetrate the thin curtains, and make my way downstairs for a hearty breakfast prepared by mum, who then promptly heads off for a morning with her watercolour group. She appears to be just as busy in retirement as she'd been as a primary school teacher, which is reassuring.

I leave soon afterwards and catch a train to Hove. I'm there earlier than necessary, but, unlike the last time I visited, I don't kill time in a pub today. Instead I walk briskly through the suburbs until I reach Vanessa and Richard's house. As usual I'm struck by how large it is – a sizeable detached property supplanted by numerous extensions. Vanessa's little mint-coloured Fiat is parked on the drive, but Richard's big 4X4 is nowhere to be seen.

I ring the doorbell.

Vanessa answers. She looks as pretty as ever, but slightly stressed at the same time. Olivia is clinging to her blue denim dress and stares up at me, as usual not giving any sign that she knows who I am.

"Charlie, hi. You're early…"

"Yeah, I stayed at Mum's."

"Well, come in… Livvi, say hello to Uncle Charlie."

"Hello," says Olivia, before skipping off towards their massive kitchen. I follow them into the house. Benji is sitting at the kitchen table drawing something with felt tips. It always amazes me how Vanessa's other two children are able to concentrate so fully on a task, unlike the one she had with me, who's a whirlwind of unfocused activity…

"Say hello to Charlie," says Vanessa again. Benji looks up at me and nods, a bit like a middle-aged work colleague might.

"Hi."

"Have a seat," says Vanessa, and I pull up a chair at the large table and sit next to Benji.

"What are you drawing, mate?" I ask.

"Daddy."

"Oh, are you missing him?"

Benji nods.

"He's away working, isn't he Benji?" says Vanessa, before adding for my benefit, "at a dental conference in Belgium. Back on Friday."

Belgium… a coincidence.

"Oh, right."

Reminds me, I must check in with Devon soon…

"Lennie's just getting ready upstairs" says Vanessa. "I'm about to feed them, do you want something?"

"Er, yeah, if that's OK?"

"Well I'm doing tuna and avocado pasta."

For the children?

"Yeah, sounds great."

*

Lennie bounds down the stairs a few minutes later, announcing his arrival with a series of thuds. He enters the kitchen and smiles when he sees me, which is reassuring. He runs right up to me and laughs, bouncing up and down on the spot a few times. This means he's pleased to see me. I offer him a high five and he returns the gesture. He doesn't really do hugs…

"Hi Lennie," I say.

"Hi dad."

He laughs again, and bounces some more, adjusting his clothes as he does. He's wearing black trousers, a white shirt, which is slightly too big for him, and a red clip-on tie. He looks very smart, but I can tell he's uncomfortable out of his usual uniform of jogging bottoms and a T-shirt. I wonder what powers of persuasion Vanessa used to achieve such a level of neatness…

"Doesn't he look smart?" she says, nodding at Lennie.

"Yes, very dapper," I reply. I notice that he's also shaved the downy beard he sported last time I saw him. His hair could do with a cut, but I guess Vanessa has to pick her battles…

Lennie is swiftly placated with a cartoon on his tablet and a plain cheese sandwich. We all sit around the table, and I enjoy tuna and avocado pasta with the others. I wonder if this is what I was seeking all along by turning up early… a small slice of normality alongside Lennie and Vanessa, with Richard safely out of the country. It's certainly a rarity, and a peaceful moment in a fortnight that has been anything but.

After lunch Vanessa gives me the keys to her car along with a brief rundown on what to do at the college, before shepherding the other two out of the house to walk to some playgroup or other. For a moment, I feel as though I'm in some alternative future, in which Vanessa and I stayed together, had more children and somehow managed to buy a massive house in Hove.

I snap out of my daydream and open the Fiat for Lennie to jump eagerly into the passenger seat. He seems happy enough. Within minutes we're heading out of the city with Lennie breathlessly telling me about some new computer game he's become enamoured with. I allow my thoughts to slide back to Straw Girl…

Today, finally, I could get an answer. I could be rich…

I really need to catch-up with Devon…

I decide to call her when we reach the college. I turn into a slip road and look into my wing mirror, waiting for the right time to join the traffic. A large, black 4X4 brakes sharply and flashes its lights, allowing me to pull out in front of it. I wave to the driver in my rear-view mirror, but his face is obscured through the tinted windows.

I drive on.

15

Devon wakes early, in fact, she's not entirely sure if she slept at all. All she remembers about the previous night was a long time spent lying on her back, staring at the dark ceiling, thinking about today. But she isn't tired. If anything, she's exactly the opposite. She feels awake; alert...

She checks her emails. Still no reply from the De Boer Institute. Oh well. She'll just have to turn up unannounced...

She takes Straw Girl out of the bed. The painting slept alongside Devon last night; still in its suit bag. As weird as it might seem, it felt like the safest place. She takes the painting downstairs and it sits with her as she enjoys a black coffee and croissant in the hotel dining room.

Suitably refreshed, she steps out into the street and the bitter cold hits her immediately. There are a few specks of snow dancing in the wind, and she regrets not bringing any warmer clothes with her. Come to that, she regrets not bringing any clothes with her, other than what she's standing up in.

She shrugs off the cold and pulls her green bobble hat on. The snow looks like it's beginning to settle. She trudges through it as she makes her way across the Grote Markt.

Devon doesn't notice him, but a man is making his way diagonally across the square; winding his way through knots of tourists, on a course destined to bring him into her path. He's large, with muscular arms under a leather jacket. His face is red and his bald head hatless, despite the weather. As he nears Devon he pulls out his phone and checks it, and – seemingly oblivious to his surroundings – wanders right into Devon's path.

Devon feels like she's been hit by a brick wall. She instinctively strengthens her grip on the suit bag, but doing so causes her to lose her balance. Her free hand plants down in the cold snow and she falls onto her knees.

The man bends over her and grabs the handle of the suit bag.

"No!" shouts Devon.

16

Lennie has spent the last half an hour telling me about the development of the computer games industry in the 1980s. His level of knowledge is impressive, but, as usual, it's quite a one-sided conversation... all I do is inject the odd "yes," or "oh!" which seems to satisfy him.

He stops his monologue to say "here it is," as we pull into the grounds of the agricultural college. It looks a nice place; rolling fields, small farm buildings and plenty of students in wellington boots looking hard at work. I'd have hated it, of course, but it looks like somewhere Lennie could make himself useful and learn a few life skills, which I guess is the point.

After we've parked, I give Devon's mobile a call, but it goes to her voicemail. I shove my phone back into my pocket and we make our way towards the main building.

"Dad, may I have a doughnut?" asks Lennie as we pass the coffee shop. I gently remind him that his reward for attending the interview, and dressing so smartly, is going to be a McDonald's. He seems to accept this.

*

Lennie claps his hands together in front of his chest. He's excited...

"Do you like being called Leonard or Lennie?" asks Bob. Lennie looks at me and chuckles.

"We always use Lennie, don't we?"

"Yes," he says.

"So, Lennie, have you always liked animals?" asks Marion.

We're sitting at a round table in a small classroom with posters of various farmyard animals on the walls. In front of as are a lecturer (Bob) and a woman from the learning support department (Marion). Both are friendly, but I'm a little concerned about what Lennie's about to say to them...

"Yes," he says quietly, looking at me, rather than Marion or Bob.

"Tell them about Kiwi," I say.

Lennie smiles.

"He's two years old, and he's got a black patch on his head, and he's called Kiwi because that's the national bird of New Zealand, and New Zealand wear black to play rugby, and also cricket sometimes."

"Yes, but what kind of animal is he?" I ask.

"A guinea pig."

"That's great," says Marion. Lennie smiles and briefly meets her eye. I smile too.

"So, Lennie, do you have any questions you want to ask us?" says Marion.

"Mmm, well, er"

"Go on," I say, encouragingly.

Lennie looks up at Marion, then at the table.

"Have you heard about the video game industry crash of 1983?"

*

The rest of the interview goes well, despite Lennie's sometimes bizarre conversational shifts. I guess the staff are used to that kind of thing. Bob tells us about the content of the course and Marion tells us about all the support Lennie will receive. It's always a bit hard trying to comprehend how he's feeling, but he seems happy enough.

I try Devon again. Voicemail, again.

"Right," I say to Lennie. "McDonald's?"

He starts bouncing.

17

Devon's shout grabs the attention of several tourists, who turn to see what's going on. She clings to the handle of the suit bag as if her life depends on it. The bald man senses this and relaxes his grip.

"Pardon," he says, "I was only, er, trying to 'elp you up."

His French accent is strong, but his English is good...

"It's fine, thank you" says Devon.

"I am so sorry, I was looking at my Google map, I, er, failed to see you."

Devon gets to her feet and brushes some snow off her tights.

"Don't worry about it."

She slings the suit bag back over her shoulder. The Frenchman is still hovering around apologetically. Devon walks away from him briskly. She needs to get to the De Boer Institute promptly.

She doesn't need any more tedious interruptions from oblivious tourists…

This is her big day. Her big chance.

Nothing, and no-one, is going to blow this for her now.

18

I head towards the nearest McDonald's, from memory it isn't far, but the traffic on the road is picking up as we get towards rush hour. Lennie still seems cheerful, but despite my attempts I'm unable to get a meaningful sense of his opinion on the college.

"Do you think you'll enjoy it there when you start in September?"

He shrugs.

"They seemed nice though, didn't they?"

"Yes."

"You might make some nice friends."

He fiddles with the radio.

"Mmmm."

He manages to tune it to a classical radio station. Dramatic strings swell and fill up the car. Lennie shrieks and turns the dial briskly, eventually settling on low-level white noise.

"Too loud," he says.

We pull up behind a queue of traffic at a set of lights. My phone, which I placed in the little plastic crevice between the front seats, makes a loud, insistent buzz. I reach down and read my text…

Hi Charlie. I've just been to the De Boer Institute. They received Dr Agnew's letter and will look at the painting tomorrow at 10am. Could take all day. Will keep you updated. D.

Someone behind me beeps their horn. I look up and notice that the lights have turned green and the rest of the queue are moving over the junction. Except me. I throw my phone back down pull away, but I move too quickly and stall the engine. Lennie jerks forwards into his seat belt.

"Ouch!"

The drive behind me has had enough, and pulls into the opposite lane of traffic to overtake me. As he does so he lowers his window and offers a frank appraisal of my driving skills…

"Twat!"

"What did he say?" asks Lennie.

"Never mind."

Several more cars have overtaken me by the time I get the engine started. As I finally pull away, I glance in my rear-view mirror to see that the only car now behind me is a large, black-coloured 4X4. It has dark-tinted windscreens, similar to the one I saw earlier, its driver hidden behind them. I drive on, along the single-carriageway country road, keeping to a sensible speed for someone who hasn't driven in over a year and has his only child on board. The black 4X4 pootles along behind me, seemingly content with my sedate pace.

Eventually we come to a wider stretch of road with enough space for the 4X4 to overtake, which he does. He starts off by pulling up close behind us. I see an indistinct, largish shape behind the tinted glass. The car then pulls alongside me with a loud rev of its engine, but instead of speeding off into the distance, the driver veers back in front of me and, totally without warning, slams on his brakes. The 4X4 comes to a complete stop, and I see its red brake lights heading towards me, getting bigger... I stamp on my brakes, but I'm unable to stop completely, and I smack sharply into its bumper.

Lennie and I jolt forwards in our seat belts and spring back at the same time.

"Shit!" I yell.

There's a moment of stunned silence, which is broken by Lennie grabbing his head in his hands, rocking and moaning.

19

I put my hand on Lennie's shoulder.

"It's OK mate," I say. "No harm done."

He keeps moaning.

My first thoughts are that it's some sort of insurance scam... the kind you read about, where the scammer deliberately draws you into a minor crash. I'm just glad Lennie is OK, even though he still seems to be in shock...

"It's fine mate," I say again. "Let me just sort this out then we'll get some food..."

I open the glove compartment and fish out the fidget spinner that Vanessa put inside. I hand it to Lennie and he starts manipulating it as I get out of the car. I glance at the front of Vanessa's Fiat; there doesn't look to be too much damage.

Surprisingly, the passenger door to the 4X4 opens first, so I walk round to that side as a young, pale-skinned woman with jet black hair gets out. The driver's side doesn't open.

The woman is in her mid-twenties, wearing blue jeans with a black fleeced jacket.

"Are you OK?" she says, in an eastern European accent.

"Yes," I say, "you?"

"Yes," she says, "it was our fault, sorry, let me give you our details…"

"OK," I say, wondering if this is how the scam is supposed to work.

I assumed they'd blame me…

She takes a pen and notebook from her side of the car and writes something in it. I glance towards the 4X4. There's a gap where her door has been left open, but I can't see the driver through it.

"My name is Maria," she says, handing me the piece of paper she's pulled from the notebook.

"Charlie," I say, taking the paper and the pen. I look closely at what she's seemingly just written…

It's unintelligible. Lines and lines of what looks like Arabic or shorthand or something. I scan through it, and my eyes fall upon one sentence towards the bottom of the page. The only part written in English. In capitals…

YOU WILL GIVE US OUR PAINTING.

I look up in shock. Maria smiles at me. I see the glint of a gold filling in her top row of teeth. I wheel around instinctively to see if Lennie's OK. But there's someone behind me, blocking my view of the Fiat. A large, muscular, bald-headed man. Someone I've seen before.

Grant...

And he's holding a gun.

"No!" I shout.

For a minute I'm convinced he's going to shoot me. *So, this is how it ends,* I think. But instead he lifts the heavy-looking pistol into the air and brings the handle down firmly into the side of my head.

I stagger to one side in pain and shock. Then everything goes black.

20

I wake up slowly, my thoughts segueing from a series of weird dreams into a general awareness of my surroundings. I'm in a dimly lit room. There's a dark blue light seeping across the bed I'm lying on, and around me on all sides are shadows.

My head is throbbing; the pain radiating from my left temple and creeping around my brain.

I don't know where the hell I am.

I must be hungover…

I try to remember what I was doing last night. Was I out drinking with Tim Anderson? I can't recall him being there… but his presence usually leads to malaise on this scale…

I try and order my thoughts.

I'm pretty sure something bad happened…

Was I sick? Did I embarrass myself? Did I get in a fight?

A light clicks on and the room is bathed in bright yellow, accompanied by a low buzzing sound. I open my eyes wider; my bedclothes are blue, my bed is framed in metal and I'm surrounded on three sides by plastic curtains.

I'm in a hospital…

I hear a man's voice.

"Charles? Can you hear me?"

To the right of my bed is a blurry, person-sized, seated shape. I rub my eyes and it comes slowly into focus. It's Sheridan Strauss. He's sitting with his legs apart and his sizable gut spilling over his belt. He's wearing a suit jacket which looks far too tight to button up, and I turn my head sideways to glance up at his red face and shock of greying curly hair.

The idea of Sheridan watching me sleep fills me with unease, but the feeling soon subsides and is replaced by a sharp panic as the memory of what I was doing earlier hits me like a thunderbolt. I was with my son, and now I'm not.

I sit upright in the bed.

"Lennie!"

*

"Where is he?" I shout, "where's Lennie?"

I sit up on the side of the bed. I'm still in the beige chinos and blue shirt I was wearing earlier – an effort to look smart, for the college meeting. I notice a smear of blood on my trousers.

"We don't know," says Sheridan.

"What do you mean?"

"We don't know where the boy is. We were hoping you could shed some light on that question?" says Sheridan.

"Me?"

"Well, you were with him last."

"Sheridan, look, I don't even know what happened. I don't know how I got here. I don't even know where I am."

"Well, you're in Royal Sussex County Hospital, Brighton, old chap."

Don't 'old chap' me…

"Look, where's my son, what's happened?"

"You tell us Charles" says Sheridan, seemingly calm. "I mean, one minute you're taking him to his college thingy, the next you're found lying by the side of the road with blood all over your face, and the boy's nowhere to be seen."

At that point, it all comes back to me…

Maria.

YOU WILL GIVE US YOUR PAINTING.

Grant.

The gun.

I get out of the bed and pace around the curtained cubicle looking for my shoes.

"I've got to do something. I've got to go."

"Not just yet," says Sheridan, "the doctors reckon you're concussed. I've been keeping a watch on you for them, but there's some other folks here in the building who've been waiting for a word with you when you come around."

"Eh? Who?"

"The police."

"What, here?"

"Yes, Charles. This is a police matter now. Vanessa's going out of her mind with worry. What the hell have you got mixed up in?"

"Me? I'm not mixed up in anything…" I say, aware that this isn't strictly true.

"Come on," says Sheridan, staring at me with his piggy, deep-set eyes. "What was it then, a carjacking, where they just happen to forget to steal the car? No. Something's going on here, chum."

I'm tempted to hit him. I just want him out of the way; I need to solve this. I need to find Lennie. I don't need Sheridan hindering me…

"I have to go," I say.

"Not yet," says Sheridan, blocking my way. "You've never been anything but trouble for Vanessa. Pregnant at 19. Mother to a retarded son before she'd even graduated. It was downhill sharp when she met you. And now this."

I stare back at him.

"What the fuck did you say about my son?"

I clench my fist and steel myself to hit him; but then I glance over his shoulder towards the door.

299

There's a knock…

The door opens, and two stern-faced police officers make their way into the room.

21

The police treat me fairly gently, probably due to the fact that my head is bloody and bandaged and my son is missing. They are a man and woman, both extremely young, which is a bit of a cliché, and they note down my version of events diligently. They also tell me their names, but my brain can't or won't, commit them to memory. Seconds after they've told me, I've forgotten.

I tell them everything that happened, of course, minus a few details. I neglect to tell them about Maria's *YOU WILL GIVE US YOUR PAINTING* message, and Grant and his gun. Instead I say I was hit from behind and collapsed.

And when they ask:

"Can you think of any reason why anyone would want to take your son?"

I say:

"No, not at all."

They don't appear to suspect me of anything, which I suppose is good. But I just want to get rid of them. I want to get out of hospital, so I can concentrate on getting Lennie back.

I know what I need to do. It's obvious… I have something they want, and they have something I want.

It's a no-brainer.

"Have you got somewhere to go?" asks the female police officer, "We'd appreciate it if you could stay locally, just while we continue our investigation."

"Well, I could stay at my mum's… in Shoreham," I say, and they note down the address.

"We appreciate the time you've taken to talk to us," says the male officer as they stand to go. "You can be sure we're doing everything we can in order to find your son."

"Thank you" I say.

Within minutes of them leaving, I'm running down a series of hospital corridors. I can't wait to be discharged officially. I want out.

I burst through the main doors onto the darkened street and reach for my phone. I call Devon's number and as I hold the phone to my ear I realise that my hand is shaking.

She answers, eventually, and sounds distant and tired…

"Charlie, hi."

"Hi, are you OK?"

"I was asleep."

"Asleep? What time is it there?"

"Just gone ten."

I glance at the display on my phone. It's past 9pm. It dawns on me how long I've been unconscious for.

Lennie's been missing over five hours…

"Look" I say, something's happened. You need to come home, now… with the painting."

"What?" she says, "didn't you get my message? The De Boer board are going to look at it tomorrow."

"It doesn't matter anymore. I need it back."

"But, why?"

"They've taken my son" I say, my voice shaking, "they've got Lennie."

"What? Who have?"

"The people who've been following us; the guy who stole my phone, and some woman he was with. They knocked me unconscious and now they've taken Lennie. I have to give them the painting."

"But, but, we're so close…" says Devon, still sounding a bit confused.

"It doesn't matter!" I shout, "can't you see, I don't care about the bloody painting anymore. I just want my boy back."

My voice cracks, and tears fill my eyes.

"OK, OK" says Devon. "The first flight back isn't until nine in the morning. I can't do anything till then, but I'll come back. Have you tried speaking to these people? To find out what they want?"

"No. They haven't been in touch, but it's obvious they're after the painting."

"Well why don't you try to speak to them? Find out their terms?"

"Well, how?"

Then it dawns on me. 'Grant', whoever he is, still has my old phone. I can get through to him straight away.

"Shit, yes, I can call them. OK, I'll do it now. Speak soon."

"OK Charlie. Take care."

I hang up on Devon and immediately call my old number. As it rings, I walk along the street heading west, intending to catch a bus back to Shoreham, but not knowing quite what I'll do when I get there.

Again, my phone rings for ages. I'm on the verge of hanging up when a familiar gruff voice answers.

"Hello, Charlie boy."

"Is Lennie OK?" I shout.

"Well, good evening to you too."

"Don't mess me about…" I say. My voice sounds high-pitched and shaky. "Tell me he's OK."

"He's fine. Maria's good with kids."

"You have to give him back to me. Tell me what you want me to do."

"It's very simple" says Grant. "I want your painting."

"OK," I say, "you can have it. Just don't hurt Lennie."

"He won't be hurt, Charlie, as long as you give us what you want."

"OK."

"And, of course, as long as you say nothing to the police about all this; although I would have thought that goes without saying."

"Yeah, sure."

There's a silence.

"It didn't have to be like this," says Grant. "Remember last time we spoke? I said that if you gave me the painting, I'd never take anything from you again. Well you didn't do it, did you? You didn't listen. You made us do this. It's such a shame..."

I run my hand through my hair, pulling it. I'm incensed... angry with him for taking my son, and with myself for not taking his threat seriously.

"The painting's with Devon. My, er, colleague. In Belgium."

"Belgium?"

"Yeah, but she'll bring it back tomorrow."

"Well, make sure she does. When you're ready to make the swap, give me a call. Until then Charlie..."

"Wait," I say, "let me speak to Lennie. "He'll be terrified. I need to tell him things are going to be alright."

"Nah," says Grant, flippantly. "He's asleep now. He was a bit overexcited earlier, so Maria gave him something to calm him down."

"What?!"

"He's fine, Charlie. Fine. Speak tomorrow."

Click.

The line goes dead.

22

I try calling my phone back again, but there's no answer. I walk hurriedly along the street, looking out for the nearest bus stop. There's one just down from the hospital, so I stand at wait for the next Shoreham bus. Luckily, there's one in five minutes.

I wonder what I'm going to do when I get to my mum's. Sleep seems impossible, yet there's nothing practical I can do till tomorrow. I briefly toy with the idea of going to see Vanessa, but I can't face seeing her in the distraught state she's bound he be in. I also know that – even if she won't say it outright – she'll blame it all on me.

Then again, perhaps I am to blame...

As soon as I heard about the potential value of the painting, that was all I'd been concerned about. That, and the life of luxury it would afford me. I pushed the fact that there were clearly unsavoury characters after it to the back of my mind. I never dreamed that anyone except myself would be at risk.

I never thought they'd target my son...

The bus arrives and I trudge on wearily, like a zombie, lost in my thoughts. I buy a ticket to Shoreham and take a seat.

I don't want to see the painting again. I don't care how much it's worth... I don't want to know about it.

I just want to see my son again.

The bus winds its slow way through Brighton, picking up and putting down late-shift workers and students on their way to the pubs and clubs. I remain oblivious to them all; staring out of the smudged window, thinking about my son and praying he's going to be OK.

Eventually we're coming out of the city and heading along Hove seafront, in the direction of Shoreham. The moonlight is reflected in the sea and the pin-prick red lights of distant ships sparkle on the surface. The journey continues to be stop-start as we regularly pause to allow passengers off and on.

I gaze towards the dark water and think back to when Lennie was born. I'd been so proud back then. I knew we were far too young, but a mixture of pride and youthful optimism gave me lofty ambitions; Vanessa and I would be a perfect, successful couple, and Lennie the first in a line of high-achieving, well-rounded children.

We might have barely out of our teens, but we would cope.

We just needed to graduate first...

In the kitchen of her shared student house in Brighton, Vanessa had told me her parents wanted her to move back home after the baby was born, so they could help care for him, whilst we continued studying for our degrees. It seemed like a good idea.

But gradually, I was phased out. I started seeing and hearing from Vanessa far less, which was always going to happen, I guess. She had a child to care for, essays to write... Our nights down the pub and cinema visits almost completely stopped.

When I wanted to see my son, it had to be on Vanessa's terms, although in reality, it was more often down to her parents. They always seemed to know what was best...

After I'd graduated I started applying for a variety of jobs in the film industry, hoping, naively, that I would soon be earning enough to set up home with Vanessa and Lennie. A year later, I was still unemployed. Reluctantly, I took a part-time job in the local library.

Soon after that Vanessa gently informed me that, although we would stay in touch for all things related to Lennie, our relationship was effectively over. The news wasn't exactly unexpected, but I took it hard. It didn't help that it was around the same time my father had his first heart attack...

As if to confirm the cliché about things happening in threes, Vanessa sat me down shortly after my father had passed away and told me that Lennie was showing signs of 'developmental delay' – not reaching milestones that other children would at the same age. Talking. Making eye-contact. Gesturing. That sort of thing.

When she first mentioned the word 'autism' I had to look it up.

My life gradually began to follow a familiar routine. I moved jobs from the library to the council offices. Bored by the 9-5 routine, I took a graduate course in screenwriting, but ended up back at the council, working part-time and writing film scripts in my spare days.

Needless to say, none of them set Hollywood ablaze…

It was supposed to be different in London… Meeting Siobhan had been a huge slice of luck. She was ambitious, hard-working and, for some reason, tolerated my idleness.

She also worked in the film industry. In marketing…

Moving to London was supposed to be my big chance to break into the industry. Siobhan had contacts. My scripts could finally be seen by the right people. I could combine part-time work with writing; using the most exciting city in the world as my inspiration.

Somehow, it had got me here…

With Lennie in peril; and me the only hope of saving him.

*

The bus finally reaches Shoreham. I disembark by the bridge and trudge up to my mum's. The house is dark, and I assume she's either asleep or out at some church function. I let myself in and snap on the kitchen light. I help myself to another generous glass of mum's cooking brandy, making a mental note to replace it for her tomorrow, seeing as it's now seriously depleted.

I head upstairs to my bedroom, turn on the lamp and take my laptop out of my bag. I boot it up and am relieved to see there's still a bit of battery left.

Sitting back on the bed, I open up a word document and start typing:

There are many stories I want to tell, but this isn't one of them.

I don't really want to have to write this at all, but it's becoming ever more pressing that I put it all down on paper - or in this case, on a laptop - and make sure it gets somewhere safe.

I pause and look out of the window, thinking of the next line. All I know is I need to document this… to make sense of it all…

I stare at the ceiling, and suddenly it changes colour. The gloom of my bedroom is flooded with a bright white light. I stand up and walk over to the window, peering out over the street.

Two headlights, set to full beam, are shining towards the house. A car sits, engine running, on the threshold of mum's driveway.

I cover the glare with my hand and squint, trying to make out whose vehicle it is. I try to focus on the silhouette in the driver's seat through the blinding light.

Then the horn beeps. I duck down.

Can they see me?

The driver beeps again.

23

Devon throws her phone down onto the hotel bed, pulls back the covers, gets up and strides across the room.

So much for an early night...

So much for tomorrow.

She looks back at the bag containing Straw Girl, tucked under the covers on the other side of the double bed.

"Shit!"

It had all been going so well. She'd visited the De Boer Institute earlier that day and had, after a considerable wait, had been greeted by a young lady named Hester, the personal assistant to Gerard De Boer – the current director of the institute.

Hester was able to confirm that Gerard had received the letter sent by Dr Phil Agnew and was very much willing to look at Straw Girl.

Just, not today...

Nor tomorrow...

Hester - round-cheeked and amiable – had explained that Gerard was very busy, as were the necessary expert colleagues he needed to assemble before considering the painting. It had taken over an hour of back and forth negotiation, with both sides using Hester as a conduit, for Gerard De Boer to give in to Devon's pleas and agree to consider Straw Girl at such short notice. Apparently, the intervention by Dr Agnew and the clout possessed by the Cowdrey Institute had swung it for her.

The appointment was set for 10am the next day...

Devon had treated herself to a smoked salmon sandwich and a long look around the De Boer gallery before taking a snowy walk around Antwerp. She'd been elated.

And now this happens...

Kidnap. Charlie's son being held hostage.

It scarcely seems possible, and Devon wonders for a second if she's dreaming. She pinches her arm.

She isn't.

She looks back over at the painting on the bed. She envisages carrying it back onto the plane tomorrow morning. Leaving Gerard De Boer and his panel hanging. Flying it back to London and handing it over to a bunch of crooks.

That in itself would be criminal. A lost work of art by a seventeenth century Flemish master, one that she could have saved and brought into the public consciousness, would instead be spirited away by the kind of people who could snatch a child.

But sadly, she can't see any other alternative. Not when there's a human life at stake.

With a heavy heart, Devon opens her laptop and starts looking up plane tickets for tomorrow morning. Again, she's going to need two...

24

I can't hide any longer; the driver of the car knows I'm here. I've been seen...

Another beep. The neighbours will be getting involved at this rate...

I reluctantly decide that my only choice is to go and see who it is. I close the laptop and make my way downstairs. I briefly consider arming myself with some kind of weapon, but decide this might look a bit hostile. Or, it might end up being used on me. Instead I make my way out into the night slowly, peering around the front door as I open it.

The light isn't quite so blinding outside. The car seems to have dimmed its headlights. My car knowledge is limited, but I can see it's a small vehicle; some sort of hatchback, dark in colour and reassuringly different from the menacing 4X4 which intercepted me earlier.

I walk around to the driver's side. It's still too dark to make anyone out.

I hope it's not Grant between the wheel… I don't fancy running into him again. The window slides down. The driver flicks on the interior light. Her face is bathed in a yellow glow. Her dark hair is tied back and her brown eyes meet mine.

"Hello, Charlie."

"Sunita?"

She looks serious, composed, yet still concerned.

"Please, get in the car."

"What?"

"I'll explain. Please get in."

"What is this?" I say, wondering why the assistant from Victor Botham's solicitors would be paying me a visit at this time of night. Especially with all this going on…

"Please, Charlie."

Sunita looks up, her dark eyes imploring me to do as she says.

"I… I don't understand."

"Then get in."

She switches off the ignition and looks around her, as if to make sure the street is empty of people.

"Charlie, if you want to find out what's going on… what all of this is really about, I can help. But you need to get in."

"I, my son…he's been taken…"

"I know. I can help you get him back. But get in."

How does she know this?

I look around me. Split decisions have never been my forte, and getting into a virtual stranger's car is something I usually try to avoid. But Sunita Sharma surely can't be a threat...

I walk back towards the house, retrieve my keys and lock the front door. Then I open the car door and get in. I settle in my seat next to Sunita and fasten my belt.

*

Sunita reverses out of the drive slowly and steers us away in silence. Her driving is an extension of her persona – at least, the persona she presents to the world; she moves the car slowly, watchfully, peering intently at the road, the tendons in her thin neck tensed.

We drive out of the town and join the bypass. Sunita picks up speed slightly but her pace remains sedate.

She remains silent.

"So, what's happening?" I ask, "like, where are we going?"

"I can't say."

"What?"

"It's not for me to explain, Charlie."

"But you said you could help me get Lennie back... you said I could find out what this is all about..."

"I said I could help you. And I can. But it's not for me to explain how."

"Well, who is it up to?"

"I can't say, Charlie. I'm sorry. But I can take you to the person who can explain everything, and things will become clear. But I can't say anything until then."

"Right. OK."

I decide not to push it.

"How long's it going to take?"

"A while," she says. "If you're feeling tired, I'd suggest getting some sleep."

"Sleep?" I say. "Are you serious? My only son is being held prisoner, by some pretty vicious people. How am I supposed to sleep?"

Sunita glances at me.

"Sorry. But do try to rest. I can help. *We* can help. But I can't answer any more questions. Not till we get there."

"Where's there?"

Sunita looks at me again, apologetically, purses her lips and looks back towards the road. It's like questioning a brick wall.

I give up and look out of the window instead. We're making our way along the bypass, back towards Brighton. To my right I can see the lights of the city twinkling in the distance. To my left the undulating wildness of the South Downs is shrouded in darkness.

Despite my protestations, the soft rhythms of the engine and Sunita's steady driving style coax me into sleepiness. I rest my head in the small cradle between my seatbelt and the window and close my eyes.

Within seconds I'm fast asleep.

25

I wake up, some period of time later in confusion. My head is numbed by the soft vibrations of the car window. Classical piano music is playing quietly from the car radio. I pull myself up in my seat and look out of the window; we're now on a much wider road than we had been when I'd closed my eyes.

I blink a few times.

"Where are we?"

"On the M25. Not long now."

"The M25? We're back in London? What the hell…"

"Just north of it actually, Hertfordshire."

"So, do I get to know where we're going now?"

"We're going to my house. It isn't far."

"Your house?"

"Yes."

"But, why?"

"I can't say any more."

"No, right. I forgot."

This is rapidly becoming her catchphrase…

I fish my phone out of my pocket. I haven't charged the thing since I bought it the other day, and it's down to 21%. I squint at the display and work out that someone's left me a voicemail. After a few minutes of trial-and-error button-pushing I work out how to listen to the message.

The raspy voice is grimly familiar. It's from Sheridan.

Charlie. Where the hell did you go? I came back to the hospital ward and you'd vanished. Just been to your mother's and she hasn't seen you either. What the hell are you playing at? Vanessa's going out of her mind with worry and you've done a runner. Then again, you've always run away from everything, haven't you?

He pauses, and I think he's going to hang up, but he continues

Give me a call back as soon as you get this, Charlie. You've got some questions to answer. After all, you were the last person to see the boy before he went missing. You don't want the old bill turning their suspicion on you, do you?

There's another pause, and I hear him breathing heavily before he evidently decides to hang up. I shove my phone back into my pocket.

"Wanker," I mutter to myself.

"Sorry?" says Sunita.

"Oh, nothing."

I note the lack of concern Sheridan expressed for Lennie in his voice message. As usual, I conclude, it's all about him, his family, and how things *appear*. How it all looks to an outsider… He's never given a shit about Lennie. Nor has his father. Both Sheridan and Leonard have always seen him as an embarrassment; a defective gene, introduced by me, tainting their perfect family line.

No. Sheridan has no concern for Lennie. He's just playing the role expected of him; the role of the loving uncle.

Well, sod him…

I look up at the overhead road sign we're about to pass. A black sign tells me we're approaching junction 18. An arrow points off to the left.

A404 – Chorleywood.

Sunita turns her left indicator on, and I assume this is our destination. Chorleywood. I've never been there, and I know it only as some minor commuter-belt town at the far end of the Metropolitan Line. I wonder what could possibly await us here… and what it could possibly have to do with Straw Girl, Grant and Maria, and Lennie's kidnapping.

I suppose I'm about to find out…

We pull off the motorway and join a series of smaller, tree-lined roads with few streetlights. Sunita switches off the radio and seems a bit tense. I sense we're nearly there…

We turn into a quieter road lined with big houses set back from the road, nestled behind more greenery. This road doesn't even appear to *have* streetlights... either that or they all get turned off at a certain time. We drive right to the end of the road, and I realise that we're in a cul-de-sac. Facing down the rest of the street is line of hedgerow with a gap in the middle. Above the top of the hedges the headlights pick put the top of a house. It's detached and made of red brick with a row of large sash windows, only one of which, I notice, has a light on behind it. We drive through the opening in the hedgerow and onto a gravel drive, which dissects a spacious lawn. I can see the house fully now, with its burgundy front door framed by a white-pillared porch.

Sunita turns off the engine.

"We're here" she says, fairly unnecessarily.

We get out of the car and I follow her, crunching through the gravel as we approach the door. She puts her car keys in the pocket of her cream coat and enters a code on a display next to the door, which enables her to push it open.

She steps in, and I follow.

We make our way into a long hallway with a shiny wooden floor, doors on both sides and a staircase at the far end. The house is eerily quiet, and I feel almost as though we're breaking in. I walk quietly, trying to make no sound as I move across the hall. I follow Sunita as she moves to the right of the staircase, opening a door at the far end of the hall with a key. I follow her through, it and she snaps a light on.

We're in a large, windowless room, and the air is slightly musty. The floor is also wooden but less shiny than outside – an intricate parquet pattern that could do with a good polish. The walls are painted in a plain magnolia which is chipped in places. In the middle of the room is a full-sized snooker table, and at one end is a collection of easy chairs gathered around a retro cocktail bar – the kind with leather padding and a glass-fronted cabinet.

It all seems functional rather than luxurious, almost like a slightly-faded bar room in a 1970s hotel.

But then my eye is drawn to the paintings...

They line the walls; a series of portraits and landscapes, over two dozen of them. I look around, trying to take them all in. They grab my untrained eye as expensive, masterly-painted works, not the output of an eager amateur...

I look at a random painting near me. It's a rural scene, depicting a clearing in the middle of some woods, populated by a stag and some small peasant figures.

"A Gainsborough..." says Sunita.

"What?"

"This was the double garage, originally. But my father was never into cars, so he had the space converted to house some of his favourite paintings, and as a kind of... entertaining room."

I look around again.

This is some man cave...

"Who is your father?" I ask, "do I know him?"

Sunita looks towards the door.

"You tell me."

The door opens, and a figure emerges from the darkness of the hallway. I see his face as he steps into the light of the room. I recognise the wayward white hair and the lopsided grin. I take an involuntary step backwards, grabbing onto the snooker table for support.

In front of me is a ghost. A man who, until now, I believed to be dead.

In front of me is Victor Botham.

26

Botham is not dead. Far from it. In fact, he looks as fit as a fiddle. He is dressed in red corduroy trousers and a mustard V-neck jumper, under which I recognise the familiar red and yellow stripes of an MCC tie.

He also appears to be wearing slippers. Soft leather moccasins.

"Charlie, my dear old boy!"

That familiar, fruity voice…

I don't know what to say. I'm still trying to wrap my head around what's in front of me and what it all means…

"You're alive?"

"Last time I checked, certainly."

"W… what's going on?" I say, looking around me.

"Fancy a port, Charlie? Looks like you could use one," says Botham.

"Er, yeah," I nod.

Is this some sort of joke?

Some sort of trap?

Or am I dreaming?

Victor walks past me towards the bar and leans down below it, producing a dusty bottle of port and pulling out the cork. He roots around in the cabinet and produces a couple of mismatched glasses. He inspects one and obviously rejects it, placing it back in the cabinet.

He turns to Sunita.

"Posie, would you mind getting a couple of clean glasses from the kitchen?"

She nods and leaves the room.

Posie?

"So, you're Sunita's father?" I say.

"Indeed. A very proud father too. Take a seat."

He gestures to one of the chairs by the bar. I perch in it, not wanting to get too comfortable. Botham reaches under the bar again and, to my surprise, pulls out a slim, shiny electronic cigarette and puffs a cloud of vapour across the room.

"I've always enjoyed a cigar, but I was browbeaten into giving up the real things when I started getting chest problems. So Posie... Sunita... got me this little thing one Christmas. It's not a bad substitute."

"Yes, I use one too..." I say, producing mine from my pocket.

"Ah, well feel free to puff away," he says. I do. The nicotine is relieving.

"Have you given up the real things too then?" he asks.

"Er, not quite."

He laughs.

"Not an easy business is it?"

Sunita walks back in with a couple of glasses in one hand and a mug in the other. Victor takes them off her.

"You're not joining us, sweetheart?"

"No, I'm having a coffee."

"Very well," says Botham, "all the more for Charlie and I."

He pours two generous glasses and hands one to me. I swallow a warming gulp and take another puff on my e-cigarette. Victor settles down into one of the chairs facing me, while Sunita leans against the snooker table cradling her coffee close to her chest.

"I expect you've, quite naturally, got a few questions you want answered?" he says.

"You could say that," I reply. "I thought you were dead. What's going on?"

"I can, and will, explain everything."

Yes, I keep getting told that...

I gesture to Sunita.

"She said you could help me get my son back... can you do that?"

"Yes. But I must start at the beginning."

"The beginning?"

"When we first met. At the National Gallery. It was no accident that I collapsed in your room, Charlie. I did it to get your attention."

I sit forward in my seat.

"What? You weren't sick? Have you actually got cancer, or is this all just some fantasy?"

"Oh, I've got cancer alright. In my lungs. And several other places too now. It's not going away and I haven't got long left. Which is why I wanted to get the painting to you. But I needed a reason. An excuse for my gratitude. I mean, it would look a little peculiar for some old chap you don't know from Adam to turn up on your doorstep with painting, wouldn't it?"

"But, why me? Why did I have to get the painting? What am I to you?"

"My dear boy, it's not so much what you are to me, but what your Grandad was to me."

"My Grandad?"

"Guy."

His words from the gallery burst into my mind again.

You're a good man, Guy, a good chap.

When he had supposedly been lying on the gallery floor in confusion, Victor had called me Guy. I'd wondered at the time if there was some connection, but quickly dismissed it from my mind.

"You knew my grandfather?"

"I did indeed. He was one of the finest, bravest men I ever met."

I sip some more port.

"I don't know very much about him. All I was ever told is that he died in the Second World War; before my father was even born."

"Yes. That is, at least, partly true," says Botham through a cloud of sweet-smelling vapour. "Your grandfather died during the second world war. We were on a mission together... it's a night I'll never forget. But the mission itself wasn't directly part of the war."

"How do you mean?"

Victor rises and walks back over to the bar. He digs around in the cabinet.

"Have you ever seen a photo of your grandfather, Charlie?"

"I think so, donkey's years ago though."

He passes me an old black-and-white photograph. It shows Guy in his army uniform and cap. He looks like a typical soldier – the kind they'd put on a recruitment advert – strong-jawed with determined eyes and a neat moustache.

"I can definitely see a family resemblance."

I laugh.

"I'm very flattered, but Guy must have been in his twenties here. I'm a bit past that."

"Oh, everybody's young to me," says Victor with a wave of his hand as he settles back into his chair.

"So, what was this mission all about, if it wasn't to do with the war?"

"Well, it was after Belgium had been liberated. Hostilities had ceased. Your grandfather and I were stationed in Antwerp at the time..."

Antwerp...

The home of Vanderschoot.

Where Devon is, right now...

"Right."

"Well, the story really starts a long time before that. It starts with a family of German origin. A family of hoteliers. A family who were once rich enough to buy a painting by the great artist Jan Vanderschoot; the Flemish master who spent his best years roaming around peasant villages and painting the characters he found there."

"Straw Girl?"

"Indeed. Arguably, one of his finest works. But not a work that has ever been published in an official catalogue raisonnè."

"Why not?"

"Because of its somewhat chequered history. It was privately owned in Antwerp for many years, before being purchased by the hoteliers. However, their firm went bust in the German depression of the twenties, and Straw Girl was among the assets sold off. The painting was bought by a family called the Levys. They owned it until the war, but when the Germans invaded Antwerp, it was seized by the Nazi occupiers."

Victor eyes me closely.

"The Levy family were Jewish. They never made it to the other side of the war. Nor did any of their relatives."

I nod solemnly.

"After the liberation, the assets of the Levy family were auctioned off. It was a chaotic time, and any provenance Straw Girl might have had was lost. But this wasn't enough to put off a budding art historian such as yours truly. I did some research, and came to the conclusion that it was more than likely the real thing. I was able to buy it for a knockdown price. A real bargain. It was the opportunity of a lifetime. But it was all to turn sour…"

"How?"

"A chap named Josef. A Nazi sympathiser and son of the previous owner – the hotelier. He was still in Antwerp, and he stole the painting from me."

"He stole it…?"

"Yes. Him and a bunch of his cronies stormed into my digs one night and took it at gunpoint. Apparently, he believed it was rightfully his, and wasn't about to let a little thing like legal ownership stand in the way."

"Clearly not."

"Your grandfather was with me that night. When I filled him in on the background, he was disgusted, and promised to help me get the painting back. Whatever it took."

"OK, and what did it take?"

Victor glances over at Sunita. She's put her coffee down on the edge of the snooker table and is wandering round it, scrolling through her phone. It seems to me that she's heard this story many times before...

"It took his life Charlie. I discovered that this man Josef was planning to ship the painting out of Antwerp, so Guy and I ambushed the van and took back what was mine. But it came at a price."

I lean forwards; intently.

"The young man we enlisted to help us got a little trigger happy. Shot one of Josef's men. In the struggle that followed, they fired back, and your grandfather was wounded. Fatally, it turned out."

"My God..."

"He died for me. And he died for the painting you've been carting about with you for the last week or so."

I'm lost for words. Straw Girl hadn't just been gifted to me through chance. It had once been saved by my own Grandfather. He must have looked at it, touched it...

Died for it...

"So that's the reason I was given the painting? For what my grandfather did during the war."

Victor eyes Sunita again. She frowns at him.

"Well, partly, old boy..."

I'm confused.

"What do you mean... partly?"

Victor sips some more port and I notice him meet Sunita's eyes again. I try to gauge what unspoken communication flies between them, but I can't grasp it.

"Well," says Victor, "your brave grandfather isn't the only connection you have to the painting. Remarkably, there's another link."

He puffs some more vapour into the air.

"It concerns Josef. The hotelier. The Nazi sympathiser who stole Straw Girl. After the war, he fled to London, where he married and had a son. He called the boy Leonard..."

"Leonard...?"

"Yes," says Victor. "You may have noticed that I haven't told you his surname yet..."

"His surname? Why... what is it?"

Botham looks up at me.

"Strauss. The family name is Strauss."

27

I'm up on my feet, pacing around the snooker table, scarcely able to comprehend what I've just been told. I grab a red ball in my hand and grip it tightly; looking up I see portraits looking down on me from the walls, making me feel tiny and useless.

"So, you're saying that Sheridan Strauss... has my son?"

"Yes."

"He's kidnapped his own nephew?"

"I'm afraid so."

My head is spinning from a cocktail of new information, stress, and a lack of sleep. I almost feel as though I'm not really in the snooker room at all; rather that I'm spiralling through some never-ending bad dream. I pinch my own arm – not so much to test whether I'm dreaming, but rather to bring myself back into the moment.

"He wouldn't do that", I say. But I don't know if I believe it. In fact, I don't believe it at all. I wouldn't trust Sheridan as far as I could throw him, which isn't far. But his own nephew... his flesh and blood. Would he really kidnap him?

The nephew he never cared for. Who he described as retarded.

The nephew his father views as an embarrassment to the family...

"I'm afraid he would," says Victor, "although, not directly. It seems he's had some bouncer and a Polish girl do all the dirty work. It's unlikely your son is aware that his own uncle is his captor."

The bouncer and the Polish girl. Surely Grant and Maria...

I stare at Victor.

Can I trust this man? After all, he lied about being dead. Maybe he's still lying?

I run my hands through my hair, thinking how I could murder a cigarette.

"How do you know all this? I mean, why should I believe you, when two weeks ago you told me you were dead."

Victor rises to his feet.

"Yes, I did. And I'm sorry, but that was a necessary lie."

"Necessary?"

"Yes. But you can believe everything I say regarding all other matters. Trust me, I know exactly what's going on."

"But how?"

Victor looks over at Sunita, who still doesn't look happy.

"Posie, please fetch Mr Milburn."

Sunita nods obediently and leaves the room.

"Who?" I ask, but before I get an answer, the door to the snooker room opens again and Sunita walks back through it, followed by a thin man in a brown suit. I'm sure I've seen him before, but in a different context. I rack the depths of my brain, trying to place his gaunt face, goatee beard and slender frame.

The man extends a hand in my direction.

"The name's Milburn. Finn Milburn. Nice to see you, again."

I instinctively shake his bony hand.

"What do you mean, again...? Have we met?"

"Not formally," says Milburn, and I detect a hint of a Scottish accent in his soft voice... "The last time our paths crossed was at Battersea Park Railway Station."

"Eh?"

Milburn pulls a red baseball cap out of his jacket pocket and pulls it over his eyes.

"Ring a bell?"

"Oh, Christ..."

The train spotter, or so I thought. The man I pushed to the ground on the platform...

Milburn flings his cap across the room and chuckles to himself.

"Look, I'm, I'm sorry about what happened..." I stammer.

"Don't be, Mr Marks," he chuckles, "it's an occupational hazard in my line of work."

"Sorry?"

"Finn here is a private detective Charlie," Victor chips in. "One of the best in the business. He's been my eyes and ears over the last few weeks. Thanks to him and Sunita I've kept up with all developments from my armchair, mostly. After all, I can't be running around much in my condition."

Victor pours a glass of port for Finn and hands it to him.

"Cheers," he says, taking a seat.

I sit too, wearily, and swallow some more port.

"Why would Sheridan do this?" I say.

"Desperation and pride," says Finn. "A dangerous mixture."

Victor nods.

"Let me fill you in from the start, Charlie. Or, at least, from when I rescued the painting. When the war was finally over, I left the army and brought Straw Girl back to England with me. I started my art dealership business in the late 40s, and throughout the 50s I made several attempts to prove Straw Girl was a genuine Vanderschoot. Unfortunately, all of these were ultimately fruitless."

"Why was that?" I ask.

"Well, forensic techniques weren't quite what they are now, and there was a lack of real provenance linking the painting back to seventeenth century Antwerp. As my art collection grew, other works began to take up more of my time. Straw Girl became little more than a decorative piece to hang on my walls, but I never forgot its history."

"In that case," I say, "why is everyone after it now?"

"A combination of factors. Firstly, after the war, Josef Strauss fled to London, where he attempted to rebuild his life. He started going by the name Joe Strauss, ditched his Nazi connections and joined a firm of stockbrokers. He did well, by all accounts. Married an English girl, fathered Leonard, bought a big house in Sussex, and in the mid-60s he founded his own firm of stockbrokers. Strauss Securities."

I roll my eyes. Countless times I've heard various members of Vanessa's family prattling on about Strauss Securities. I've never particularly known nor cared what the company did, except that it clearly kept the family in big houses, 4X4 cars and swimming pools.

"Yes, I've heard of it" I say.

Well, Josef never forgot about Straw Girl. He still viewed it as his family's property; but he was a respectable man by this time. A wealthy man. He came to see me once, at my Marylebone dealership. 1967, I believe. Offered me a King's ransom for the painting. Almost half a million, in today's money."

"Blimey…" I say.

"A huge amount for a work not listed in the official Vanderschoot catalogue raisonnè. Nevertheless, I told him what he could do with his money. He was insulted. Strauss believed he could buy anything he wanted, but not Straw Girl. It always eluded him."

Victor, a born raconteur, seems to be enjoying telling his story. But I'm growing impatient – eager to know how this all leads to Lennie. I lean forward and meet Victor's eye.

"So, what's all this got to do with what's going on now?

Victor continues…

"Well, Josef grew infirm and eventually passed the company on to his son, Leonard, in the 80s. Seems he also passed on the story of Straw Girl – the family heirloom that was rightfully theirs. But there was no way I was giving it up, and I think the Strauss family reluctantly accepted that. They had their own riches to console themselves with. Anyway, at around the same time, in the eighties, I met my future wife, Indira…"

"My mother," says Sunita, the first time she's spoken in a while.

"Yes. She fell in love with the painting and became determined to prove its veracity. Sadly, she was about to embark fully on the project when she passed away in tragic circumstances whilst visiting the states. If I tell you the date she died, it might explain how she met such an untimely end. It was the 11th of September, 2001."

I notice Sunita now has her head in her hand. She runs her forehead and looks towards me. I try to look sympathetic.

"I'm sorry."

"Anyway," continues Victor, "time marches on, and eventually Leonard passed most of the running of Strauss Securities onto his own son, Sheridan."

He looks towards me.

"We're coming towards the present day now..."

"Good," I say.

"Now, around this time I first began to notice odd things happening. Unsettling things. Suspicious people hanging around at the gallery. People following me. An attempted break-in here at the house. After this I upped my security, but things were still worrying me. That's when I turned to Finn."

He nods in the direction of Finn Milburn.

"Aye," says Finn. "My first job was to dig around in Sheridan Strauss's business affairs. The results were quite illuminating, you might say. It seems the global financial crisis wasn't kind to Strauss Securities. Not kind at all. Then the uncertainty of Brexit came along... You could say they've never fully recovered."

I sit up.

"They're in trouble?"

"Big trouble. After much investigation, it seems clear to me that the firm is on the brink of insolvency."

"So, Sheridan's going after Straw Girl to pull himself out of a financial hole?"

Finn looks at Victor, who finishes his glass of port.

"Spot on."

28

I'm pacing around the snooker room again, trying to get things straight in my head.

It's not proving easy…

"So, you're telling me that Sheridan is behind all of this… the stalking, the attempts to steal the painting, the kidnap of Lennie?"

"Yes, with encouragement from his old man…"

Leonard's in on it too? Hardly surprising really, knowing the old bastard. But surely the conspiracy can't go any further?

"What about Vanessa?" I ask, praying that she's not involved.

Finn answers me.

"I can't find any evidence to suggest that Vanessa Strauss is aware of any of this. It seems to have been cooked up by the male side of the family."

I breathe a sigh of relief. But while I'm relieved that Vanessa isn't involved, it makes me detest Sheridan even more. What kind of man would put his own sister through such trauma? I slump back into one of the chairs.

"I've never liked Sheridan, or his father. They're horrible people. But abducting one of their own family…"

"The threat of destitution makes people do odd things, Charlie," says Victor. But they believe Straw Girl can rescue them, especially if the million pound plus price tag is accurate."

I run my hands through my hair. I think back over the events of the previous few weeks; in particular the man who assaulted Devon outside the pub. He'd been tall and lean, by her description. Hardly likely to have been the man-mountain Grant…

"He hasn't been acting alone though," I say, "do you know who his accomplices are?"

"Well" says Finn, "the bouncer and the Polish girl are hired hands. Career criminals from the Brighton area. He'll be paying them a one-off fee."

"And the tall man who mugged Devon?"

"Yes, well he's someone you might be familiar with too. An old friend of Sheridan's. Arnie Russell."

"Arnie Russell?"

I'm genuinely shocked by this. Arnie always seemed rather harmless… someone whose main crime was periodically boring me at family celebrations.

"Yup," says Finn.

"How is Arnie involved?" I ask.

"Sheridan has paid off Arnie's gambling debts on more occasions than he can probably remember. The man owes him. Plus, his army experience makes him good at stealthy operations… such as breaking and entering."

I think back to the break in at the flat… the black handprint smeared on the cream sofa, which I still haven't sorted out yet…

"Arnie was the one who did over my flat? He was Mr Black Hand?"

"Indeed," says Finn. "He was also behind the break in at the storage facility."

"Bloody hell."

I stare into my drink, still trying to wrap my head around it all, when a new question pops into my head.

"So, why *now* then? Why leave the painting to me when you did?"

Victor looks around, glancing at Sunita and Finn, then speaks, quieter than usual…

"When Indira died, I lost my zeal for the painting. I suppose it reminded me of her too much… I kept it safe for years, but I barely looked at it. Then I fell ill. Can't complain about that, I suppose, after all, 96 is a good innings. I made arrangements in my will for all my other paintings, but Straw Girl continued to bother me… its unofficial status was an ongoing niggle. I suppose you could say it was unfinished business. So, I made my decision. I'd give it to one of Guy's relatives, but he or she would have to do something for me in return."

"And that was?"

"Prove the painting was genuine."

"And you chose me specifically to do that? Why? I mean, he has other relatives... I've got cousins..."

"Yes, well I had Finn here do a bit of research. According to him, you seemed like a fairly determined chap, but also, one who could use a few extra quid."

Not far off...

I nod, but I'm quite uneasy with the idea of Finn digging around in my private life...

"Of course, he also found out that you worked in the National Gallery, and that strengthened your case. It was a fair bet that you had at least a passing interest in art. But then the clincher came... the extraordinary coincidence, you might say, of your link to the Strauss family. When all that came up, it was obvious you were my man."

He smiles at me – his familiar crooked grin – and I feel a flash of annoyance. It all seems like a game to him; a pursuit he's orchestrated from his comfy, commuter-belt armchair, surrounded by paintings and port. But Lennie is still missing, and that's real...

"Right. And you didn't think that I might not want to be dragged into all this? Break ins at my flat, assaults in the street, my son being bloody kidnapped! What if I hadn't wanted any part of it?"

"The painting's worth over a million, Charlie. Would you really have turned it down?"

"If I knew my son's safety was at risk, yes, I probably would've done…"

I stand up, my voice rising in volume. Victor offers a conciliatory hand gesture.

"That's, of course, is my biggest regret in this whole thing, Charlie. I considered all possible outcomes. But your son is a Strauss. I never considered that Sheridan would use his own nephew against you..."

"Well, he has."

"I know. But we're going to get him back safely, I can assure you."

He glances at Sunita and Finn in turn. Sunita frowns again…

"How?" I ask, "after all, I talked to Grant, and all their terms were pretty bloody clear. The painting, in exchange for Lennie."

Victor nods.

"Yes, obviously their terms will be the exchange of the painting..."

Victor looks at Sunita again.

"Or at least, what they *think* is the painting."

29

It's late now, past one in the morning, and Victor has shuffled off to bed after going through his plan several times. The way he explains it, it all seems to make sense. But then, it's not *his son* being held hostage...

Sunita leaves the snooker room to see Finn Milburn out. I close my eyes and rub them vigorously. I could quite easily fall asleep, but an equally big part of me feels guilty about resting while Lennie is still being held against his will. I hear the sound of Milburn's engine, followed by Sunita returning, and open my eyes.

"I'll show you were you can sleep tonight," she says, "would you like another drink? Or some water?"

I blink with my heavy eyes.

"Could I have a coffee?" I ask.

"Sure," she says, "follow me."

We leave the snooker room and follow the hallway to the kitchen. I rest against the large breakfast bar while Sunita makes coffee.

"I have to tell you Charlie, I was never in favour of this idea," she says.

"I'm sorry?"

"I didn't want my father to do any of it. I didn't want him dragging you into it. I didn't see why he couldn't just leave you the painting in his will, like any normal person. But he insisted on doing it this way. I think he just wanted to be alive to see Straw Girl proved genuine. And to get one over on the Strauss family."

"I see. So that's why you came to see me at the flat, to make sure I was safe?"

"Yes."

A thought crosses my mind.

"Do you really work for Mr Hussain?"

She shakes her head.

"No. Since I graduated, my full-time role has been as my father's assistant. I'll be taking care of his art collection when he... passes away. Hussain is the family solicitor, and an old family friend. He's in on it, obviously. It was decided that by posing as his assistant I could keep an eye on your progress."

I nod. It seems like everyone's been lying to me, but I can't really bring myself to be angry with Sunita. Her father is dying, after all, and he seems like a difficult man to say no to… so I just smile.

"Does your father have any other children?" I ask.

"Yes, three. All by his first wife. But I'm the only one he trusts, apparently."

I nod.

"Anyway," she says, "it seems like his plan is the only one we've got."

"I guess so."

"I'm sure your son will be fine" she says.

I smile again.

"OK," she says, handing me a mug of coffee, "let me show you your room."

*

In any other circumstance, Victor's guest bedroom would be a pretty luxurious billet. It boasts a soft carpet, fresh towels and an inviting four-poster bed. Unfortunately, relaxation is the last thing on my mind.

I pull out my phone. It's on 18% battery now, but nevertheless, I unlock it and call Devon's number. It rings for a while before she picks up.

"Charlie? Hi."

She sounds groggy.

"Hi. Sorry, were you asleep?"

"Yeah, just dropped off."

"Oh, I'm sorry."

"It's OK. I've been sorting out plane tickets for tomorrow. I fly back at nine in the morning."

"Right," I say, "the thing is, you might want to cancel them..."

"Sorry, what?"

"You're going to have to cancel the plane tickets and stay in Antwerp. Go ahead with the meeting at the De Boer Institute tomorrow."

"But...but why? Is your son safe now?"

"No, it's a long story, but there's another plan."

"What?"

I fill her in on the latest developments: that Victor Botham is alive, that Lennie's own uncle is the one who's holding him hostage, and that Victor thinks he has a sure-fire way to sort things out... Devon takes it all in, and there follows a long pause. I have to interrupt her silence to make sure we haven't been disconnected...

"Hi... Devon?"

"Yeah, hi, still here."

"So, what do you think?"

"Well, to be honest Charlie, it sounds pretty implausible."

"Oh..."

"I mean, this friend of Victor's late wife..."

"Clara Swann."

"Yes, he really thinks she can paint a perfect copy of Straw Girl in 24 hours?"

"Yes, apparently he's pretty confident. She's some kind of genius by all accounts – like a sort of savant..."

"A savant?"

"Yeah. Apparently she lives alone in some little town in Scotland, with her cats, like some sort of hermit, but she has an amazing talent for mimicking famous artists."

"Seriously?"

"Yeah... she studied with Sunita's mother at St Martin's. Her house is full of perfect copies of Turners, Van Goghs, Monets.... you name it."

"So, what is she, some sort of fraudster?"

"No, not at all. She does it all as a hobby, not for profit. But she's prepared to do this, to help Victor out... and to help save the real Straw Girl."

"OK. I just don't see how she can do it so quickly... I mean, a faultless reproduction of a Vanderschoot... it's not painting by numbers..."

"I know. But apparently this is what she does..."

"But Sheridan and his accomplices, won't they notice it's not the original?"

"He shouldn't do. He's a stockbroker, not an art expert, and these people he's got doing his dirty work are small-time crooks and an old army mate. Besides, if they do decide to get it checked out properly, by the time they find out it's a fake we should have proved ours is genuine and sold it off to a gallery."

"Well, yes, hopefully. Depends how tomorrow goes."

"Are you confident?"

"Well, quietly. I think we have a good case, with some solid forensic research. But we're lacking in provenance actually linking the painting to seventeenth century Flanders…"

"But you think we have enough?"

"I think so. I don't know, it's hard to say. I've never dealt with the De Boers before. I'll know more this time tomorrow… that's if you're sure this is what you want to do?"

"It's the only thing I *can* do, if I want to keep the painting and get my son back."

"Well," says Devon, "you could always tell the police that you know who has your son…"

I shake my head.

"No. I can't risk that… I'm not sure if Sheridan would harm Lennie, but I don't know anything about this Grant man, and he specifically warned me not to involve the law."

"OK. So, I'll go to the De Boer tomorrow and keep you updated. What's your plan?"

"Well, apparently Clara is already working on the painting. Sunita's going drive up to Prestwick and collect it tomorrow, then I'll arrange a time and place to exchange it… for Lennie."

"OK," says Devon. "Well, I'm going back to sleep. I have to be up in a few hours. I suggest you do too…"

"Sure. Night. And good luck."

"Good luck to you too, Charlie. Sleep well."

I hang up, turn off my phone to conserve the battery, then lie down on the top of the bed and stare at the ceiling. I don't plan on sleeping at all, but within minutes I drift into a confused and troubled slumber. I wake up sometime later with a violent jerk. The lights are still on and I'm fully clothed and covered in sweat.

I can't remember what I was dreaming about, but I'm sure it involved Lennie.

30

A new day comes around, and it's one that Devon, until hours ago, fully expected to be one of disappointment. She had just about reconciled herself to the necessity of Straw Girl having to be brought back to the UK and handed over to a gang of criminals. She had just about accepted that her big chance to make her name in the art world had been taken away from her.

But then came a last-minute reprieve...

On waking up, Devon had wondered whether Charlie's early-hours phone call had been a wildly hopeful dream. But a brief check of her phone confirmed that he had indeed contacted her in the early hours of the morning.

There's a new plan...

The Antwerp morning is bright but bitterly cold; a weak winter sun failing to warm the cold streets as Devon makes her way through the city to the De Boer Institute. She has her now-ubiquitous suit bag draped over her back, making her progress through the Grote Markt significantly sluggish. She stares down at her Dr Martens boots as she trudges through the town square, wondering if she ought to have bought something a bit smarter to wear in front of the De Boer panel.

Oh well, too late now.

Looking up, she glimpses of a stack of Gazet van Antwerpen newspapers on a vender's stall, which tell her it's the first of February; the month of her birthday. She hadn't realised until now…

It's a short walk to the De Boer Institute, and once she reaches it she stands outside for a minute or so, mentally preparing herself. It's an imposing place; set back from the road behind a set of tall metal gates similar to the ones across Downing Street. Through the gates is a small courtyard framed by three wings of grey-stone buildings.

She identifies herself and is let in. As she passes through the gates she breathes in sharply and tenses every muscle in her body.

This is it…

31

I sleep again for a few hours – fitfully and uncomfortably, waking up around seven in the morning. I lie still for a few minutes, but it already seems pretty obvious that sleep isn't returning, so I drag my weary body out of bed and walk across to the curtains. Parting them allows a bright burst of morning sun to flood into the room, and as I squint out at the driveway I realise that Sunita's car is already gone.

I turn my phone on and realise two more things: that it's the first day of February, and my battery is now at 11%.

I make my way downstairs in search of coffee. To my surprise, Victor is already up. He's perched on a stool at the breakfast bar, dressed in a silky maroon dressing gown. In front of him is a plate of scrambled egg on toast and a folded-open copy of the Daily Telegraph. Radio 4 is on in the background. He looks as though he hasn't got a care in the world; whilst Lennie is being held in God-knows what kind of conditions. Anger starts to well inside me, but I try my best to suppress it…

Come on, Charlie, the man's dying. Unless that was just another lie…

He glances up and spies me.

"Good morning old boy," he barks. "Sleep well?"

"Not really."

"Oh, well. There's scrambled eggs and bacon for breakfast – get some food inside you, and some coffee."

"Has Sunita left?"

"Yes. About an hour ago. It's a 12-hour round trip to Clara Swann's place. Traffic-permitting, she should be back here with the painting by seven or eight this evening."

"So what do we do?"

"Sit tight. Wait. Speak to the kidnappers and tell them we'll be able to make the transfer in due course. And in the meantime, eat breakfast."

I shovel some eggs and bacon into my mouth and wash it down with a black coffee. I mention my phone problem, and Victor tells me that there's a stash of old electrical equipment in his wardrobe, which might include a charger that works, so I follow him upstairs.

His bedroom is just as exactly as his taste in loungewear suggests it might be. The white carpet is so thick my whole foot melts into it. The four-poster bed is even larger than the one in my room and is decorated in expensive-looking silky fabrics. A leather chaise longue sits in one corner, and the walls are decorated with even more paintings. One which I recognise immediately is The Birth of Venus by Sandro Botticelli.

"Don't tell me this is an original too, Victor?" I say, "I thought the Italians had it…"

He laughs.

"The original is indeed in the Uffizi in Florence, and about three times the size of this. No, what you see here is a genuine Clara Swann copy. She made this for me and Indira as a wedding present."

"Blimey. Most people get a toaster…"

I look closely at the painting. To my untrained eye, it's beautiful… a perfect imitation of the original, which admittedly I've only ever seen in photos. But still, its sheer brilliance gives me greater confidence in what Clara Swann can achieve.

"She's bloody good…" I say, almost under my breath.

"She certainly is. I'm not sure how you would define genius, Charlie? Perhaps there has to be an element of creativity involved. What would you say?"

"Er, yeah, I suppose. Like, no musical genius ever spent their whole career copying other people's songs, did they?"

"No. And Clara is very much a copyist. Her original work was never quite as strong. But when it comes to reproductions such as this, she's in a league of her own. And her ambition knows no bounds; for example, she was more than willing to make a life-sized copy of the Birth of Venus. Six foot by nine. It was only our lack of wall space that convinced her to scale it down. But I have no doubt she would have done it… and in next to no time, just like any other painting she turned her attention to. That's surely a form of genius in itself?"

"Well, I guess."

Another picture catches my eye – a photograph this time – showing a woman who I immediately assume to be Indira. She is very beautiful… coffee-skinned with long black hair and a smiling, heart-shaped face. There's a definite resemblance to Sunita; but her daughter's fragility is absent, replaced instead by a magnetic confidence that seems to leap down the lens. She's wearing what looks like a traditional Indian dress, with an ornate necklace and earrings.

"Your wife?" I ask.

"Indeed. A beautiful woman, wouldn't you agree?"

I nod my head, not quite sure how enthusiastically I should answer…

"She was a hugely fond of Straw Girl. I often wonder how differently things would have worked out, if she hadn't caught that damned flight back in 2001. Straw Girl might already have been authenticated."

I nod again.

And Lennie wouldn't have been kidnapped… Then again, neither would I be in with a chance of owning a million-pound painting.

If I'd been asked a month ago if I could put a price on my son's life, I would have dismissed the idea as crazy. But here I am, hatching a plan to get him back safe whilst preserving the asset that could make me a fortune. Basically, I want to have my cake, and to eat it.

Am I just selfish… do I care more about myself than my son?

Or no… maybe this is a chance to build a closer relationship with Lennie… to have the money to see him more often, to take him to those places I could never afford….

Victor's voice stirs me from my revelry.

"Do you think one of these buggers will work?"

In his hand is a spaghetti-like mass of tangled electrical cables and plugs.

"Er, possibly."

*

It takes a good half hour of untangling, followed by another half hour of charging, before I feel confident in using my phone to get in touch with Grant. Victor sits back on his chaise-longue and watches as I make the call. I tap in the number of my old phone and listen as it rings. Like last time, Grant leaves it to the very last second before he picks up… just enough for a nausea to build up inside me.

"Morning Charlie," he says.

"Hi," I say, in as neutral a tone as I can muster, given that I'm talking to someone who has my son's life in his hands.

"Got the picture for us then?" he says in his familiar growl.

"It's on its way. Should be with us this evening."

"Fine. We'll collect it tonight then. No point delaying. I expect you want to see your boy?"

It's more of a statement than a question.

"Yes. How is he?"

"He's fine."

"Can I speak to him?"

"Not right now."

"Please. I just want to check he's alright…" I say, trying to suppress the anger bubbling within me. How dare this man tell me that I can't speak to my own son…

"Like I said, he's fine. You'll see for yourself tonight, won't you?"

"I'd rather speak to him now…"

Grant chooses not to hear this.

"Do you know Shoreham Tollbridge?" he asks.

As it happens, I do. Very well. It's an old wooden bridge near my hometown, which used to carry the main road over the River Adur, before the Shoreham bypass was built. Nowadays it's just used by walkers and cyclists. I must have crossed it hundreds of times in my youth…

"Yes, I know it."

"Be there at eleven tonight with the painting. We'll tell you what to do."

"Fine."

"And remember, no police. Any sign of the old bill, and the whole thing's off, and obviously, you don't get to see your boy again."

"OK... I get it."

Grant breathes in heavily... I can almost smell it.

"See you tonight Charlie."

He hangs up. I turn to Victor, who looks unusually pensive.

"OK," I say. "It's on."

32

Devon approaches the receptionist and places the bag on the floor in front of the desk.

"Can I help you?" asks the receptionist in accented English. To Devon's ears, the question almost seems to be a challenge... code for: 'what kind of business can someone like you possibly have in a place such as this?'

Devon's used to this kind of attitude. It could be the fact that she's wearing Doc Martens, purple tights and a denim dress under her parka. It could be the fact that she has a well-travelled Marks and Spencer suit bag with her. Or it could be something to do with the colour of her skin. That happens, sometimes...

"Hello," she says, "I have an appointment this morning... with Gerard De Boer."

"OK" says the receptionist, raising an eyebrow at the name of the Institute's esteemed director, "and your name is?"

"Devon Lamb."

"OK. One minute, Miss Lamb."

The receptionist makes a call and asks Devon to take a seat, handing her a visitor's badge on a yellow lanyard. She shuffles backwards and perches on a hard stone bench, looking around the room. As lobbies go, it's certainly one of the plusher ones she's been in. The floor is a shiny marble, a chandelier hangs from the ceiling and the walls are, naturally, lined with paintings. Devon notices a Rubens. A modern clock sits on the wall above the receptionist, and Devon stares up at it, watching the seconds tick by.

After a minute or so a familiar, friendlier, face enters the lobby. Hester - the moon-faced personal assistant to Gerard De Boer - smiles widely beneath her glasses, which puts Devon at ease.

"Ah, hello again Miss Lamb. Please, follow me."

Devon paces after her through a maze of cramped corridors and up a steep, wide spiral staircase. She looks down at the ever-increasing void in the middle as she follows Hester's sharply clicking footsteps and gulps. Heights have never been her thing...

At the top, Hester leads her along another corridor and knocks on a double door at the end.

"Come in."

The room they emerge into is every bit as imposing as the lobby, if not more. The carpet is a deep luxurious red, the highly polished oak-panelled walls are again lined with paintings, and at one end is a huge window offering a panoramic view of Antwerp. Devon can see the Scheldt River and the acres of flat city sprawl extending out under the weak winter sun. The view is so impressive that she focuses on it first, before turning her attention to the three figures sitting behind the desk...

In the middle of the desk is Gerard De Boer. Devon recognises him immediately, having looked up his photo on the internet back in the hotel. He is a compact man, with an angular, tanned face and short silver hair swept backwards.

He speaks...

"Good morning, Miss Lamb."

His voice is as silkily sophisticated as she might have imagined. She replies in kind and approaches him, shaking his hand before moving on to the two people on either side of him. She then takes a seat facing the desk; just like she's at a job interview.

"Please allow me to introduce my colleagues, Dr Felix Van Dijk and Dr Arianna Verdi."

Devon smiles and nods. Van Dijk, the man, is much larger than De Boer, with a high forehead, red nose and vaguely sweaty sheen. Verdi, the woman, is petite and more Mediterranean-looking, with dark curly hair and olive skin.

De Boer continues.

"We understand you have a painting to be considered by the Jan Vanderschoot committee?"

"Yes, I do," says Devon.

"Is the painting in the bag?" asks De Boer.

"It is."

"Very well. The painting will be examined by forensics and other experts here at the institute, but as the incumbent members of the Vanderschoot Panel, any final decision on the painting's authenticity will be made by us alone. You understand?"

"I do, yes."

Ariana Verdi speaks. As Devon suspected, her accent is Italian.

"You have a dossier of evidence for us to consider?" she asks. Devon nods, gets to her feet and hands over the cardboard folder carrying the report she's spent most spare minutes in the last fortnight compiling. De Boer looks down at it with an expression Devon can't quite read.

"I have also emailed a hard copy to your assistant, of course," says Devon, retreating back to her chair. De Boer passes the report to Ariana Verdi on his left, who starts leafing through it.

"You are staying in Antwerp?" asks De Boer.

"Yes. Nearby."

"OK. So, this is how the process works. We will study your painting today, along with the evidence you have provided. The painting will be available to collect from us at closing time this evening – that's six pm. We will not enter into any further meetings or discussions with you regarding the painting. We will make our considerations, and write to you with our decision, which is of course final. It might take up to a week for this letter to arrive."

"Right, OK. Thanks."

A week?

Devon hadn't considered that it might take this long... she was expecting a decision today, or tomorrow at the latest. She wonders how it could possibly take them so long... it's a yes or no thing, surely. She smiles at the panel; Verdi offers a weak smile back, Van Dijk drinks some water and De Boer peers back over his high cheeks. She's never been the best at reading expressions, but even Devon can tell his one isn't the most encouraging.

"OK, Miss Lamb. Hester will show you out."

Devon rises and backs away from the panel. She realises too late that the strap of her bag is caught on a chair leg, and as she retreats she drags the chair over with an embarrassing clatter. She feels her cheeks reddening.

"Oops, sorry."

Hester smiles sympathetically and holds the door open.

33

The rest of the day is, frankly, interminable. I've never known minutes pass so slowly... not even in university examinations or my days spent sitting in the corner of the National Gallery did time drag quite like this.

Victor does his best to entertain me and keep my spirits up. When the clock has finally crawled round to 11 a small, middle-aged Asian woman arrives, and it transpires that this is Victor's housekeeper, Betty.

I've never met anyone with a housekeeper before...

Betty makes us some tea and biscuits and Victor shows me around what he refers to as his 'games room' – the converted garage where I first encountered him last night, seemingly back from the grave. He talks me through a few of the paintings on the wall. There is indeed a Gainsborough, as Sunita mentioned, as well as some pictures by more recent British artists; a William Nicholson still-life, a Graham Sutherland portrait. There are even a few efforts by his late wife Indira; landscapes mainly. To my untrained eye, they look pretty good.

Victor regales me with the history of each one, but I barely take in a word he says. His plummy tones fade into background noise as I think about Lennie; being held God-knows-where… no doubt upset and confused. I'm unable to relax, unable to concentrate. I mentally cross my fingers and wish for everything going to plan – Sunita's collection of the decoy painting, the meeting with Grant and Maria, Devon's meeting with the De Boer panel. There are so many variables.

Victor challenges me to a few frames of snooker, but even this is not enough to stop the endless loop of thoughts in my head. I manage to pot a few balls, but I can't keep up with the score and keep losing track of my breaks. At one point I pot one red ball after another.

"You OK old chap?" asks Victor.

I nod.

"Yeah, just weary."

"Well, by all means get some rest this afternoon. I won't object if you head upstairs for a kip. We could have a long night ahead of us." He says.

I don't doubt it.

A few shots later my phone rings. It's Vanessa. I let it ring until she gets fed up and hangs up. I can't face speaking to her now;

she'll be upset, probably hysterical, and I won't know what to say.
I text her back: **Sorry, can't talk now, have spoken to the Police. I'm sure everything will be OK, speak later. Xx**

Then I turn my phone off, put it on a side-table and miss an easy black into the corner pocket.

"Not your day so far, is it?" says Victor.

34

Devon smiles goodbye to Hester and walks back through the opulent reception area. She emerges into the public part of the De Boer Institute, on the other side of the courtyard, which features an art gallery and a coffee shop. With no other plans for the day, she heads into the café, orders a latte and takes a seat at a table in the corner. She retrieves her laptop from her bag and sets it up in front of her.

Immediately she notices the man looking at her. He's sitting across the café at a table with another man; who appears to be busy doing some sort of maintenance on an expensive-looking video camera... polishing it and unscrewing various bits, oblivious to his colleague. The man smiles at her. Devon meets his eye and looks back at her laptop. A few seconds later she finds herself glancing back towards the man; he's drinking from his latte cup but still looking in her direction. She stares back at her laptop. Out of the corner of her eye, she notices him get up and walk towards her. This is all she needs...some idiot coming over to chat her up. She mentally, and physically, rolls her eyes.

Then again, on second glance, Devon notes that he looks quite friendly. He's tall and slim, dressed in black jeans and a brown suede jacket. His hair is dark and in need of a cut, and his eyes are hidden behind thick-rimmed glasses. In fact, there's definitely something of the Louis Theroux about him...

"Hello miss," he says in a Belgian accent, "mind if I join you?"

Devon glances up at him then back at the laptop.

"Er, sure."

"You're English?"

"Yes."

"I thought so. I saw you in reception... you work here?"

Devon glances up at him, cautiously.

"No, I'm just visiting."

"Me too... My name's Marcel."

He proffers his lanyard. She looks at the attached ID card:

Marcel Courtois. Canvas TV.

"I'm here for a couple of weeks, making a documentary about the De Boer Institute, hence the camera crew..." he gestures towards his mate, who is now eating a croissant.

"OK," says Devon. There's a slight pause.

"May I ask what brings you to the gallery?" asks Marcel.

Devon looks up at him, dubiously.

"Work."

"Ah," says Marcel, "so you work in art?"

Devon looks up from her laptop again. She meets Marcel's eyes briefly. He does seem quite nice, actually, and she doesn't have any pressing work to do. She could just humour him for a few minutes...

"Yes. I'm a trainee curator at the National Gallery in London."

Marcel raises his eyebrows.

"Cool! What did you say your name was?"

"I didn't," says Devon.

"No, so may I ask what it is?"

"Devon Lamb."

"It's a pleasure to meet you, Devon," says Marcel.

"Er, yeah," says Devon, "you too."

Marcel smiles.

"I work for Belgian's leading cultural TV station, we make a range of documentaries about all areas of the arts. The De Boer has allowed us access for filming... but limited access. Today is apparently a very limited day. Hence why we're stuck in the café right now."

Devon nods, and notes how good Marcel's English is. There's almost a transatlantic tone to his accent.

"So, what kind of work are you doing?"

Devon sips some coffee.

"I'm here with a painting. I'm representing the owner, who is trying to get it approved by the De Boer committee as a genuine work by a particular artist."

Marcel raises his eyebrows.

"Oh, you mind if I ask which artist?"

"Jan Vanderschoot."

Marcel raises his eyebrows higher - they almost poke out above the frames of his glasses.

"Vanderschoot, my word, a fellow Antwerp boy! I love his work, especially his rural scenes. Hey, I'm sure our viewers would be interested in this story... would you consider appearing in our documentary? We could film an interview with you today..."

Devon shakes her head.

"I'm sorry, no. I'd have to check with my employer, but the National Gallery are generally disinclined to work with TV stations, so I'm pretty sure it would be a no."

This much is true, but Devon neglects to say that she isn't working for the National Gallery on this particular case. Still, it's an easy excuse not to have to appear in front of a TV camera, which is an idea she loathes.

"Oh, shame..." says Marcel.

"Yeah, sorry."

"Still, off the record though, your story fascinates me. What can you tell me about the picture?"

Devon sips her coffee. Although her natural instinct is to be cautious, it's quite nice to be able to talk about her passion with a man who appears genuinely knowledgeable about the subject. It certainly makes a change from Charlie's cultural naivety, or listening to colleagues like Tom from the gift shop droning on about hipster folk bands. She allows herself to relax a bit.

"It's a picture of a young peasant girl in a rural setting, gathering straw. It was probably painted around 1640, but it has a fairly chequered history. It was last recorded as being sold by a bankrupt hotel owner in 1925, then it disappeared off the radar, until my client inherited it... or at least, a painting I consider to be it."

"Wow, do you have a strong case?"

Devon nods.

"I think so. I've had forensic research done... the dimensions are the same, there's evidence of extensive repairs and overpainting..."

"And who overpaints a forgery?" asks Marcel.

"Exactly. I also had an analysis done on the pigments used. There's no substances in the paint that wouldn't have been available in the seventeenth century."

"So if it is a forgery, it's a very accomplished one?"

"Yes, although there are master forgers out there who make sure they use contemporary techniques and materials... so it's not out of the question. But I also asked for a comparison between the pigments on my painting and those of a genuine Vanderschoot

owned by the Cowdrey Institute in London. It demonstrated that they were chemically virtually identical."

"The same paints?"

"Yeah, exactly."

"Cool, so your case is pretty strong."

"Forensically, yeah. But there are gaps in the provenance trail. As far as we know, it was painted in the 1640s and was in private ownership in Belgium for centuries, being exhibited at the Salon De Paris in the 1840s. Sometime after, it was sold to a hotel owner and then in turn to a Jewish family, but the war came along and, since then, it's been unaccounted for. There's nothing linking this particular picture to either Vanderschoot or Antwerp in the seventeenth century."

Marcel nods.

"I see."

"Anyway, I'm just hoping what I have is enough, but Gerard De Boer is notoriously hard to please."

Marcel smiles ruefully and nods towards his colleague, who is slumped at his table idly scrolling through his phone.

"So it seems."

He fiddles with the cuff of his suede jacket and Devon suspects he's thinking of another question – a true documentary maker – just like Louis Theroux.

"So, if this painting proves to be the genuine article, do you know what it's likely to be worth?"

Devon shrugs. There doesn't appear to be any harm in telling Marcel, but the real answer is that she doesn't know.

"It's hard to say," she replies, "but to put it in context, a Rembrandt, unseen in public for half a century, sold for twenty million at auction a few years ago. Vanderschoot's not exactly in Rembrandt's league, but a previously undiscovered Van Dyck recently fetched three million. That might be a better indicator. You can never tell for sure, but my estimate is that it would be worth well over a million. Maybe two."

"Wow."

"Yeah, exactly."

Marcel gestures towards the café roof, presumably indicating the bigwigs of the De Boer panel.

"So, this painting, they're looking at it now?"

"Yeah, they've got it all day."

"Well, I'm certainly intrigued, do you have a picture or a print I could look at? Purely out of interest?"

He smiles at her; it's an engaging type of smile, and, she has to admit, one belonging to a handsome face. She does have a printed copy of Straw Girl in her bag, and she wonders what real harm it can do to show this unconnected foreigner...

"OK," she says, finishing her latte and delving into her bag. She finds the copy of Straw Girl, which is ensconced in a plastic wallet, and pulls it out reverentially, passing it across the table to Marcel. He stares for a second in silence, and then takes off his glasses and looks closer. He extends his neck until his nose is almost touching *the paper, then sits back and rubs his eyes, as it he can't quite comprehend what he's seeing.*

"My God..."

"You like it?" asks Devon.

"Yes, but it's more than that..."

"What do you mean?"

He looks back up at her.

"I think I know where this was painted."

35

Half an hour later, against all her natural instincts, Devon finds herself in the passenger seat of a stranger's car, in a foreign country, heading through the suburbs of an unfamiliar city in search of some unknown destination. She clutches the printed copy of Straw Girl in her hands as Marcel continues to make amiable conversation as he drives. Meanwhile, his cameraman colleague Olaf slumbers in the back seat.

Antwerp rushes past outside the car as city centre bustle turns into low-rise housing and then commercial sprawl; boxy factories, out-of-town hypermarkets and the obligatory IKEA. Soon the landscape changes again – into fields dotted with wind turbines lining the straight main road. Devon wonders how far they're going, and if this was a good idea, after all. Straw Girl, her number one priority, is back with the De Boer people, and she seems to be moving further away from it.

At this point Marcel indicates left and turns off the main road.

"Nearly there," he grins, "I'm looking forward to you seeing this!"

Devon nods.

"Yep. Cool."

A crossroads looms ahead. Marcel waits for the lights and turns into a narrow-street lined with tidy houses. A blue sign at the side of the road reads:

PUUTS

"Where's this?" asks Devon, hoping it's their destination and not another part of the journey.

"Puuts" says Marcel, unnecessarily, following it with: "the home of my grandparents. A place I visited often, as a boy."

"OK."

Unimpressed with this trip into his colleague's past, Olaf begins to snore loudly in the back. Marcel ignores him and makes his way through the small, neat town, which is a curious mixture of the modern and the traditional. A centuries-old church is dwarfed by its nearest neighbour - a steel and glass shopping centre, and a quaint town-square is overlooked by a modern block of flats.

Before Devon can form much more of an impression of Puuts, they appear to come out the other side, into the countryside, on a narrow road dotted with occasional farm-like dwellings. Marcel turns again next to a whitewashed house and drives up a small track, barely big enough for a single car. Half-way along, he stops.

"Here," he says.

"Here?" asks Devon?

"Yes. This is where he painted it."

Devon peers out of the window, but she can't quite see it, whatever it is... She steps out of the car, and the vista becomes clearer. She's in the middle of flat, open fields with a large grey sky bearing down on her.

"That way," says Marcel, joining her and pointing towards the horizon.

Devon holds the print up and moves it around. She sees how the fields converge on this point from left and right, making a slight depression on the landscape. To the left, creeping towards the horizon, is a distant wooded area. To the right is a mound, which, despite being fairly small, stands out amidst the flatness surrounding it. Devon's eyes flit from the print to the real-life view, then back again. She closes her eyes and imagines the grey day she's in being flooded with the blue skies of the picture. She imagines the peasant girl herself kneeling in the middle of her view, collecting straw from the ground.

A shiver creeps along her spine. Countryside does have a tendency to look the same, but the similarities here are obvious. This really could be it...

"It's the mound that convinced me" says Marcel. "It's an ancient burial mound. This part of Belgium is flat for miles around, there's no other hill like this anywhere..."

Devon looks to the print and back at the view again. The mound on the print is bright green and dotted with sheep. The mound today is a dirtier, muddier green, and the sheep seem to have gone elsewhere to graze, but apart from that, it's identical. So are the fields; the way they slope into each other, the subtle lines they create in the terrain, the angle of the horizon to the sky. But there's something else: a feeling she can't quite define... a tingle of electricity crackling across the centuries, a nameless static, which tells her that the young peasant – Straw Girl herself – once stood on this very spot; long ago in a lost moment that Vanderschoot managed to freeze in time, forever.

"This really could be it..." says Devon.

"It is it," says Marcel. "I'm sure."

"How can you be certain?" she asks.

"Please, get back in the car" he says, "I have somewhere else to take you."

Devon takes out her phone and captures a few photos of the landscape, before following the sound of Olaf's snores back to the car.

*

It doesn't take long to get where they're going – barely a minute's drive up the same narrow road. They pull in next to a wall behind which lies a cluster of small buildings. Off to the left of them – almost slightly estranged, is the spire of a church.

Marcel turns off the engine and gets out. Devon follows. Olaf stirs.

"Stay here, Olaf, get some rest" says Marcel. His colleague groans.

"He was out on the beer last night…" says Marcel, with a hint of disapproval.

Devon nods. They pass through a small gate in the wall and walk over a field towards the church. It's a modest building, with whitewashed walls and a plain, unobtrusive spire. As they get closer, Devon notices that the land in-between the church and the rest of the village is dotted with headstones.

A graveyard…

It is towards this graveyard that Marcel leads her.

They make their way across the damp grass past a series of headstones of varying condition and age – most are vintage; their lettering faded by the elements and overgrown with centuries of moss. Some are newer and easier to read, and a few are even decorated with fresh flowers.

Devon looks around solemnly. She has the same feeling that she gets when visiting her father's grave in Brixton; a feeling of oppression, of being held down by the invisible force of all the lives that once were. Marcel leads her towards one headstone in particular… it's newer-looking than most, made of what looks like black marble with prominent grey lettering. The text is in Dutch, of course, but the key details stand out to Devon… the dates, and the name.

She reads the parts she can understand:

JAN VANDERSCHOOT (1609 – 1656)

"Contributed by the people of Puuts, 2014," Marcel reads.

"My God," she says, "he's buried here…"

"Of course," says Marcel, "Puuts was his home town – although it was little more than a collection of small villages and farms in those days. The locals paid for this new headstone a few years back. The old one was in a state of decay, so they raised the funds for this."

Devon is lost for a suitable response. She looks at Vanderschoot's stone, and then around at all the others… the older ones crumbling, listing, overgrown with moss. Does one of these belong to his subject… to Straw Girl?

He was here. She was here.

"Bloody hell…" she says.

"I thought you'd like to see this," Marcel says.

"Yes," says Devon, "thank you so much."

"What for?"

Devon takes out her mobile and captures a few shots of the gravestone, despite the uneasy feeling it gives her.

"This is just what I need."

"Sorry?"

"This is the evidence I need. This is the missing piece linking the painting back to Antwerp in the 1640s… I've got the forensic evidence, but I was missing something like this. The location of the

painting was in the same village that Jan Vanderschoot grew up in… minutes away from the church in which he's buried. This is what I was missing. Nobody else would have painted this. This is the smoking gun!"

"The what?" asks Marcel.

"The provenance," says Devon.

"Well," says Marcel, "I'm glad I could help."

"Me too. Oh, what time is it?" asks Devon.

"Er, it's almost one."

"OK, we need to go back to the De Boer Institute, now. Please."

"Right, sure. But why the hurry? I thought maybe we could get some lunch…"

Devon tenses her hands and presses them against her green woolly hat…

"No. I need to write up this evidence and submit it to the panel. That's if they will still accept further evidence after studying the picture… I need to get it to them as soon as possible."

"OK" says Marcel, "let's go."

36

Wednesday afternoon continues to pass as quickly as an ice age. In fact, I have to look up which day it is on my phone, as they've all started to merge into each other; shorn of the routine occurrences that give them their usual identity... sort of like what happens at Christmas.

In no other way is this like Christmas...

I take Victor's advice and head to my room for a sleep, but as expected, any hope of rest is optimistic. I lie still on the bed for a half an hour, puffing on my e-cigarette. Eventually, to add insult to injury, it runs out of battery.

I make my way downstairs and sneak out of the house. I've no idea what kind of town centre Chorleywood has, but if they don't have an e-cigarette shop, I surmise that they will at least have one that can supply me with a packet of old fashioned fags.

Giving up can wait, for the time being…

I walk for ages through a tree-lined sea of featureless, affluent suburbia until I realise I'm completely lost. My new budget phone lacks a mapping app, so I resort to the traditional method of asking someone the way. I approach an elderly man whose meticulous approach to car-washing suggests he might be able to point me in the right direction, and he does. Following his instructions, I soon reach the railway station and from there it's a short distance to the modest shopping street and nicotine.

I sit on a bench and smoke my first cigarette slowly. Unsurprisingly the first intake of smoke precipitates a coughing fit, but after that the welcome influx of nicotine makes me feel both calm and alert. I get lost on the way home again, but this time it's partly deliberate. I want to be lost. I want to be away from everything, if only for a while.

Eventually I make my way back to the Botham residence. Betty opens the door and Victor greets me in the hallway. He's dressed now; resplendent in red trousers and a mustard-coloured jumper, but looks unusually concerned.

"Charlie, boy, where the blazers have you been?"

"Just into town," I say.

"Town? Whatever could you want there?"

Sheepishly I produce the fag packet from my pocket. Victor grins.

"I see. Needs must when the Devil drives, I suppose. Speaking of which, I've just had a call from Sunita. She's collected the copy of

Straw Girl from Clara Swann and is en-route back to London. She says it looks magnificent; indistinguishable from the real thing."

"Well, that's good."

"Quite. Incidentally, I was thinking we ought to come up with some sort of code word for Clara's version of the painting. We should be careful about referring to it out loud as 'the copy' – if you know what I mean?"

A code word? This is all a bit James Bond...

"OK, " I say, "er, what about Elvis?"

"Elvis? As is Presley?"

"Yep," I say, "you said Clara Swann lives in Prestwick…"

"Near it, yes."

"Well, Prestwick is the only place in the UK that Elvis ever visited. A stop over at the airport when he was returning from military service." Victor looks at me oddly.

"Well, bugger me" says Victor, "you learn something new every day! OK, well in that case, Elvis should be with us by seven, at which point we head to Shoreham. Fancy a cuppa?"

He turns on his heels and heads to the kitchen, seemingly remarkably relaxed – chipper even - about the whole affair.

But then again, it's not his son whose life is at risk….

*

By seven o'clock, Elvis is in the building.

Sunita carries him to the door and I offer a helping hand into the house. We take him into the living room where the blanket he's been wrapped in is whipped away, revealing the painting underneath, which is propped up against the sofa.

Sunita was right… it is magnificent. If anything, it looks better than the original; shinier, sprightlier, more vibrant. The colours leap from the canvas. Straw Girl's eyes reach towards me; more delicate and poised than before. I assume this is because the picture is fresh and not worn down by four centuries of wear, tear and grime, and I sincerely hope that Sheridan Strauss lacks the innate art knowledge to be able to tell the difference.

Either way, the painting only has to convince him for long enough to let Lennie go free. If - or rather when - he subsequently finds out it's a fake, well that makes no difference to me…

Victor creaks to his haunches and peers at the painting through his spectacles.

"No… no, Clara's not lost her knack, I'm pleased to say. Another triumph. How was she?"

"She seemed well," Sunita replies, "I couldn't stay for long though. Had to get back on the road."

"Indeed."

He pulls himself back up to his feet with admirable agility for a man of his vintage and turns to face me and Sunita.

"Right" he says, with a hint of old military bearing evident: "here's what we're going to do… the three of us will drive down to Sussex with Elvis in Sunita's car. Finn Milburn will follow us in his own vehicle and keep an eye on things from a distance - in case anything goes awry. That kind of thing's his forte. We'll meet the kidnappers at the suggested rendezvous. Apart from that, if we all remain calm, everything's likely to go OK."

Likely… doesn't exactly fill me with confidence.

Victor continues:

"When we have the boy back safely…"

"Lennie," – I interject.

"When we have *Lennie* back" Victor corrects himself, "Sunita will take him to the local police station and explain what's happened," he turns to her – "as much as you can, darling, of course."

Sunita nods.

"Charlie and I will head back to London and await the return of Devon and the genuine painting. If Strauss somehow discovers that Elvis is a fake, then there could be reprisals. Of course Charlie, when you manage to sell the original Straw Girl there won't be anything he can do about it, but until then it might be best to lie low."

I nod, but the idea of lying low doesn't sound too appealing. I had hoped all of this was coming to an end.

And Siobhan will be back soon…

"Right then," says Victor, with the vigour of a much younger man, if there are no further questions, then I suggest we hit the road." With that he turns and exits the living room.

There are no further questions. No more deliberations. Just something that has to be done.

I follow.

37

Devon grips her bag to her chest as Marcel drives them back through the centre of Puuts and out towards the motorway. She wills him to drive quicker, even though being in a speeding car usually makes her anxious. This time is different; she needs to get back to Antwerp and submit her latest findings as soon as possible…

It has suddenly become imperative.

As soon as she'd seen the real-life view that Vanderschoot had painted - and visited his grave not even a mile away - Devon had lost all faith in the case she submitted to the De Boer Institute only a few hours ago. Without this latest piece of evidence, all her carefully-assembled forensic work suddenly seems flimsy and circumstantial.

Gerard De Boer and his sidekicks need to see this…

Marcel steers them up a straight road between two flat fields and stops at a junction to a slip road, which leads back onto the motorway. As he waits for the lights to turn green Devon notices that the car is vibrating slightly more than seems healthy. Just as the light fades from red into amber the vibrating stops and the engine shudders to a halt. Marcel turns the key in the ignition, but nothing happens. The light turns green. He thumps the dashboard and tries again, but this clearly doesn't help. He tries one last turn of the key and presses hard on the accelerator, but nothing happens.

"Ah, shit…" he says.

Olaf stirs to life in the backseat.

"You're going to flood the engine," he mumbles.

"Oh, go back to sleep," Marcel says, adding something that Devon assumes to be a Dutch expletive.

"What's happened?" asks Devon.

"This engine's been playing up for weeks. I can usually get it started again though," says Marcel, turning the key yet again.

"I'm telling you man, it's fucked" says Olaf.

"I think he's right," says Marcel.

"You're joking," says Devon.

"I'm afraid not," says Marcel, "think it's finally given up."

"Well, what are you going to do?" Devon asks, her concern growing.

"The car belongs to the TV station. If I phone them they'll send out a mechanic."

393

"OK, and how long will that take?"

Marcel shrugs.

"He'll have to come from Brussels. About an hour, maybe more."

"Shit. Shit!" Devon thumps the door to emphasise her profanity. Marcel looks a little shocked.

"Let's get this thing out of the road," he says, noticing that another car has stopped behind them. Olaf reluctantly drags himself off the backseat and helps Devon and Marcel push the car to the side of the road. Once the highway is clear, Devon pulls her laptop out her bag and starts it up; thankfully, the battery is almost fully charged. She opens the car door and settles onto the backseat.

There's nothing else for it; she's just going to have to write her report up here...

*

After an hour of solid typing Devon stops and re-reads what she's written. It all seems to make sense, which is fortunate, given the circumstances. Luckily, despite being in the middle of the Flanders countryside, she finds she has a good enough mobile signal to be able to send the images she took of the Straw Girl location and Vanderschoot's grave to her own email address, inserting these into her word document. When it all looks reasonably presentable she looks up the number of the De Boer Institute on her phone and calls it.

Outside, Marcel and Olaf sit silently on a grass verge and look on in amusement as Devon turns the car into her own private office.

After a few minutes spent alternating between patient explanations and being put on hold, Devon manages to get through to Hester, who is quite possibly the only permanently friendly and helpful member of staff on the De Boer Institute's payroll. She promises to print the document Devon is about to send her and deliver it personally to Gerard De Boer. Devon breathes a sigh of relief and checks her phone. It's just gone three o'clock.

Hopefully she's not too late.

*

The mechanic arrives shortly afterwards and after a spot of tinkering with the car decides that Olaf's earlier diagnosis was pretty much correct; it needs to be towed away for further investigations. A taxi is duly summoned to take Marcel, Olaf and Devon back to Antwerp, and by the time they arrive at the De Boer Institute it's getting on for five o' clock.

"Thanks," says Devon to Marcel as they make their way back into the lobby, "that was a great help, despite the car trouble..."

"Yes, sorry about that, I thought it was just playing up. So, what are you doing now?"

"I've got to wait here till six, then I can have the painting back."

"And their verdict?"

Devon shakes her head.

"I hope that'll come soon, but apparently it could take up to a week."

"Oh, so what will you do?"

"Take the painting back to England and wait for their decision, I suppose."

"When will you leave?" asks Marcel.

Devon hasn't really thought about this.

"Er, tomorrow, I guess."

"I see. And, so, do you have any plans for tonight?"

Devon hasn't even considered this evening either; so focused has she been on the events of the day.

"Um, I don't know, not much…"

"In that case," says Marcel, "perhaps you'd like to join me for dinner?"

Devon stares at him. Her natural instinct is to say no, of course. Men are distractions, at best, and more often than not, irritants.

Although, Marcel does seem different… a world away from gift-shop Tom. When she thinks about the conversation they might share over dinner, she can almost imagine it being interesting… Marcel knows about art and culture; there are actual things they have in common. It wouldn't be like the lunchtimes at work, spent feigning interest in trendy folk singers and microbreweries. She might even enjoy herself.

She realises that she's still staring at him.

"Sure," she says, "that would be quite nice."

"Great," says Marcel.

Numbers are exchanged, Marcel and Olaf knock off for the day and Devon takes a seat in the corner of the lobby and waits. The clock ticks round to six o'clock, then quarter past, and Devon starts to get that job-interview sick feeling in the pit of her stomach. Part of her wants to get the painting back and go, but an equally big part of her wants the panel's deliberations to last as long as possible. After all, no news is good news...

At half six the door to the right of reception opens and Hester emerges into the lobby. Her face is difficult to read; she's neither smiling nor frowning. With her is a man in an overcoat, and between them they are carrying Straw Girl in her suit bag.

Hester notices Devon, and now she smiles.

"Hey. Sorry for the wait," she says, proffering a clipboard, "I just need you to sign this form to show you've taken the painting back."

Devon signs in the space. Straw Girl is handed over.

"Thank you for all your help," says Devon, "any idea when the panel will reach a decision?"

"Yes," says Hester, confidently.

"Oh?" says Devon.

Hester holds up a plain white A5 envelope.

"They've just done it."

"Oh... right. That was, quick..."

"Mmm hmm," says Hester neutrally.

Devon turns the envelope over in her hands. She reads the front: it's addressed to the painting's owner, of course.

Mr Charles Marks - Private and Confidential.

"OK," she says to Hester, "well, thanks again."

She stoops to pick up Straw girl, slips the letter into her parka pocket and heads out into the Antwerp evening.

38

All the time we're travelling, it doesn't really feel like it's going to happen. It's possible to look out of the car window at the darkening skies and imagine we're on a different journey altogether, with some other, kindlier destination.

But we're not.

I think back to that Friday morning in January. It was only a few weeks ago... but it seems like an age.

Specifically, I think back to the split second before Victor Botham approached me and asked me to read him the label beside The Execution of Lady Jane Grey. In that moment, I'd been bored and idle; another minimum-wage worker with unrealistic dreams in a city stuffed with them. I'd been self-absorbed and unchallenged, obsessed with my own ambitions and with enough time to indulge them. Goodness knows what I was thinking at the time... my thoughts extended to little more than what I was going to eat and drink that evening.

And yet all of *this* was there… just out of my field of vision, waiting to engulf me.

Perhaps the painting itself had been a sign. Perhaps Victor had engineered it that way. Lady Jane; pale, disorientated, reaching blindly for the block – the last place her head would ever rest.

The final moments of a life; before everything changed forever.

Yes, it must have been a sign.

Before long we're skirting around the top of Brighton and I catch occasional glances of a dark expanse of sea off to my left, identifiable only by the lack of lights compared to the twinkling shawl that envelops the city. It quickly disappears as we head down out of the hills and west towards Shoreham. I'm heading home again, and the air feels different already. I can almost taste the salt…

Sunita drives in her customary sedate manner; her neck muscles taught as she peers forward at the road. I stare out of the window at the passing countryside, and Victor continues to chunter away, making little jokes, embarking on rambling anecdotes and occasionally humming notes of opera. After a while I stop listening and he becomes little but background noise, and I wonder whether it's some kind of defence mechanism – some characteristic response to stress – or if nothing *really does* bother him that much.

Maybe that's just what happens when you get into your nineties…
life loses its jeopardy.

Well, Lennie's only nineteen… and it's his life at stake.

We get to Shoreham early. It's just gone ten, and there's still an
hour till the meeting time. We stop at a McDonald's, of all places,
and sit in the car drinking coffee. Mine tastes like cardboard. I take
a stroll around the dark car park and smoke a cigarette, which
doesn't quite soothe my nerves, but at least takes away the taste of
the coffee. The temperature has dropped away and the February
night air is bitingly cold, so I'm grateful when I climb back into the
warmth of Sunita's car.

Then it's time to go.

We arrive at the tollbridge at a quarter to 11 and park up by the
side of the river Arun. We sit for a minute in silence; even Victor
seems to have lost the stomach for small talk. I look at the scene
around me; the river is calm and inky black under the clear,
cloudless night sky. The bridge stretches out across the water; its
hump-like shape and crowded wooden beams protruding into the
sea are instantly recognisable from my youth. It looks eerie, lit
solely by the bright moon, with the imposing Gothic edifice of
Lancing College visible in the background.

There's not another soul to be seen, and I'm grateful for the
dramatic drop in temperature, which seems to have discouraged
late-night walkers. If Finn Milburn is here too, overseeing things,
then he's doing it very surreptitiously. But I guess that's his job…

Suddenly the light changes, and I look forwards, as do Victor and Sunita. A pair of headlights is shining at us from the other side of the bridge.

They're here.

"OK" says Victor in a hushed tone, "get out, and fetch Elvis."

The three of us step out into the freezing cold of the night air. I glance ahead along the length of the bridge. I'm unable to make out anything at the other end, only the bright glare of the headlights. I open the back of the car and lift Elvis out. He's still wrapped in the tartan blanket in which he arrived from Scotland. I tuck him under one arm as best I can. He feels lighter than the original Straw Girl...

Victor, Sunita and I walk towards the bridge.

"Posie, wait by the car," hisses Victor.

"No," says Sunita.

"It might not be safe," he replies.

"Well then you stay back, you're 96, after all..."

"Look," I whisper, "both of you stay back. I'll go."

I walk onto the bridge and carry Elvis towards the headlights. I'm aware of Sunita and Victor hovering behind me in the shadows.

"Stay calm, old chap," says Victor.

I walk steadily. The wooden bridge creaks below my feet. I still see nothing in front of me, except the brightness of the headlights. I can't look directly at them. I hold my hand up to shield my eyes.

"Who's there?" I shout.

The light changes again. The headlights are dimmed and I can now make out another shape. I squint. There's a large, dark 4X4 vehicle parked at the end of the bridge. In front of it is a human shape silhouetted against the yellow light. The shape is tall, solid and muscular... it's clearly Grant.

And in his right hand I can make out the shape of a gun.

39

Grant walks towards me and I'm now able to make out his features – the bald head, ruddy face and narrow, hostile eyes. He's dressed in a long black leather coat and holds the gun to his side, pointing it towards the water as he paces closer. I walk towards him, until I can almost see the faint scars on his pitted cheeks.

"Good evening Charlie," he says.

"Where's Lennie?" I ask.

"He's in the car," he says, nodding behind him. "You got the painting then?"

"Obviously," I want to say. Instead I hold up the tartan blanket with Elvis wrapped inside. He nods, then turns around and makes a hand gesture towards the car, which is still nothing but a black shape to me. I can't make out a thing... Lennie could be in there, or somewhere else entirely.

The passenger door opens and another figure gets out. He's also dressed head to toe in dark clothing – a brown suit jacket over a black polo neck – but is shorter than Grant and clearly not in the best of shape. I can make out a portly gut expanding over his belt. He's wearing a black balaclava with a single slit for the eyes to look through, but despite this, I know who it is…

It's Sheridan Strauss.

He has no idea that I know it's him, which is pretty much my only advantage at the moment…

Sheridan stops a few paces behind Grant and peers at the painting through his eye slit.

"OK," says Grant, "give it here."

"No," I say, "not yet."

He glances back at Sheridan.

"What do you mean?"

"Show me Lennie first. I need to know he's alright."

Grant and Sheridan exchange another glance. Sheridan nods slightly, and Grant makes another gesture towards the 4x4. The back door opens and a slim, dark-haired figure climbs out.

Maria.

The internal light flicks on briefly and I catch a glimpse of the driver. He's wearing a scarf pulled up to his nose and a flat cap angled down over his eyes, but I can guess who it is. It's Arnie Russell. He's been on my case ever since I visited Victor in hospital…

I look back at Maria. She extends her arm back into the car, like she's grabbing onto somebody's hand; coaxing someone out from the backseat...

I can make him out now, just about... With every second and every squint my eyes are adjusting to the light. Lennie emerges from the car. He's wearing a blindfold, and still in the clothes he was wearing for the college interview; smart trousers, a white shirt and his red clip-on tie - which I'm quite surprised has remained in place.

I can't see his eyes, but I can see that he looks weary, pale, but otherwise OK. I wonder what he's been through, and try to imagine what's been going on in his head. It's hard enough to do this at the best of times, but now...

Maria keeps a hold of his arm as she walks him towards the bridge. He looks a little unsteady on his feet. When they're in my sights they stop, and Maria removes his blindfold. I smile at Lennie and wave. He raises a hand and waves back at me, but has clearly been told to remain quiet. The closer I get to him the more frightened he looks...

"OK," says Grant, "let's see it."

He gestures towards the painting. I walk forwards and pass the blanketed bundle to him.

This is it. Everything hangs on this moment. If they can tell it's a fake, the whole thing is over. The consequences don't bear thinking about...

I feel like I could be physically sick. Grant pulls back the blanket and peers at the corner of the canvas. His face doesn't give anything away. He walks backwards - with one hand still on his gun - and passes Elvis to Sheridan.

Sheridan seems to struggle with the painting's weight. He wedges it against his knees in an ungainly manner, breathing heavily, before easing it onto the ground. He pulls the blanket back to the side so the canvas is visible, but I'm not sure what he expects to see in the moonlit gloom. I'm suddenly grateful they chose to do this at night…

Then he pulls out a torch.

Oh dear.

Sheridan sinks to his haunches and aims his beam at the painting.

Clara Swann's fake painting…

'Elvis'…

I realise that my hands are trembling, and I pray that Grant assumes it's simply the cold. I try to force myself to look up at Lennie on the other side of the bridge, but my attention keeps switching to Sheridan, who's now shining his light on every inch of the surface.

Oh Christ – he's looking for something… something we've overlooked that will give the game away…

I look back at Lennie and force a grin.

Come on Charlie… he's not an art expert, he's a sodding banker. Have faith in Clara Swann. It's going to be OK…

Shit!

Sheridan seems to focus in on something at the bottom of the painting. I assume it's Jan Vanderschoot's signature – or rather Clara Swann's inch-perfect forgery of it.

I can see Sheridan's porcine eyes squinting through the hole in the balaclava, looking up and down. Time seems to slow to a crawl.

Come on… come on!

With a sharp movement Sheridan rises to his feet. I hear his knees click. He looks back towards Maria and raises a single finger of his gloved hand. Maria nods at the signal, bends down to Lennie's level and says something to him. I try my best to lip read…

It looks like she says "*walk slowly.*"

Lennie begins pacing forwards across the bridge - as usual, taking his instructions very literally - walking at a glacial speed; one step at a time.

Meanwhile, Sheridan wraps the tartan blanket back around the painting and turns towards Grant. He nods at his accomplice and walks back across the river in the direction of the 4X4. He passes Grant, who still has his gun trained firmly on me. I stand still where I am, my eyes fixed firmly on Lennie as he continues his slow journey across the bridge.

For some reason, Grant suddenly catches my eye. I glance from Lennie to him just as Sheridan passes. Grant almost looks like he's smiling… he then looks away from me and wheels around until he's facing towards Sheridan's departing back. He almost seems to move in double time at first, but then I see everything unfolding in slow motion...

He extends his right arm, his tensed muscles visible through his jacket. He takes a few steps forwards, straightens his aim and begins to pull the trigger. I can see what's happening. I could shout, or push him away, or otherwise create a distraction, but I do none of these things...

Instead I stand in shocked silence and watch as he puts a bullet right into the back of Sheridan's head.

*

He's dead, clearly. There's no debate about that. Sheridan lies face-down on the bridge with an expanding pool of blood seeping from his skull into the wooden slats of the bridge. In the moonlight it looks like thick, black tar. I'm amazed by how much there is. While I stand in helpless rigidity, Grant walks towards Sheridan, clearly unfazed by the gore in front of him. He bends down onto his knees, removes the painting from Sheridan's dead hands and walks away.

Maria moves at exactly the same time, as if part of some pre-rehearsed ambush, which is exactly what this seems to be. She strides up to the black 4X4 and pulls out a gun of her own. The engine stutters into life as Arnie Russell tries desperately to get away, but he's barely able to get the thing into gear before a burst from Maria's gun shatters the windscreen.

A constant blare from the horn confirms that Arnie is slumped against the wheel, dead, presumably.

I'm not sure whether it's the sound of the horn or the gunshots, or most likely a combination of both, but Lennie is shocked out of his slow progress and begins to sprint across the bridge, screaming and holding his hands over his ears.

"Lennie," I shout, "it's OK!"

He doesn't hear me. He runs straight down the middle until he sees the hulking figure of Grant coming in the other direction; the painting under one arm and his gun in the other. Lennie panics, looking desperately from one side of Grant to the other, but there seems like no safe route past. He lets out another piercing scream before taking the only option available to him...

He leaps up onto the side of the bridge and jumps straight into the thick blackness of the river.

40

The first thing I notice is how cold it is. Every part of my body tenses with shock. I sink under the surface and freezing water shoots up my nose and into the back of my throat. It feels like it's up to my ears on the inside. I throw my head back and stare at the moon, thrashing my hands around in a desperate attempt to stay afloat.

I can hear Lennie doing something similar several metres away, coupled with high-pitched screams which fade in and out as he dips under the surface. Everything is noise and cold and I can feel my heartbeat reverberating around my head.

I can't do this.

I have to do this…

I force myself onto my front and swim towards Lennie. It's harder to move than I thought; my muscles seem drained of energy by the cold, but eventually I reach Lennie. He's not screaming now, but is floating on his back, bobbing up and down; his head going in and out of the river, spitting water out every time he comes up for air.

"Lennie," I say, my voice almost swallowed by the blackness of the night.

"D… dad. Help!"

"It's OK mate, I'm here."

I put my hands around his waist, but it's so cold I struggle to get a grip. My legs are kicking furiously; instinctively trying to reach some solid ground but never finding any. I'm conscious of losing energy, fast…

"Hold on to me," I say, "grab my back."

Lennie puts his hands on my shoulders.

"Move your legs slowly," I say.

"I'm scared…"

"It's OK."

I'm vaguely aware of a sound coming from the other side of the river – doors slamming, an engine revving, wheels spinning – but then my head dips under the water and everything goes silent. All I can hear is my heartbeat. It's fast…

I turn onto my front and attempt to swim with Lennie holding onto me. I'm not sure what stroke I attempt, but I'd say it's some sort of cross between doggy paddle and a mad frantic thrash. Progress is slow. I feel myself getting colder and more tired. I look up at the side of the river. It must be only ten metres away, but it might as well be a hundred, with the speed we're moving.

I can now hear voices coming from the riverbank.

"Come on Charlie. Not far now!"

"Keep going!"

It's Victor and Sunita. I kick and thrash harder, but it doesn't seem to do any good. I feel like I'm in one of those dreams; the kind when you're escaping from someone, or running towards something, but it feels like you're wading through a sea of invisible treacle. Your legs move, you expend energy, but you keep moving backwards... while the fear and desperation grows.

I had a dream like that once, shortly after Lennie was born. I was holding him; he was tiny, helpless, and some unknown *thing* was chasing after us. I couldn't see it, of course... it was just a feeling... an entity. I remember glancing behind me and sensing a vast blackness. A void. I moved my legs like pistons but still didn't move a single inch, and the blackness was closing in on me.

The next time I turned around the blackness was almost touching me. And when I looked in front of me, Lennie was no longer in my arms.

He's not a baby anymore though, he's a nineteen year-old boy, and I feel his grip on me slipping away. He starts screaming again, in-between sharp intakes of breath.

"Hold on," I say.

"I can't!

"Hold me!"

I'm sure I'm almost at the side of the river, but in the darkness I can't quite tell. I can hear Victor and Sunita, but I can't see them.

413

And I don't think I can move any more…

My limbs feel hollow. I breathe in, but the air seems to catch in my throat and stings before it gets to my lungs. Lennie is like a lead weight, dragging me downwards. I feel faint. I close my eyes - I can't help it - and my head disappears under the water. Lennie is thrashing and screaming. I poke my head above the water level.

"I'm sorry…"

Then I'm dragged back under.

This is that dream again. This is what it meant. This is where the darkness finally catches me.

The object hits the water with a sharp slap, spraying water over us. I push my eyes above the water line, which is a huge effort, and see a thick black circle bobbing on the surface. A tyre.

"Grab it," shouts Sunita.

I reach up and put both hands on the tyre. My body breathes a sigh of relief at no longer having to support itself. I pull Lennie towards it and he holds the other side. We look at each other, illuminated by the moonlight, gasping huge gulps of air.

The tyre jolts to the side. Sunita is in the water now, pulling on the tyre. I can hear Victor on the bank, shouting…

"Careful Posie, careful."

She drags the tyre towards the sound of her father.

"Can you touch the ground?" she asks. I push my feet down and can just about feel my toes hitting the riverbed. Relief floods over me. I push myself onto firmer ground and help her pull the tyre and

Lennie over the long reeds at the side. I scramble up onto the muddy bank, dragging Lennie behind me by his cold hands. When I'm sure we're on dry land I collapse onto my back and stare up at the sky; my stomach rising and falling sharply as I desperately try to get air into my lungs. Above me, the moon disappears behind a layer of cloud and the night gets a little darker. I don't move. I don't think I can. I look to my left and see Lennie lying next to me; his stomach going up and down.

I close my eyes.

41

The Antwerp night is cold, but Devon feels warm. In part, this is due to the agreeable temperature inside the little Italian restaurant, but, she has to admit, the company is having a warming effect as well. Marcel is both funny and interesting. He's just finished telling her about a documentary his company made last year in Rome – investigating the artworks of the Vatican – and he's now moved onto anecdotes about growing up in a large family in Antwerp, with an art historian father and piano-playing mother.

The tales of an artistic, bohemian and slightly chaotic upbringing resonate with her, reminding her of her early life in Brixton. And while this makes her feel a little sad, especially as Marcel's dad didn't pass away when he was only four, he manages to make it funny... he intersperses his story with little jokes and humorous observations. Devon sips her coke – her second of the night – and looks into his green eyes. This is quite possibly the longest time she's spent talking to one man in isolation for quite a while, and she isn't anywhere near bored yet. That, in itself, is something of a miracle.

When the pasta is finished they order desserts and take their time to eat them, such is the flow of the conversation. Marcel finishes his red wine and orders them coffee, and they keep on chatting until the restaurant staff begin making hints about needing to close up. Devon looks around and notices that she and Marcel are the last diners in there. It's just gone midnight. She smiles.

They leave the restaurant and step out into the cold night; a few specks of snow are falling around them. It's beautiful and quiet. Marcel offers to walk Devon back to her hotel and links his arm into hers as they walk along the quiet street. The continue talking as they walk, and their conversation carries on for a good half an hour once they're standing outside the Hotel Schubert. Marcel asks Devon about tomorrow; she explains that she'll get a flight back with the painting and return to work the following week.

"When do you expect to find out if it's the real thing?" asks Marcel.

"I already have." Says Devon.

"What?" asks Marcel.

"It's in here," she says, holding up the envelope.

"They've made their decision?" says Marcel. Devon nods.

"But you haven't opened it?"

"No," says Devon. "It's addressed to Charlie. I'll need to open it with him, or at least seek his permission, and I haven't been able to reach him."

What Devon doesn't tell Marcel is that there's another reason she hasn't opened the envelope. Sure, Charlie has a right to find out what it says at the same time as her. But the speed at which the De Boer Institute reached their decision was hugely disheartening…

One day. That was all…

Deep down, Devon suspects that the letter contains bad news. If the De Boer people had intended to verify Straw Girl and include it in the Vanderschoot catalogue raisonnè, they would surely have spent much longer debating its relative merits. Days. Weeks even.

A letter brusquely handed over on the same day as Devon bought it in leads her to one conclusion…

They're not convinced.

This is why Devon has left the painting back in the hotel room, where previously it had journeyed everywhere with her. This is why she hasn't even bothered to contact Charlie yet. She might be wrong, but her thoughts lead her to one sorry conclusion…

It's over.

Suddenly Marcel is talking again…

"I'm coming to London soon. For work. Perhaps we could meet up when I'm there?"

"Yes. Sure."

Devon smiles.

"I'd like to know what happens to the painting."

She nods.

"And to see you again, of course."

She nods again.

"Well, you have my email address."

"Yes, I do. OK, Devon, I'll say goodnight."

"OK, goodnight."

Marcel is uncharacteristically silent for a moment, then he moves towards Devon, leans forwards and kisses her on the mouth. Devon kisses him back, and as she does he puts an arm on her shoulder. His touch is light and gentle. After a few moments he moves away slightly and smiles at her.

Devon smiles back.

It was a nice kiss. Definitely. It was also her very first one.

But she doesn't tell Marcel that.

42

As planned, we drop Sunita and Lennie off at the nearest police station. Lennie is drained, cold and compliant and I hope the first thing the police do is to warm him up. After that, Victor takes the driver's seat and we head back to Chorleywood. He drives surprisingly fast for a man in his 90s. I spend most of the journey huddled in a blanket with my wet clothes piled on the backseat and the heating on full. Despite my discomfort, I'm happy. Lennie is back in safe hands. Anything, including Straw Girl, feels like bonus now.

It's gone one in the morning when we get back to Victor's house.

"I'll get you some clean clothes," he says as he guides me into his living room, "and a large port. Looks like you could use one."

I nod.

Victor duly furnishes me with a drink and some pyjamas. I sip my port and it makes me think of all the blood that flowed from

Sheridan's head a couple of hours ago. I still can't quite believe he's dead...

"They betrayed him," I say to Victor. "I didn't see that coming."

He shrugs his shoulders.

"You know what they say: dance with the devil and get pricked by the horns. Strauss had no choice but to involve a couple of career criminals to do his dirty work. Seems he paid the ultimate price for that."

I nod.

"Do you reckon Grant and Maria will notice that their painting is a fake?" I ask. Victor shrugs again.

"They didn't look the most intelligent of types. But who knows? Perhaps they might, but not until they try selling it. By which point you might already have sold the original and there won't be anything they can do about it."

"I guess."

"Besides, it's definitely not ending up with the Strauss family now, and that's a reason to be cheerful if I ever knew one."

"I'll drink to that," I say.

We sit and sip our ports together for a while, the silence eventually broken by a phone call from Sunita. She tells us that Lennie is being checked out at the local hospital but seems fine. Apparently his mum is on her way to see him. I'm pleased to share in Vanessa's relief. I fully expect the police to want to talk to me, and there's bound to be some explaining to do in due course...

But not yet...

*

Finn Milburn arrives at the house shortly after Sunita's call. Victor welcomes him in with his customary port and he takes a seat. He's still in his brown suit and smells strongly of cigarette smoke as he sinks slowly into the sofa. He looks tired and gaunt, but then again, he's looked tired and gaunt every time I've seen him. He rubs his hands against his temples…

"So, I don't know if you saw, but I was watching proceedings from the other side of the river…"

I hadn't seen him…

"Grant and Maria pulled Arnie Russell's dead body out of the car and dumped him in the water. All rather unceremonious. Then they took the 4X4 and made off. I would have thought Sheridan was offering them a hefty slice of the profits to stop something like this happening - but how ever much it was, it can't have been enough. Him and Arnie were sitting ducks really. Anyway, I decided to follow them, seeing as you folks were out of the woods…"

Out of the woods? Had he seen Lennie jump into the water? I guess he hadn't…

"Anyway, I soon lost them. But I managed to tip off an old mate from Sussex Police – told them what they were driving and where they'd headed. They were picked up just outside Gatwick. They're safely in custody now. Along with their fake painting…"

"Blimey…" I say.

Elvis is back in the building.

"Indeed," says Finn.

"Talking of the painting," says Victor, "any word from Antwerp yet?"

"No idea," I say, "my phone went into the river with me. It's knackered. I've no idea if Devon's called or not."

"Into the river" asks Finn, raising an eyebrow.

"Yeah, my son panicked. He's fine now."

"Well, let's give her a call now," says Victor.

"It's almost two in the morning" I say.

"Well, this is rather urgent," he says, "don't you want to find out if there's been any news?"

I do. But then again, I don't. After all the stress of the past few hours, I almost can't face the possibility of Straw Girl being declined by the De Boer Institute. It would render everything we'd been through pointless... I'd be unemployed again. Penniless. Back to square one. How would I explain it all to Siobhan?

I don't want to know. Not now. Not here. I want to remain in suspense for a little longer. To prolong the dream…

Victor gets up and walks across the room. He returns with the phone and hands it to me.

"Let's call her."

*

Devon lies on her hotel bed, staring at the ceiling. She's tried to sleep, but the soothing balm of unconsciousness has remained stubbornly out of her reach. There's too much going on in her head. She looks towards the window. The skies are dark outside, but the lights of the city night are still bright enough to cast her room in an eerie orange glow. She looks over to the desk again. The letter's still there. Unopened...

She can't bring herself to look inside, but neither can she sleep with it sealed. She closes her eyes and rests her head back on the pillow.

Then her phone rings.

"Devon? Hi. It's Charlie. Sorry to call you so late."

A lump tightens in her throat.

"No worries," she says. "I wasn't asleep anyway. You OK?"

"Yes. It all went well. Lennie's safe, and the exchange went... fine. I'll tell you more when you're back."

"OK," she says, "cool."

"I don't suppose there's been any news about the painting then?"

Devon clears her throat.

"Actually, there has."

"What?"

"The panel came to their decision this evening."

Silence.

"What? Already? What… what did they say?"

"I don't know. I haven't opened the envelope yet. It's addressed to you."

"What? You mean, you haven't read it?"

"No. You want me to open it now?"

"Well, yeah. I guess."

"OK."

This is it, then. Devon sits up on the edge of the bed, then stands, rubs her eyes and walks over to the desk. She turns the light on and opens the envelope. She slides the letter out and reads it.

*

I hold the phone away from my ear and look at Victor and Finn.

"She's opening it."

I press the phone back to my ear. I can't hear anything.

"Devon? You there?"

Nothing. Victor and Finn sit forward in their seats. Then I hear Devon's faint voice…

"So, do you want me to read it to you?"

"Yes!"

"OK…"

Epilogue

.

London, May 2019

I get off the Circle Line at Westminster and the first thing I see as I emerge from the underground is Big Ben; jutting into the blue spring skies and swaddled from head to toe in scaffolding like a wounded patient. I turn right down Whitehall and make my way towards Trafalgar Square – the same route I used to take to work. Every day.

I haven't taken this route for a while now…

Everything seems the same – the buildings, the tourists, the anonymous suits rushing head-down to their jobs running the country – but still, things are different. Far different to when I used to walk this way to work every morning. I notice more… I notice the architectural details on the top of the buildings, the way the pigeons swoop and scatter, the crispness of the spring air. I feel awake.

I enter the National Gallery through the Sainsbury Wing, stopping to have my bag checked by security, but instead of heading straight through into the staff area I make my way up the sweeping staircase and take a brief stroll around the gallery. Nobody seems to recognise me as I make my way around the rooms. It's like I never worked there at all…

I eventually end up in Room 44. Where it all started. I stand in front of the Execution of Lady Jane Grey. The drama of the picture captivates me once more; just as it used to do when my job was to sit there minding it.

I feel a hand tap me on the back. I turn around and see a man dressed in the same dark uniform that I used to wear.

"Charlie? Is it you?"

"Abdul, hi!"

He slaps me harder on the back.

"Long time no see! What are you up to now mate?"

"Ah, this and that" I say, "mainly just working on my writing."

Abdul smiles and we chat for a few minutes before he slinks back to his post and I make my way to the café.

Devon is there, waiting for me in a corner. I order an espresso and a glass of tap water and join her at the table. She looks smarter than usual. Gone are the Dr Marten boots, purple tights and parka.

Instead, she's wearing a smart grey trouser suit and her wayward curly hair has been tied back in a bun.

"You look smart…" I say.

She rolls her eyes.

"It's Sotheby's, Charlie. I assume you've heard of them?"

"Yes, I have."

"You don't turn up there looking like an art student. Well, you might, but I'm not going to. I've got a higher profile now."

"Oh yes," I say, congratulations on the promotion."

"Thank you," she says, smiling.

"So, what time does the auction start?" I ask.

"Midday," she replies, narrowing her gaze, "you are sure you don't want to come?"

"Absolutely," I say, "I can't be doing with the tension. I've had too much of that recently. Anyway, there's something else I need to do."

"OK," she says "you're the boss. But I'll let you know what happens as soon as I know."

"Thanks. Are the National Gallery going to bid on it then?"

"They are, but I haven't been told anything – there could be a conflict of interests seeing as I'm selling it on your behalf."

"OK. I'd like the gallery to get it though. It would be nice to still be able to come here and see her, now and then…"

"Yeah," she says. "I hope we get him too."

"You put the reserve on?" I ask.

"I did. You still don't want to know the estimate price?"

"No, no," I say, "don't tell me. I don't want to be disappointed…"

Devon smiles.

"I'm sure you won't be."

I finish my espresso.

"How's everything else with you?" I ask.

"Oh, yeah, fine," she says. "I'm going back to Antwerp next weekend. Holiday."

"Oh, nice."

"What about you? How's Lennie?"

"Oh, he's great. Still looking forward to starting at the agricultural college. He's been doing some work on a local farm. Volunteering. Seems to have gotten over it all quite well…"

I hope this is true… it's hard to tell.

"How's your girlfriend?"

"Siobhan? She's good. Busy as ever."

This, at least, is true. Siobhan had barely got back from California before another business trip came up in Rome. This weekend, she's off to Paris…

"That's good."

I nod.

"Yep."

"And what about you? Are you still working on your film scripts?"

I shake my head. The truth is that I haven't been able to find the inspiration recently, not since real life took on more drama than my imagination could ever have conjured up.

"Nah, not so much. I've been thinking I might park the screenplays for a while. Actually, depending on what happens at the auction today, I've been thinking about investing in a bit of art. I'll miss Straw Girl if it sells. Might look to pick up a few other bits in its place…"

Devon looks a little surprised by this news. I think she still has me down as a slovenly philistine. Which might well be somewhere near the truth….

"Well," she says, "if you find you need some advice, you know where to come."

"Of course."

Devon starts to slide some of her papers into a leather folder.

"I'd better be off soon," she says.

"OK, cool," I say, watching as she gathers together the last of the documents.

"By the way," I say, "do you have the letter with you?"

"Of course," she says.

"Can I see it one more time?"

"Yeah, sure." She digs around in her folder and finds the letter. I hold the envelope, as I've done so many times before; trying to convince myself that it's real. That it really exists.

I take out the letter, fold it open and lay it in front of me. I read it through.

*

The De Boer Institute, Antwerp, Belgium

Dear Mr Marks,

After careful consideration, we are pleased to inform you that the committee have unanimously approved your painting 'Straw Girl' for inclusion in the Vanderschoot 'Catalogue Raisonnè. A certificate will be issued within the next few weeks.

Yours sincerely,

G.P De Boer

It was real. It happened.

*

I bid farewell to Devon, wishing her good luck, and make my way back to the tube station. From there I head across London to Euston and catch a train going to the north. I settle into my seat, knowing that a long journey awaits me, but I'd rather be out of London today. I want to be so far away from the auction that it's almost possible to forget it's taking place. I want to see rolling countryside and little towns I've never seen before and somehow convince myself that nothing's going on back in London.

Besides, there's someone I need to say thank you to…

The train is warm to the point of stuffy, and after a while I fall into a deep sleep. When I'm finally jolted back into consciousness I realise we're almost in Scotland. The landscape changes and takes on a rougher feel.

I change trains at Glasgow Central station and take a slower-moving local service through a series of little towns. It doesn't feel like spring anymore. Up here the skies are grey and a cold wind seeps through the rattling windows of the carriage I'm in. It's mid-afternoon by the time the train arrives in Prestwick, and the clouds are thickening with the threat of rain.

It doesn't take me long to walk from the station to my destination. I follow the route on my new smartphone and find it pretty easily, up a long straight road and left into a little maze of residential streets. The first specks of rain begin to fall as I locate the right house. It's a bungalow to be precise; a neat, anonymous building with white walls and a spacious but overgrown front garden. The lettering spelling the house name (Halcyon) is in a retro style and some of the white paint is chipped. I make my way up the little path and knock gently on the door.

Behind the frosted glass I can see a small, blurred figure moving towards the door. It opens. Standing in front of me is Clara Swann.

"Hello there," she says in a soft Scottish accent, "can I help you?"

"Yes," I say, "um, I'm Charlie. Charlie Marks. I wondered if I could come in?"

She fixes her bright blue eyes on me and smiles.

"Charlie!" she says, "of course you can."

Which is a relief, given how far I've come...

*

I'm shown into her front room by way of a small hallway. We pass two cats on the way, one black and one tortoiseshell. Both are introduced to me...

"This is Roddy and this is Julio."

I struggle to sense a theme with the names...

The front room is comfortable but old-fashioned. The armchairs and sofa are dark green and the carpet an indistinct, threadbare beige. The walls are papered in what I suspect is a genuine rather than faux 70s pattern of orange and brown. Photos of unknown family and friends occupy most of the surfaces. I take a seat next to another cat (Lizzie, white) and Clara brings me a coffee in a china cup.

"Thank you," I say.

Clara is partly how I imagined her to be, but different at the same time. Despite the hermit-like, anachronistic existence she clearly lives, she's no confused old granny. There are books everywhere, and most subjects seem to be covered; art, literature, science.

Above the electric fireplace is a large seascape of rolling waves, painted – no doubt – by Clara herself.

"You're most welcome," she replies, sipping her own coffee. She's tiny. So tiny I imagine she could get away with wearing children's clothes to save money. The faded denim dungarees she's sporting may well have been with her since she was about 12. Over them she wears a baggy light blue shirt with a liberal amount of paint splodged all over it. Her bright-red hair stands out against the blue; curly and wayward with the odd streak of silver.

"Scotland's a long way for you to come," she says, sitting down opposite me.

"I was at a loose end, and I fancied a bit of a journey… and I thought it was about time I came and thanked you in person."

"Ah, there's no need," she says.

"There is. If you hadn't finished that painting so quickly, I don't know what might have happened. My son might not be here today. I'm grateful. Very grateful."

"Well, I'm just glad I could help."

"So am I."

"Ah, it's just what I do," she says. "If it hadn't been your painting, it would have been something else I was working on. I don't sleep much at night."

"Well, I just wanted to, you know, express my thanks" I dig around in my bag, "this isn't much, but it's something…"

I hand her the present I've carried up from London – a tote bag with a seagull pattern on it. Inside is a bottle of Tanqueray gin... her favourite tipple, or so I'm reliably informed.

"Aha, you've clearly had some advice from Victor!" she says, "and the bag's lovely, thank you."

"You're most welcome."

"How is he, by the way? Victor I mean..." she asks.

"He's OK. I went to visit him in hospital the other day – he's still having the chest problems, but he seemed in good spirits. The cricket season's started now, so that's keeping him occupied."

Clara laughs.

"Ah, he'll probably outlive us all!"

"Yeah, wouldn't surprise me."

"And how's Posie?"

"She seems fine. I always find it a bit hard to tell though."

Clara nods.

"Yes, she was always a very reserved child. I do wonder if she'll come out of her father's shadow, you know, when he's not here anymore..."

"Mmm," I say, not quite sure of an appropriate response. I look to my side and catch Lizzie's suspicious feline eyes.

"Anyway," I say, changing the subject, "I was very impressed that you managed to complete the copy of Straw Girl so quickly. What was it, 24 hours... do you always paint so fast?"

"Well, yes…" she says, an almost mischievous smile playing on her lips, "but I had a bit of an advantage with Straw Girl…"

"Oh," I reply, "what was that?"

"Well," she says, "I have copied that painting before."

"I'm sorry, what?"

*

I follow Clara down a narrow corridor. She shuffles along in front of me in her moccasin slippers, another cat hovering at her feet. At the end of the corridor is a plain white door. It's padlocked. Clara pulls out a key from her dungarees and opens the lock. She swings the door open and descends down a staircase. I follow. We emerge into a basement lit by a single bright light bulb. Around the walls are piles of canvases. Pots of paint and easels are lined up everywhere and a large table sits in the middle; covered in sketches and jars full of brushes. The smell of paint is almost overwhelming.

There are paintings hanging up on the walls too. Portraits, seascapes, landscapes. Some I would probably recognise, if I looked closer, but I don't, because my eyes are drawn straight to one painting in particular, hanging at the far end of the basement. I walk towards it in awe and confusion. It's almost like looking at a ghost…

It's all so familiar. The green fields. The sheep on the hill. The blue skies. The girl in the middle; crouched with a bundle of straw under her arm. I look at her blue eyes... her golden hair.

Straw Girl.

I turn round to face Clara. She has an odd grin on her face.

"Bloody hell," I say, "it's... it's another one."

"Sure is."

I look back at the painting. It's the same - exactly the same - as the one I'd carried around for weeks. The one I risked my life to save. The one that's now in Sotheby's, being auctioned as we speak...

"What... why?" I stammer.

"It was Indira's idea," says Clara. "She was a very perceptive lady. One of the cleverest people I ever met. When she first took an interest in the painting, she foresaw the fact that the Strauss family might one day try to take back what they saw as their rightful property. So she came to me, and asked me to make a copy. She thought it would be a way to deceive them; to cast doubt on which one was the original. A form of insurance, I suppose."

"Bloody hell."

I'm not sure what else to say...

"She asked me to make it as close a copy as possible; using only authentic materials that would have been available in the seventeenth century. She was my best friend, so of course, I did what she wanted. She took one of the paintings home to Chorleywood, and left the other here."

"Oh, right… so…"

I'm not sure what to say. There's a question I want to ask, but I'm not sure how to phrase it. Or what the answer would mean…

"So, did anyone else know about this? What about Victor?"

She shakes her head.

"As far as I know, she was the only one who knew. A few months later, the 9/11 attacks happened. I don't think she ever told Victor what she'd done."

In that case…

I look down at Clara – I meet her ageless blue eyes.

"So… in that case, how could Victor be sure his version of Straw Girl was the true original?

She shrugs her shoulders and smiles.

"I guess he couldn't."

"So, what you're saying is, the one that's currently selling in London could well be the copy, and this… this could be the original?"

My words are coming out shakily…

"It's a possibility."

"OK, but you must have an idea, surely?" I gesture towards the painting… "Clara, do *you* know if this is the original?"

She winks at me.

She winks.

"I might do. But that would be telling."

*

I walk away from her cottage in a state of shock. A maelstrom of thoughts are spinning in my brain… I'd asked her again, of course, but she wouldn't tell me. She still wouldn't break Indira's confidence.

She'd given her word.

I stare up at the skies. The clouds are dispersing. A ray of sun breaks through.

My phone is ringing.

Devon calling.

"Hi," I say.

"Hi Charlie."

She sounds excited.

"You alright?"

"Yeah. It sold, Charlie!"

"It sold?"

"Yeah, a few minutes ago. Are you sure you're OK?"

"Yeah… I'm fine."

"So, do you want to know how much it went for?"

"Er, yeah, I guess."

Devon clears her throat.

"One. Point. Two. Million."

THE END

ABOUT THE AUTHOR

Steven F. Galloway is an author from West Sussex, England. He has previously published three ebooks: The Lake, Sarah Dee Was Here and Being Waterproof. In his spare time, he enjoys cycling and drinking beer. You can follow him on twitter, if you wish. @StevenFGalloway.

46993016R00263

Printed in Poland
by Amazon Fulfillment
Poland Sp. z o.o., Wrocław